The Third Parent

The Third Parent

ELIAS WITHEROW

THOUGHT CATALOG
Books

BROOKLYN, NY

Cover photography by © Ammy Design.

Published by Thought Catalog Books, a publishing house owned by The Thought & Expression Co., Williamsburg, Brooklyn.

First edition, 2017

ISBN: 978-1945796708

Printed and bound in the United States.

10 9 8 7 6 5 4 3 2 1

This one is for my brother, Pete.
You're one hell of a dude. Love you, man.

Thanks for sitting in the rain with me.

And one last thing:

This book is not for the faint of heart

Transcript of a 911 Call

Date: October 3rd, 1992

Address: ———

Caller Identification: —— ———

Time of Call: 9:37 pm

Original Transcript

911 Operator: Nine-one-one what's your emergency?

Woman: There's a man in our house.

911 Operator: Are you in immediate danger?

Woman: Yes, I don't have much time.

911 Operator: Do you know the identity of the man?

Woman: He's downstairs with my husband…(static)…with my children.

911 Operator: Ma'am, is it possible to leave the house?

Woman: No…no he won't let us leave…

911 Operator: Has he hurt anyone?

Woman: Oh yes…yes, my husband…(static)…there was so much blood…

911 Operator: Ma'am, I need you to give me your address. I'm going to patch it through to the police and get you some assistance.

Woman: He's going to kill me for this.

911 Operator: Is the intruder armed?

Woman: *(soft laughter)*….no…he doesn't need to be.

911 Operator: Your address ma'am, please, I need you to give me your address.

Woman: *(whispered)* This was such a mistake. I shouldn't have called…*(panicked)* Oh no, I shouldn't have called you.

(Distant scream)

911 Operator: What was that? Has someone been hurt? Ma'am?

Woman: *(whispered)* He's going to hurt all of us…he's going to hurt us until we learn…until we do what he says…(crying) there's nothing we can do to stop this…

911 Operator: Ma'am I need you to hide until the police arrive. But first, you MUST give me your address.

Woman: (frantic) Oh no…oh no, he's coming…he knows I'm on the phone!

911 Operator: Is there somewhere you can hide?

(long pause)

911 Operator: Ma'am? Hello!?

Woman: *(faint)* I'm s-sorry…I'm didn't mean to…please…

911 Operator: Hello?! Is the intruder in the room with you?!

Woman: *(crying)* Please don't do this…please, I'm sorry, I'm so sorry, Tommy…(static)….no! NO! LET ME GO! NOT THAT! PLEASE, OH GOD, PLEASE, NOT THAT —

(Unknown noise)

(Silence)

911 Operator: Ma'am!? HELLO!?

(static)

911 Operator: Is someone there?!

Unknown Male: Hehehehehe…

The First Five Years

Chapter 0

The man with the plastic grin still haunts me. I can picture him perfectly in my mind's eye. I can smell him. I can even hear him. I can hear that toxic laugh of his. I feel if I were to ever gaze into his eyes again, I would go blind. He is the most poisonous being to ever walk the earth. He is the hell on my shoulders and the thunder that follows.

I should back up.

Words…that's what I'm here to offer. Words. Explanations. Answers. But don't expect to find reason here. No…reason left me many years ago. And so I give you words. Words to formulate and shape your own conclusions. But there's something we should agree on and I'll just get that out of the way right now: words can't give justice to the hell that monster put me through. And yet here I am, writing down words with hands not quite steady. I don't even know where to begin.

Looking back on my life, I feel myself growing claustrophobic. It's like walking down a long hallway with rooms filled with memories. Each time I reach a doorway and peer inside, I'm greeted with fear and horror that leap out at me with jagged teeth.

And this hallway is endless and I am left alone to trod down it.

I poured myself a generous drink before writing this and I'm quickly discovering I'm going to need another. But I have to get this out. It has hovered over my soul like a crow, its sharp beak striking down and tearing away pieces of myself. Will this help? I don't know. I pray it will.

My name is Jack Williams. I have a sister, Katie. She's three years older than me. Growing up, she was my protector. A shoulder to cry on. Someone to share sadness and joy with. We were close—very close—and I love her fiercely. My father, Michael, was married to my mother, Penny. They were wonderful parents. The best a kid could ask for. Strong, loving, and supportive. They encouraged my sister and me to follow our dreams and did their best to make sure we had the structure to achieve them. I owe them my life in more ways than one.

My dad, who everyone called Mike, worked at the bank. He was a businessman in every sense of the word. He liked schedules, planning, preparation, and professionalism. He took his coffee black and his eggs over easy. He wore the same cologne for twenty-five years and bought a new tie every six months. When we went on family vacations, he made the arrangements well ahead of time, paid all the expenses, and made a little countdown calendar a week before the trip. He told us this was part of the fun—the anticipation we felt before the vacation. He loved his family. He loved us. It was hard to remember a time when he didn't have a smile on his lips. He wasn't a strict father, but he lived by a moral code: the American Dream. He always told us to work hard, respect others, and tuck your shirt in. If you remembered to do that, everything else was apple pie and Sunday Night Baseball.

My mother, Penny, was his constant support. She was a quiet woman but filled with warmth. Submissive, but outspoken when she needed to be. She loved my father but was always the first to correct him when he got bent out of shape (which wasn't much, but hey, it happens). I think my father really respected that. I think it's what really glued them together. When he left for work, my mother would send us off to school and then teach a yoga class in the basement of our house. After two years of redesigning and remodeling, she had converted it into a studio in which she could work. It pumped in the extra income to elevate our family into the middle class. Lazy is not ever a word I'd use to describe my mom. When we came home from school, she would usually be finishing up her final class for the day. She'd make us a snack, ask how school was, and then start preparing dinner. That was something she firmly believed in. Having a home cooked meal together with her family.

Looking back, we really were the poster family for the American Way. We lived in a small residential neighborhood lined with neat little houses all bordering the road like soldiers standing at attention. Our house was at the end of the cul-de-sac, the last of the troops staring down the barrel of the long street. It was a gentle community, friendly and rhythmic. Husbands went to work, kids went to school, and mothers made it all happen without flaw. There were cookouts in the summer and Christmas caroling in the winter. Everyone mowed their lawn on Saturday, drank beer during the evenings, and went to church on Sunday. And that routine was practically sacred in our neighborhood.

Our house, the lone soldier at the end of the street, had a pool in the backyard and a tall, white fence around the border of our lawn. The Murphys were the only other family on the street that had a pool (and they weren't quite as well off as us) so we usually had an annual pool party on the Fourth of July. Because that's just the kind of community we were.

You're probably reading this and going, "Yeah, ok, so what? Who cares?"

I'm laying this all out for you because it's important to know exactly the kind of life we lived. Not just my family but the neighboring families, as well. We were a cozy, comfortable, happy bunch of people living life one sunrise at a time. Tragedy was just something that happened on TV. We weren't equipped to deal with confrontation and horror.

And that's why we all suffered like we did.

For five years, we suffered.

And it all started when someone arrived on our quiet street, bringing hell with him.

His name was Tommy Taffy.

Chapter 1 —1995

I sat at the empty dinner table, watching my mom bustle around the kitchen. I idly kicked my legs, trying to ignore the rumble in my stomach. Katie was helping Mom cut vegetables and my dad was preparing a plate a meat for the grill. I watched him mold the last hamburger patty and toss it onto the stacked plate to join the others. I knew that when he went out back to fire up the grill, he expected me to follow with a beer in hand. Dad always drank beer while he grilled and I always watched, slightly in awe. Even though I was only six, sometimes he'd let me take a sip if my mom wasn't looking. I didn't like the taste, but I always drank a little if he offered. Dad said that was how I'd grow hair on my chest.

"Ok, I think these bad boys are ready to go," Dad announced, picking up the plate of burgers.

I knew this was my cue and so I slid off my chair and went to the fridge. I pulled the door open and was momentarily engulfed in a rolling fog. I dug out a cold bottle and cradled it in both hands like it was a precious treasure.

"Don't forget the cheese," Mom said, putting her knife down.

Katie, who had recently turned nine, looked over her shoulder at Dad and me. "Can we toast the buns? It's so yummy like that."

"I'll toast your buns if those veggies aren't ready by the time these burgers are," Dad laughed, scooping a spatula out of the drawer.

Katie giggled and shook her head. "Don't be a weirdo, Dad. Here, take the buns out and put them on the grill, please." She picked up the bag of buns and dumped them on top of the plate of burgers.

Dad rolled his eyes. "Oh great, now they're contaminated."

"They're in plastic, though," I piped up, fingers growing cold around the bottle of beer.

Mom nodded approvingly at me. "He knows, Jack, he's just being difficult tonight."

"As opposed to any other night?" Dad chuckled.

My mom pointed her knife at him. "Good point. Now get your buns out there and grill those patties before your son freezes his fingers off."

"Yes, dear, whatever you say, dear," Dad said, tipping me a wink. A smile cracked the corner of my mother's lips as she turned back to the vegetables.

And that's when a knock came at the front door.

We all froze, exchanging looks. *I didn't expect anyone, did you? No? Then who could it be?*

"I'll get it," Dad said, placing the plate of burgers down on the kitchen table. My stomach groaned at this annoying delay, and I set my dad's beer next to the pile of meat.

"It's probably Charlie asking to borrow the mower again," Dad said, going to the door.

But when he opened it, it wasn't Charlie. I couldn't see who the guest was because my dad blocked him from view, but I could hear him. His voice was friendly and enthusiastic and it rippled inside for all of us to hear.

"Hi! I'm Tommy Taffy!"

My dad didn't move, his frame still blocking my sight, "Can...can I help you with something?"

"I'd like to come in if that's ok?" the stranger said, his voice bubbly. And without warning, the man stepped inside, pushing my father aside. He slammed the door behind him, leaving a confused look on my dad's face at this act of unwelcome rudeness.

"Hi, gang!" the man said, raising a hand to us.

Something like unease washed through me then at the sight of the unexpected guest. It was a twist in my stomach and a tightening in my throat as my eyes goggled at his features.

He was about six foot and had blond hair. He was wearing pants and a white T-shirt that read *HI!* in a red cartoon font. But it was his face that caused the unease. Something was wrong with his face. His mouth was twisted into a smile, but instead of teeth, there was just a strip of unbroken white like he was wearing a mouth guard. His nose was wrong, too. It was just a small nub rising out of the middle of his face, devoid of nostrils. And his eyes...his eyes practically glowed electric blue, twin moons of sparkling, brilliant color.

As I breathlessly took in this strange, eerie man, I noticed something else about him. His skin was perfect and completely flawless. There wasn't a single pore or blemish on him anywhere. The smooth pink was almost creamy like soft plastic. He had no fingernails, no hair on his arms or legs, and I couldn't help but draw comparisons to my sister's Ken doll.

Dad composed himself and placed a firm hand on the man's shoulder. "Hey, pal, you can't just come barging into our home.

If you need something, I'd be more than happy to help, but let's step back outside, ok?"

The bizarre man, Tommy, looked at my father's hand resting on his shoulder and then up into my father's eyes. Something pulsed in those pearls of blue and Tommy's smile tightened.

"No need for alarm," he said calmly, "I just thought I'd come stay with you for a while."

"Mike?" My mom asked, abandoning her station at the counter, concern written across her face. "Who is this?"

The man turned to her. "I'm Tommy Taffy! And I've come to live here!"

My dad firmed his grip on the man's shoulder, all signs of goodwill disappearing. "Look, buddy, this isn't funny. I'm going to have to ask you to leave. Right now."

Tommy shook his head, still smiling. "Leave? But I only just got here."

My sister slid to my mom's side. "Why does he look so weird?" she whispered. "What's wrong with him?"

Tommy's eyes locked with hers and he spread his arms. "Oh, sweetie, it isn't nice to call people weird."

"Come on," Dad said, pulling Tommy to the door. "It's time to go. Don't make me call the police."

"The police?" Tommy said, allowing himself to be led back to the door. "Why would you call the police? I haven't done anything, have I?"

"You're trespassing," Dad said, "and interrupting dinner with my family."

Tommy, still smiling, answered coolly, "You don't want to invite me to stay?"

"No," Dad said reaching for the door. "I want you to leave."

Suddenly, like lightning, Tommy grabbed my father by the

throat and slammed him against the front door. The impact was like thunder in my ears and I jumped, the pit of my stomach giving out. Mom gasped and Katie let out a squeal of fear, clutching Mom's arm.

Dad sputtered in shock as Tommy's grip tightened around his throat. "Hey, what's the big idea!? What are you doing!?"

Tommy leaned in close, his voice like burning silk. "I think you should invite me to stay for dinner. Wouldn't that be the polite thing to do?"

"I'm calling the police!" My mother shrieked, eyes wide.

Tommy, still gripping my father around the throat, shot a look over his shoulder at her. "If you move, I'll break his neck."

Mom's face went white and she remained in place, protectively wrapping her arms around Katie. I just stood in isolation, fear ripping through me. I had never seen anyone hurt my dad like this and it shattered the shield I had always thought was there.

"Now," Tommy said, turning back to my dad, "are we going to have a problem?"

I saw something change in my father's eyes and a look entered them that I had never seen before. It was a mixture of fear and anger, a rising tide of emotion that spread across his face. Tommy seemed to sense the change and only had a split second to react before my dad punched the intruder in the face.

The blow glanced off the side of Tommy's head as he jerked away, my dad's knuckles crunching into Tommy's ear. Without pause, Dad brought his other fist up, aiming another blow beneath the grip around his throat.

This time, Tommy dodged it and released my dad, taking a few steps back into safety.

"Mike!" my mom screamed, the violence erupting panic in

her. Katie had started to cry and I just stood there like a ghost, paralyzed.

Dad rubbed his throat and coughed, baring his fists again, preparing for another strike if necessary.

Tommy shook his head, chuckling, "Hehehehe..."

"Get out of my house," Dad growled. "Get out RIGHT NOW!"

"It's never easy in the beginning," Tommy said softly, "but you all learn eventually. One way or another."

Dad took a step toward Tommy and cocked his fist back, but this time he didn't have the chance to follow through. Tommy sprang forward with alarming speed and ducked low, plowing an elbow into my dad's chest hard enough to knock him to the floor, the air leaving his lungs in a painful gasp.

Katie screamed and buried her face in my mother's side as Tommy leaned down and picked up my dad by the hair. Without pause, he threw him into the wall with terrifying strength. My dad crunched against the hard surface and went sprawling to the floor once again. As he tried to stand, Tommy was back at his side. Effortlessly, he bent down and picked up my dad with one hand lifting him off his feet and then slammed his body violently back to the ground.

Gasping and dazed, Dad tried to get to his feet, but Tommy kicked him viciously in the stomach, dropping him like a sack of sand.

Smiling, Tommy leaned down. "Don't make this harder than it has to be. It's not worth it in the long run. And let me assure you, Michael, it's going to be a long run."

Breaking from her trance, Mom dashed for the phone hanging on the kitchen wall. Tommy calmly turned to her as she practically crashed into the wall, hands fumbling for the receiver, fingers tangling in the long cord.

Instead of stopping her, Tommy walked to my side and looked down at me. I felt a numb kind of dizziness pour over me as I stared up at this terrifying man, his perfect features shining down at me, his eyes like cobalt spotlights.

"Don't be afraid," Tommy said softly, smiling down into my pale face. And then he spun me around by the shoulders and pressed my back against his body, his strong hands resting on my shoulders. He reached down and took one of my hands, his fingers gripping my thumb.

"Penny," he called gently to my mom, "oh, Penny, I wouldn't do that."

My mom, one hand on the receiver, looked over at us and her eyes bugged out of her head, her mouth working silently. She looked into my eyes and I saw terror engulf her as she realized this monster had her son.

"Put the phone down, Penny," Tommy instructed.

Mom sputtered, frozen.

Tommy gripped my thumb. "If you don't put it down in three seconds, I'm going to break his finger."

"NO!" my mother screamed, slamming the phone back onto the wall. "No, don't hurt him!"

Tommy released my thumb but kept his hands planted firmly on my shoulders. He rustled my hair and I felt sick.

"Good girl. See? We're starting to learn how things work," Tommy said smoothly. "Now, why don't we all go into the living room and calm down a little bit."

"Let him go," Mom croaked. "You let Jack go right now!"

I stifled a cry as Tommy ran his hands gently over my face

and down my arms, his touch like cold velvet sprouting goose-bumps along my skin.

"There's no need for hysterics," Tommy instructed. "Let's just all take a breath and go sit down on the couch. There are some things we need to go over."

Dad was slowly crawling to his feet, a labored, pained look on his face. "Just leave…us…alone…please…"

Tommy shook his head, sighing, "Haven't you gotten it through your head yet? I'm not going anywhere and the sooner we all understand that the sooner we can stop all this unnecessary drama. Now, everyone go sit down on the couch. Please."

No one moved. The air cracked with violent tension.

Tommy's voice hardened and he pointed to Katie, addressing us all, "If you don't do what I say, I'm going to hurt her very badly. Please don't make me."

I heard my mom suck in a harsh breath between her teeth as Tommy's threat splintered our resilience. Instantly, she went to Katie and wrapped her arms around her, guiding them both to the couch. They sat down, tears running down their cheeks.

"Good," Tommy said. He turned to my dad. "Michael?"

Slowly, my dad complied and went to sit next to my mother and sister. His eyes were hard and full of fury, but there was also a very real fear in them now.

"It's going to be ok, people!" Tommy suddenly laughed, his hands still on my shoulders. I felt his body rock against me, my shoulders pressed against his stomach.

And that's when the phone rang.

We all looked at each other as the familiar jingle echoed through the now silent house. We all waited, unsure what to do. My heart was crashing into my chest and I kept expecting to wake up.

Tommy suddenly pushed me forward, his voice cool and commanding. "Go ahead, Jack. Answer the phone."

I stood frozen, staring at my mom and dad, eyes wide and unsure. I felt like I was going to pee myself.

"Go on," Tommy instructed, "but remember: If you say anything naughty, it's not going to be pleasant for your sister."

"Go ahead, son," my dad said, his voice shaking.

I slowly walked to the phone like I was in a dream. The plastic yellow brick continued to sing on the wall.

I reached up and answered, pressing it to my ear in a death grip.

"H-hello?" I croaked.

For a second there was nothing but an odd static…and then a voice filled my head, a soft, but strained male voice that trickled in through the receiver like a summer wind.

"Let me speak to Tommy."

I licked my lips and looked over at the strange, doll-like man. I extended the phone to him, hands shaking.

"I-it's for you."

Something flickered across Tommy's face, but it was gone so quickly I couldn't decipher what it was. Slowly, he walked to my side and took the phone. Staring down at me, he put it to his ear and listened.

He said nothing for a couple seconds and I could faintly hear the voice on the other end speaking.

Tommy's face never changed, but he slowly shook his head. "Hehehehe…" And then he hung up.

"Who was that!? What was that all about!?" Dad cried from the couch. "What is going on!? Who ARE you!?"

Tommy ignored him. Whatever the call had been about didn't seem to have any lasting effect on him. He placed a hand on the back of my neck and guided me toward the living room where my family waited, tense and afraid.

My mother held her arms out to me, but Tommy didn't let me go. Instead, he took us to the big overstuffed chair that sat opposite the couch. Smiling, he sat down and pulled me up onto his lap. My hands balled into fists, terrified and shaking. I didn't like this man, didn't like the way he looked or talked to us. I didn't like how he had beaten my dad, breaking the calm Saturday afternoon with shocking violence. And I especially didn't like sitting on his lap, a worm of wriggling unease coiling through my stomach.

Tommy, sensing my fear, placed a hand on my leg and stroked the back of my head. "Easy, champ, just relax. We all need to relax."

"Get your hands off of him," Dad growled, trembling where he sat.

Tommy gave him an annoyed look. "Calm down, Michael. Mike. Can I call you Mike? I think I will, it's more familiar..." He traced a finger down my cheek, causing me to bristle. "More intimate. Now, all I want is to sit here and talk this out like rational people. Can we all do that? Yes? Let's all nod our heads, ok? Great."

"Please don't hurt Jack," Katie cried, meeting my eyes and exchanging a look of sibling comfort.

Tommy looked taken back. "Hurt him? Dear girl, that's the last thing I want to do. You and sweet Jack are the whole reason I'm here!"

"What are you talking about?" Mom asked. "Just what do you want with us?"

Tommy wrapped his arms around me and laced his fingers

across my stomach. He perched his chin on my shoulder and stared at my parents. "I'm here to help you raise them."

My parents exchanged an uneasy look before my father shook his head. "We don't want your help. We don't need it. We're doing just fine, now please…please would you just leave us in peace?…I'm begging you…"

Tommy raised his head, voice hardening, "Mike, if you ask me to leave one more time I can't promise I'll remain so composed."

Dad stared pleadingly at Tommy but kept his mouth closed.

"There's a couple rules I want to go over," Tommy announced. I could feel his breath on the top of my head and it felt like a poisonous cloud descending over me. I looked to my sister for comfort and she held my eyes, lip quivering.

It's ok, we're going to be ok, they said. I wasn't sure I believed her.

"First off," Tommy continued, "Let's not get any wild ideas about the police. We don't need them. We're going to be just fine here…together. If one of you tries to call again…" he met my parent's panicked eyes, "and I'm mostly speaking to you two, but if ANY of you try to call the police then I'm afraid I'm going to have to take drastic measures. One of you will have to be punished. So please, don't make me do that; I don't want to do that. I want us all to get along and be one happy family, ok?"

"This is crazy," Dad muttered, shaking his head in disbelief.

Tommy suddenly reached down and jerked my hand up, holding it out for all to see. He gripped my thumb and I cried out in fear, babbling, crying for my parents.

"Do I need to break it?" Tommy said loudly. "Is that what I need to do for you all to understand that you're not in control anymore?"

"No! No, please don't hurt him. PLEASE!" Mom cried, half standing. Katie held my eyes whispering silent words of comfort to me, tears running down her cheeks. I felt myself crying, terrified that this monster would at any second break my thumb. The anticipation was agony as Tommy glared at my parents, my finger hostage in his grip.

"Mike?" Tommy said, raising his eyebrows, "Well?"

"I'm sorry," Dad said quickly, "Please don't hurt him. I'm sorry...you're the boss, ok?"

Tommy dropped my finger and I quickly clutched it to my chest, trembling. I wanted to run to my mom, fall into the protection of her arms, but I didn't dare.

"Boss?" Tommy said, rolling the word around in his mouth. "No...no I don't like that. I'm not your boss." He sighed and massaged the side of his head with two fingers. "You people still aren't getting it. I'm here to help you. I'm here to help you raise your two beautiful children. I'm not your boss, your master, or anything of the sort. I'm like another parent. And as a parent, I have rules that need to be followed. Simple, easy rules." He pointed to Katie. "Do you remember the first rule?"

Katie jumped at being addressed and then nodded, "We can't call the police."

"We don't need the police," Tommy said. "Good memory. I'm really proud of you, Katie. I know this is probably really confusing and frightening for you, but I'm not a bad guy. I'm going to help you. I'm going to help you grow up to be a beautiful, smart, successful woman."

"O-ok," Katie responded, not quite sure how else to answer. I looked at my family longingly from my prison on Tommy's lap.

"Excuse me," I dared, "Can I please go sit with my mom and dad?"

Tommy looked down at me, positively beaming, "Well, well, look at the manners of this young man. Of course, you can, champ. But only because you asked so nicely." But before he let me go, Tommy leaned down and kissed the side of my head.

"Good boy," he whispered in my ear.

His voice felt like a snake slithering into my ear and I scrubbed it away as I slid off his lap and practically ran into my mother's arms. She sighed with worried relief and hugged me to her chest, kissing the top of my head and squeezing me close.

Tommy clapped his hands together bringing our attention back to him. "Now that we're all a little calmer, let's finish going over the new rules, ok?"

We all said nothing, a jury of silenced peers.

"You probably shouldn't talk to people about me," Tommy continued. "It just wouldn't be right. During my time here I'll keep to the confines of this house while you all go about your day. But know this...if you do happen to confess to another about my presence here..." he smiled, shaking his head, "boy, it'll get nasty. And if you think you can outsmart me or try to escape...well...that would be your loss. Why abandon such a wonderful home? Why give up such a pleasant life? I can't stress this enough. I'm here to help. So just live life like you normally would, avoid the police, don't run your mouth to your friends or co-workers, and we'll all get along fine."

He raised a finger. "One last thing: if I tell you to do something, you need to do it. It's for your own good. Every person comes across tests in their lives. Tests that determine the type of person they are or will be. Endure these and you will come out a better person." He looked at my parents. "And if either of you try something, if you try to get rid of me before my time here is done...well...it will be your children that suffer. Remember that when you get the urge to call the police or friends. Remember that if you confess to them, I'll know. And before anyone can do anything, it will be the little ones that pay the price. Ok? There's a lot of fingers between the two of them and I can assure you...that is just the tip of a very deep and dark iceberg."

"Whatever you want," Dad said, his face a grim sheet of stone. "It's whatever you want. We won't say anything so long as you don't harm the children."

Tommy nodded approvingly. "Wonderful to have your consent, Mike. Penny? Penny, you look rather sick. Are you ok? Do you understand what I just said? Penny, nod if you understand."

Mom swallowed hard and then nodded.

"Can you say it, Penny?" Tommy goaded, "can you tell me you understand?"

"I understand," Mom croaked.

Tommy winked at her. "Oh, you're going to be a fun nut to crack."

"Why are you doing this?" Katie suddenly asked and we all froze.

But Tommy just smiled and outstretched his hand to her. "Come here, child." Katie shrank into the couch but Tommy waved his hand insistently, "Come on, it's ok. I'm not going to hurt you. The hurting is done now."

I reached out and gripped Katie's hand, silently begging her not to go, but she slid from my sweaty grasp and slowly walked over to stand in front of Tommy. I could feel my mother tense against me, her breath hitching in her chest.

Tommy leaned forward in his chair and placed his elbows on

his knees so he was staring into my sister's eyes. "How old are you, Katie?"

Katie looked back at us on the couch before answering, "Nine. I'm nine."

Tommy nodded, smiling warmly. He reached out and tucked a strand of hair behind her ear. "So young still. So innocent. What a blessing you are to this family. Do you know that? That you're a blessing?"

Katie shook her head, hands behind her back.

Tommy placed an open palm against her cheek. "You're going to break a lot of boys' hearts, I think. With eyes like those..."

"Don't talk to her like that," Dad growled, fists clenched so hard his knuckles turned white. "Please...Tommy...she's just a child."

Tommy's eyes fluttered across Katie's face and I saw his tongue slither out and wet his lips. "Yes...just a child...hehehehe..."

"Come back here, Katie," I pleaded. "Come sit next to me."

Tommy sat back in his chair as Katie returned to her place by my side, our hands finding one another. I felt a little better with her back next to me away from the strange intruder.

Tommy watched us and smiled approvingly. "Do you love your sister, Jack?"

I gripped Katie's hand tighter. "Yes."

Tommy exhaled, "Mmmm...good...that's good to hear. You should love your family. You only get one."

Mom shifted on the couch, her voice strained. "So...so what now?"

Tommy snapped his eyes over to her. "Well, from what I've gathered, you all were about to make dinner, yes?"

"Dad was going to grill some burgers," I said quietly, eyes on the floor.

Tommy clapped his hands together. "Great! Well…carry on, don't let me stop you. I know this interruption in your evening has probably made you all very hungry."

We didn't move. Food was the last thing I wanted right now. My stomach felt like a pit filled with sloshing muck. My little world had been so severely shaken that I felt sick, bile rising in the back of my throat. I glanced at Dad, at his wounds. A purple bruise was beginning to blossom along the side of his face like a flower in the spring sunlight. He was wringing his hands together and staring at the tips of his fingers. He looked unsure, scared, and most of all, he looked pained. And that terrified me.

"Come on, come on," Tommy said, standing and waving at us, "no need to look so glum. It's a beautiful day out and I don't want to spoil your evening plans. Come on, up we go!"

We rose as one, casting glances at one another. My mother gripped my shoulder with an iron grasp like she was afraid I would suddenly vanish. Katie was at my side holding my hand. I was glad for it, glad for some semblance of comfort. I felt like crying but dared not to. Something told me that would upset this strange man with the smooth face. Tommy Taffy.

"Jack, come out with me," Dad said, motioning toward the kitchen. "Help me grill the burgers. Katie, stay with your mother."

"That's better!" Tommy said cheerily, crossing his arms and watching us disperse back to our stations.

I stayed next to Dad, his hand guiding me to the kitchen table. He scooped up the plate of abandoned, uncooked meat and miserably went to the back door. I snatched the sweating bottle of beer from its lonely spot and followed. I cast a look over my shoulder at Mom and Katie and my sister gave me a sad little wave. For whatever reason, it felt like it was a good-bye. I bit my lip as tears once again threatened to erupt from my eyes, but I managed to bravely hold them back.

“Let’s go, Jackie,” Dad said, pushing the back door open and stepping out onto the patio.

The sunlight spread its luminous rays down upon us like the warm hands of a caring mother. Fingers of light stroked my face as the door snapped closed behind me.

Our backyard was bordered by a tall white fence closing us off from the woods behind the house. Since we were at the end of the street, there were no curious neighbors to hear us. The patio was a concrete slab that held a glass table and an array of chairs. An umbrella jutted from the center of the table like a flag its green cloth extending out like a forest canopy. Beyond the patio was our pool and then a swatch of grass; it was nothing to brag about but enough space for Dad and me to throw the baseball.

Dad set the plate of burgers down on the grill’s arm and bent to switch on the gas. I stood watching him, clutching his beer in both hands. There were so many things I wanted, needed, to ask him, but I felt like silence better suited the moment.

As Dad brought the grill to life, I heard the back door creak open. I turned and felt my stomach twist. Tommy walked towards us, grinning and shaking his head.

“What a great backyard, Mike, really. The pool is a wonderful touch. Bet it feels incredible during the summer, huh? On a hot day like today?”

Dad shifted his eyes and mumbled, “Uh, yeah, it’s great.”

"Do you like to swim, Jack?" Tommy asked, casually walking to my side. I saw my Dad follow him closely with his eyes.

I nodded, shifting the beer in my hands. "Yeah…so does Katie."

Tommy planted his hands on his hips. "Have you learned to swim?"

Again, I nodded, staring at my bare feet.

Tommy bounced his eyebrows. "Good, good. I guess that's one thing I won't have to teach you."

"Teach me?" I asked quietly. I still wasn't understanding who this man was or what his intentions were. My young mind spun with confusion. People didn't just barge into other people's houses. People didn't treat others like this. People didn't hurt my dad…

"There's a lot of lessons you must learn," Tommy plowed on, "important lessons about becoming a man, or in your sister's case, becoming a woman. Like I said inside, I'm going to help your parents make sure you both grow up to be successful, intelligent members of society. Isn't that great?"

"Jack," Dad interrupted, "I forgot the spatula. Can you grab it for me?"

I finally passed him the beer and turned to obey when Tommy's voice froze me.

"Mike? Didn't you forget something?"

My father looked up, alarmed, one hand clutching a limp burger.

Tommy rolled his fingers, "I didn't hear a 'please' in that sentence."

Dad blinked and then looked back at me, "Please Jack?"

Tommy smiled, "That's better. You have to lead by example, Mike. That's the most important thing a parent can go. Lead by example. Your kids are always watching, even when you think they aren't."

Dad tossed the patty onto the grill. "Sure." The meat sizzled and filled the empty hole of growing silence. I went inside with a tightness in my chest. I felt like I was dreaming, like this was some horrible bubble I was trapped in. I begged it to disperse, to free me from its walls of fear. The world felt different inside the bubble. It all looked the same, smelled the same, even tasted the same. But something had shifted, changed, and now dread had begun to fill the sphere surrounding my family.

"Jack?" Mom said, her voice shaking.

I realized I was standing in the doorway, unmoving. I shook the trance from my mind and looked at my mother. Her face was sickly pale and her eyes were bloodshot and wide. She was running on the edge of a knife, barely maintaining mental balance.

I went to the counter and picked up the spatula for Dad. Katie stood silently, watching me. Her fingers were stained with vegetable juice, the knife in her hand the murder weapon.

"Dad forgot this," I said, turning back to go.

"Jack?" Katie asked softly.

I turned, "Hm?"

Her face squished with worry before whispering, "Be careful." Her words sent chills down my back, our eyes meeting with mutual understanding.

Mom and Dad can't protect us right now.

I gave her a weak smile and crossed the kitchen. I opened the storm door and jumped out of the way before it could smack me in the face. I looked up at Dad and Tommy and felt a wave of new fear roll through me like fog in the early morning...

Tommy was gripping the back of my dad's neck, hard, and

whispering furiously into his ear. Their bodies were tense and I couldn't hear what was being said. Dad's back was to me, but I could see Tommy's face. It was twisted into a snarl, his blue eyes dangerous.

He looked sideways at me and immediately released my dad, his composure returning. "Ah, there he is. Come on, these bad boys are going to need to be flipped soon."

I shuffled over and looked up into Dad's eyes. They were brimming with tears and his jaw was locked, tendons standing out in his neck. Smoke wafted from the open grill and filled the evening air with familiar smells of summer. But there was nothing familiar about the way my father looked.

It was a look that stuck with me for a long, long time.

"Thank you, Jack," Dad finally said, taking the spatula without moving his head. He flipped the burgers, the meat sizzling loudly as flames engulfed them.

"You going to drink that?" Tommy asked my dad, pointing to the untouched beer next to the now empty plate of burgers.

"Not thirsty," Dad said quietly. His knuckles were white against the spatula.

"Go ahead and have some," Tommy encouraged. "I think you need to loosen up a little bit. It's the weekend; enjoy yourself!"

Dad picked up the beer and took a ghost of a sip before returning the bottle to its place. Tommy's face grew dark. He stared at my father, smoke rolling between them, my father's eyes trained on the cooking burgers.

Suddenly, Tommy closed his eyes and his too-smooth face broke into a smile. "What a day to be alive."

"Want a clean plate for the burgers?" I asked nervously. Dad nodded, but Tommy held up a hand, stopping me. He motioned for Dad to hand him the spatula. Slowly, my father handed it over, confusion melting his somber expression.

"I need to know you understand completely what kind of relationship we now have," Tommy said dangerously, all humor and cheer draining from his face.

"I understand," Dad growled.

Tommy shook his head, eyes twin slits, "No Mike, I don't think you do. And it's very important that we clear this up. Remember what I said about leading by example? You need to show your family that you're compliant. You need to change your attitude or you're going to make things very, very hard for everyone else."

Dad just stared at him and my heart thundered in my chest. I felt like I was watching two gunslingers sizing each other up, just like the cartoons I watched on Sunday morning before church.

"Hold out your hand, Mike," Tommy said darkly, his perfect lips a thin, white line.

"Why?" Dad asked, unmoving.

Tommy stepped closer to him, their noses almost touching. "Because I told you to."

Never breaking eye contact, my dad extended his hand, palm up.

Tommy's voice dropped to almost a whisper. "If you move your hand, I'm going to drown Jack in the pool. Do you understand?"

Some of the hardness left my father's eyes and he nodded, barely tilting his chin. I could see the blood draining from his face and again, I wanted to cry, paralyzed by the confrontation before me. Tommy scooped up a sizzling burger from the grill with the spatula, smoke rising from the cooked meat in waves that watered my eyes.

Slowly, he lowered it into my father's waiting hand.

Immediately, Dad's face went red. He clamped his jaw shut to extinguish a groan crawling up his throat. Burning hot grease dripped between his fingers and I saw his hand quiver as his skin cooked beneath the inferno.

A slow smile crept up Tommy's face as he watched the anguish ignite in my father's eyes. The seconds ticked by, the two of them silent, refusing to be the first to speak. My dad's face had taken on a sickly cherry color now and I saw sweat beading across his forehead. The hand hosting the burger was shaking violently and veins stood out on his arm.

"Stop it!" I cried suddenly, smacking the patty from my dad's hand. "It's burning him!"

Immediately, Dad sucked in a grateful breath and rubbed his hand vigorously against his pant leg, gasping. Tommy sniffed and the humor returned to his impossibly blue eyes. He looked at me and for a second I thought he was going to hit me, but instead, he ruffled my hair and went inside, leaving us both in pained shock.

"Dad?" I asked, the tears finally escaping. "Dad are you ok?"

My father gritted his teeth and clutched his hand, the skin an angry shade of crimson. "I'm ok, Jack. I'm ok. Everything is ok."

I shook my head, vision blurring, "No it's not! He hurt you! Why did he do that?!"

"Listen to me," Dad said, bent over, gripping my shoulder. "We need to be very careful around Tommy. If he asks you to do something, you need to do it. Otherwise, things could get very bad."

"Dad, you're scaring me," I sobbed, standing helplessly before him, tears streaming down my face like comets.

Emotion swelled across my dad's face and he embraced me in a hug. "We're going to get through this. I'm not going to let anything bad happen to you. Be brave."

I nodded miserably into his chest.

And that's when we heard a gunshot echo across the sky.

Dad tensed against me, his grip tightening around my shoulders. It had come from somewhere down the street. The blast faded and I felt my dad's heart drumming against my ear.

"What on earth…?" Dad whispered.

A split second later, we heard a distant scream. A woman. The shrill cry echoed again, a harsh, guttural sound full of fear that splintered the cooling air.

"Let's go inside," Dad said quietly.

"What's happening?" I asked, wiping my face.

Dad looked around, his voice low. "I don't know. I think that was Mrs. Murphy."

"Is she ok?" I asked dumbly, the scream now fading. It was replaced by gentle night bugs as evening bled across the sky.

"I don't know, Jack. Come on, inside."

He threw the burgers back onto the plate we had originally used and then I followed him into the house. The kitchen smelled of simmering vegetables and butter. Normally, it would have made my mouth water, but tonight it felt more like a disease trying to worm its way down my throat.

Tommy was sitting at the head of the dinner table, waiting for us. Katie and Mom were on either side of him, also seated. My mother's hands were folded tightly in front of her, eyes wide, staring across the table a Katie. My sister looked at us as we walked in and quickly motioned for me to sit next to her.

"Smells great doesn't it?" Tommy asked, addressing my father. Dad just placed the burgers on the table and pulled a chair out. Piles of steaming food lay before us, but hunger was an alien concept that we were all struggling with.

"Who wants a burger?" Tommy asked cheerily.

"Was that a gunshot?" Katie asked quietly. Dad snapped his eyes over to her and gave her a curt shake of the head. *Don't talk about that.*

Tommy looked at my sister, his face unreadable. Finally, he said softly, "Would you like a burger, Katie?"

Katie shook her head, a look of strained anguish peeling her lips down. "No! I'm not hungry! I don't want this! I don't want any of it! I want you to leave and stop hurting my dad!" The tears came next, great big diamonds down her flushed cheeks.

Wordlessly, Tommy slid a burger into a bun and placed it on Katie's plate. He then repeated the action for the rest of us, his face a blank slate.

"Honey, come sit with me," Mom said gently, scooting her chair out and reaching for Katie.

Tommy slammed his hand down on the table so hard that my water glass tipped over.

"She will stay EXACTLY where she is, Penny!" Tommy yelled, eyes flaring with blue lightning. "We are going to SIT here and enjoy this meal as a FAMILY!"

"You're scaring her!" Mom cried, clutching her hands to her chest. "Look at her, she's terrified!" Katie sat miserably in her spot, sobbing and rubbing her eyes. I reached out and patted her leg under the table. It was all I dared to do.

Tommy slowly stood up, his eyes blazing. "Well, if it's bothering you so much, maybe you shouldn't look at her."

"Stop, please, everyone…" Dad said weakly. But Katie just

cried harder and Tommy's face was positively burning with cold rage.

"Jack," Tommy said darkly, "pass me the mustard."

"I'm sorry!" My mother shrieked, "she's just scared and—"

"The mustard, Jack. NOW!" Tommy bellowed, extending a hand to me. Sniffling, terrified, I looked at my dad who just closed his eyes, and then handed Tommy the mustard.

Tommy walked behind my mother and placed the mustard bottle on top of her head, "When will you people learn to listen," he muttered darkly, "Why do you make me do things like this?"

He suddenly gripped my mother's ponytail and jerked her head back. Screaming, Mom flailed in a panic, but Tommy swatted her hands away like they were pesky flies. He upended the bottle of mustard and doused both her eyes with it. Dad exploded into a standing position as Mom went into agonized hysterics, kicking and thrashing in place as Tommy held her.

Tommy glared at my father, yelling over Mom's screams. "If you move, Katie gets it next! Or do you think you can stop me?" Dad went still, hands shaking, his face strained.

"No?" Tommy smiled, "Then sit DOWN!"

Dad obeyed, chest hitching, and gripped the edge of the table in helpless misery. Tommy smiled and slowly pressed his thumbs into Mom's eyes, rubbing the burning condiment deeper into her sockets. Katie had covered her face with her hands, trembling, feet pulled up into her chair. My lip trembled as I watched all this, tears flowing freely down my face. *Stop this, someone please, make him stop hurting her.*

"Penny! PENNY!" Tommy yelled into my mother's face. "Calm DOWN, Penny, it isn't that bad! You can make the pain stop! Do you want the pain to stop, Penny?"

"Yes, please GOD stop this!" Mom wept, yellow tears running down the sides of her face, thick trails of mustard extending from her eyes like tentacles.

"Are you ready to listen to me?" Tommy prodded, jerking my mom's ponytail in his grip.

"Yes. YES, PLEASE!" she shrieked.

"Then open your mouth," Tommy instructed. "Open it wide, Penny."

"Please, let her go..." Dad begged, unheard.

Tommy ignored him and unscrewed the top of the mustard bottle. Mom opened her mouth, spittle leaking from the corners of her lips. Tommy gripped my mother's hair again and then dumped the entire bottle into her mouth. Immediately, Mom sputtered and coughed, but Tommy jerked her head back violently, her mouth filling. It looked like a yellow marsh rising to the edges of the shore, a gurgling puddle of waste.

"Swallow it," Tommy chirped, "Swallow it all down, Penny."

Gagging, shaking, I watched as Mom clenched her throat muscles and forced the thick mustard down. She buckled once, threatening to vomit, but caught her breath at the last minute. Tommy chuckled and then looked directly at me.

"Can you pass the ketchup, Jack?"

Fresh tears welled in my mother's blazing eyes, a yellow film coating the top half of her face. Katie was still weeping next to me, buried in her own fear, and my father just stared at Tommy, his face so white you could cut snowflakes from his skin.

"Please, Tommy," I begged quietly, my eyes feeling thick and bloated. "Please...let her go..."

Tommy held my gaze for an endless amount of time and then finally pushed my mother's head forward, a small smile twisting his smooth lips. "Sure, Jack...anything for you, bud."

Mom gasped and blindly found her way to the sink, splashing cold water across her stinging eyes, hands shaking. Dad stood and went to her. He gently picked up a dishrag and helped her clear the remains of the mustard from her face.

Tommy sat back down at the head of the table and slowly looked around at the four of us. "You people sure do get wound up easily." I stared at my lap as Katie's cries finally began to diminish.

Suddenly, something heavy crashed into our front door causing us all to jump and momentarily forget our own misery. Tommy just casually turned his head looking almost bored.

A female voice screamed at us from the other side as she thudded on the sturdy wood. "Get out of there! Penny, Mike, get your kids and GO! Run! He's everywhere! He's hurting us! Oh God, he's HURTING US!"

Another gunshot echoed outside and the woman on the other side of the door screamed. Something huge thudded against the side of the house, shaking the foundation, and then the woman stopped screaming, her cries cut short. A third gunshot exploded outside and then I head someone yelling, a man. It sounded like Jason's dad from across the street.

"What is happening to us…?" Dad said, immobile next to my mom.

The phone began to ring. I jumped, despite all the noise, because now the source was coming from inside our house. I watched the yellow box dance on the wall, the color matching the mustard on my mother's face.

Through all of this, Tommy remained seated, an amused look plastered across his bizarre plastic features. He nodded to me and jerked a thumb over his shoulder.

"You going to get that?"

I slid from my seat, skirting a wide trail around Tommy, and reached for the phone. Trembling, I raised the receiver to my ear.

"Hello?"

At first, it was all distant static, but then a voice called to me through the distortion. It was the same voice as before. Eerily soft, yet strained.

"It's starting again."

And then the line filled with chirping static, growing so loud that I held the phone away from my ear, wincing. After a moment, the line went dead. I stared at the receiver for a second and then gently hung it back on the wall. I walked to my seat, staring at my feet.

"It was him again, wasn't it?" Tommy asked quietly. I said nothing, clamping my hands tightly together.

Tommy smiled. "Hehehehe..."

The evening fell into a state of stunned silence, shock and fear ebbing into each one of us to take root. The sun slowly dipped behind a graveyard of hills and bled a stunning painting across the sky. As the darkness snuck closer, I felt myself falling into an almost nightmarish fit of worry. I didn't like the night. I never had. I was afraid of it, afraid of what could be in it. Each night before I went to bed, I would don a pair of headphones. This was my security blanket, something my dad had thought of. If I couldn't hear the house settling or the chirp of night bugs, then the monsters would have no lifeline into my imagination. But now that Tommy was here, the night seemed ever more hostile, teeming with teeth and claws.

Tommy had reclined in the living room and stayed there for most of the evening. I noticed with unease that he had closed the curtains over the big bay window. It was like watching a prison door slam shut. My parents hovered around the kitchen, trying their best to mentally recover and put on a brave face for Katie and me. The two of us sat at the table, a forgotten stack of coloring books before us. I just stared at the floor, praying for this all to be over. Katie would occasionally shoot a look at Tommy who just smiled at her from the living room as he lounged comfortably on the couch.

At nine, Mom and Dad rounded us up for bed. Tommy watched us as we were ushered up the stairs to brush our teeth and change into our pajamas. I noticed that Dad had wrapped his hand in a white bandage and he kept it at his side. After I finished in the bathroom, I went to my room across the hall from Katie's and stood in the doorway. Katie went to her room and stopped, turning to look at me.

"Love you," she whispered before Mom gently guided her inside. Dad glanced over the balcony at Tommy and then came into my room. He turned off the light and helped me into bed. I rolled into my covers, the air conditioning humming from the vents like the cold breath of a dying iceberg.

Dad sat at the edge of my bed, his hands folded in front of him. I could tell he was heavy with thought, his hair falling across his eyes in a dark curtain. After a moment, he brushed it aside and turned to me.

"You ok, little man?"

"When is he going to leave?" I whispered, staring at the open door.

Dad gripped my leg over the covers. "I don't know. We all just need to be brave right now. Something is happening in our neighborhood that…that I don't really understand. But we're a family and we're going to get through this together. I will always do what's best for us. I don't want you to be afraid."

"He's so scary though," I breathed, pulling the blankets up to my chin.

Dad tried to smile. "He doesn't scare me, kid. He's just a bully. And bullies always get what's coming to them. He can't keep us hostage forever. Someone will say something. Until then, let's just stay safe, ok?"

Before I could answer, my heart jumped into my throat and my eyes went wide as they jerked over to the bedroom door.

Tommy stood watching us, a small smile dancing at the corners of his mouth. Dad looked up and I saw his face go white. Tommy said nothing. He curled a finger at my father, motioning to him.

Come.

Dad looked back at me, blinking furiously. He exhaled slowly and then grabbed my headphones from the nightstand. He gently slid them over my head, the severed cord just a tiny nub sticking from the side. Sometimes I liked to touch the exposed wire as I fell asleep, the simple motion lulling me into slumber.

Dad looked down at me and then kissed my forehead. I watched him stand and leave the room. Tommy threw me a wink before closing the door part way.

And so I waited for sleep. Begged for it. I just wanted to escape this hellish situation for a couple hours and forget about all the fear and pain. After a little while, my eyes wandered to the crack in my door. I saw Mom leave Katie's room and go down the hall to the master bedroom. Even with the headphones on, I heard the door slam shut. I jumped, clutching my blankets, the darkness pressing in on me.

Seconds grew into minutes and time seemed to slur before me. I was lost in the muffled silence of my padded headphones, blood pumping in my ears, heart bouncing in my chest. I waited...and waited...and waited...until I heard my parents begin to scream from their room. Horrible, piercing shrieks that echoed through the house.

I dove under my pillow, pressing the earpieces tight against my head and whimpered into the cotton. What was he doing to them? What could possibly make my father and mother scream like that? I prayed and I prayed and then I wept. The hours dragged their feet until the screaming finally stopped, leaving me alone with the darkness.

I don't know how long it was before I finally fell asleep.

But it didn't last.

Sometime during the long night, I stirred from my troubled slumber as something began to buzz in my ears. I rolled over, the headphones hot against my skin. Was I awake? I groaned softly as the buzzing grew and I realized it was static, white noise crackling like popcorn.

And then the voice spoke to me through the static like an echo.

"Tell me, Jackie...do you dream?"

My eyes snapped open and I clawed at the headphones, tearing them from my head. I lay panting, terrified, my mind spinning. What had just happened? How? I looked at the headphones in my hand like they would bite me, but something whispered to put them back on. It was a quiet voice from the back of my head guiding my thoughts.

Slowly, I slid the sweaty earpiece back over my head, the plastic band hugging my skull. The static was still there, idly waiting for me.

"I need you to remember something for me," the voice said again, almost desperate. **"Don't write it down, don't say**

it out loud, don't think about it until you absolutely need to. Remember this and remember it with furious urgency: six-six-three-five-eight-Rez."

And then the voice was gone, the strange reverb of the man's instructions lodging deep into my reeling mind. Six-six-three-five-eight-Rez? What did that mean? It sounded like nonsense, but for whatever reason, I felt it was important. I closed my eyes and repeated the strange pattern in my head until I could summon it on instinct.

When I opened my eyes again, Tommy was watching me from the crack in the door, his blue eyes glowing in the black.

"Hehehehehe..."

Chapter 2 —1996

A year passed. I don't think any of us expected Tommy to stick around for that long. But as time passed, each day compounding upon the previous, a very real dread settled over my family. After the first three months, I think we all knew Tommy wasn't going away anytime soon. And so we adjusted as best we could. It's scary how quickly you can become accustomed to misery. Instead of fearing it, you embrace it as something that's always been there waiting for you. When you wake up, when you go to bed, that awful feeling slips over you like your favorite shirt.

We did the best we could. Life marched on, the four of us living our lives around Tommy and his cruel ways. That first year we learned a lot about the bizarre intruder. He didn't like to be seen by outsiders, for one. Whenever my mom had yoga class in the basement, Tommy would melt into the shadows until it was over. Another thing was that he never ate or drank. During meals he would just sit there and watch us, smiling that smooth, eerie smile. Katie offered him something once, but Tommy just shook his head and patted her cheek.

The mental state of our family during that first year wavered greatly. It was mostly my parents who fluctuated. I don't know how they carried such a weight on their shoulders without breaking. When my father went to work he'd kiss us goodbye like he expected to come home to a house full of corpses. He would tell us to behave, listen to Mom, and stay safe. During the school year, Katie and I would leave shortly after. I didn't really have many friends at school so it was easy for me to keep my mouth shut about Tommy and what was happening at home. My teachers noticed the somber change in my personality though and asked a couple times if I was ok. I would just smile and tell them everything was great. Each time the lie escaped my lips, I would feel a sudden urge to scream at them, scream that nothing was great and that there was a monster living in my house. But I didn't. I kept my mouth shut, just like Tommy said.

The winter months came and went. Christmas was a dismal affair of false joy. But I give my parents a lot of credit because they tried...they really did. It was hard to feel genuine happiness though when their faces were so strained and hollow. Every smile felt false, every laugh a lie. It weighed heavily on me.

My own mind began to wonder if we would ever be free of Tommy. At that age, life seemed so much more infinite. I couldn't believe the police hadn't come and taken him away. But why would they? They had no reason to. They didn't even know about him because everyone kept their mouths shut. We didn't know how to handle confrontation like this. None of us did. Not my family, not the Murphys, not anyone else on the street. Because you see...something hadn't just changed in my family—it had affected the entire street. At that point, I didn't know exactly what it was...but I could feel it. Everything was quieter, more private. People stayed inside more. I barely saw my neighbors and the times I did, they would just hurry along with ghosts in their eyes. We all stopped talking to one another. The cookouts ceased, the Christmas parties, and even the morning church rush. It was as if everyone was afraid to leave their homes…or afraid of what would happen if they did.

And Tommy observed all this with cool silence. A lot of the time I could see him thinking, his mind spinning behind those shockingly blue eyes. It was as if he knew exactly what was happening all at once and knew that he was in complete control of the situation. During the evenings, Tommy would sit us all down in the living room and give us lessons on how to be good people. It was strange to say the least. His topics would range anywhere from loving your neighbor to the importance of honestly. Each time his knowledge and drawn-out talks would fluctuate from simple child logic to intense, philosophical discussion. It was weird; each night was a toss of the coin.

His acts of cruelty receded somewhat during those long winter months as well. I would still catch him whispering in my parent's ears, gripping them tightly, but for the most part he treated us like old friends. It made me sick, his smiling, almost loving pats on the head. He wasn't a part of this family and yet he acted like the most important member. But the danger never left his eyes. We all felt it. We knew that if any of us acted out, he would be swift with his punishment. Again, I don't know how my parents bore it all.

Winter melted into spring until finally, the hot summer arrived in all its blazing glory. It was during one of these scorching summer days that Tommy once again scarred our family. When, once again, we learned something terrible about our captor.

I was playing catch in the backyard of our house with my neighbor Jason Murphy. It was one of the few times I had seen him over the past year. Mom was teaching her yoga class in the basement and Jason's mom, Theresa, had brought him over to play with me.

The July heat burned down over us as I adjusted the glove in my hand and wiped sweat from my forehead. We had been tossing the baseball for about twenty minutes now and neither of us had said much. Jason looked exhausted and ragged. He was the same age as me, but his eyes looked five years older. His skin was pale and his hair hung in greasy strands across his forehead. Wordlessly, he tossed the ball to me.

"Want to go in the pool?" I finally asked, lobbing the ball back to him. Jason shook his head.

"Come on," I goaded, "you love going in the pool. You haven't been all summer."

Jason lowered his glove and sighed, "I don't have my suit."

I shrugged. "So go get it! Your house is just down the street. Come on!"

Jason looked up at me. "I don't want to go back to my house."

"Why?" I asked and wished I hadn't.

Jason looked at me for a long moment and I saw his shoulders slump. He looked at his feet and just shook his head, a frown plastered on his face.

"I don't like my house," he whispered. I went to him, tossing my glove aside. He looked up into my face and I saw fear as plain as the summer sun in his eyes.

I looked around the empty backyard and leaned in close. "Jason…is something bad happening at your house, too?"

He seemed to startle at that. "What do you mean?"

I licked the sweat off my lips. "Is there a man living with you?" I knew I wasn't supposed to talk about Tommy, knew I was wading into dangerous territory, but I couldn't help it.

After almost a year of solitude, I simply couldn't stand it anymore.

Jason's eyes welled up with tears and he slowly nodded, his lip trembling. "He's so mean to us..."

My chest felt like a deflated balloon, all the air rushing out of me in a strong gust. So my suspicions were confirmed. We weren't the only ones who had been suffering. The looks and changes in my neighborhood weren't just my imagination. In a sick kind of way, I almost felt relieved.

"I'm not supposed to talk about him," Jason whispered, looking nervously around.

"He's here, too," I said softly. "Almost a year now."

Again, Jason looked shocked. "What are you talking about, Jack? How is that possible? Don't be a dummy; he can't be in my house and yours."

I stepped closer, dropping my voice, urgency rising in my chest, "But he is!"

A noise caused us both to jump and we spun toward the back door. Katie, now ten, walked outside and over to the pool. She waved at us.

"You guys want to swim?" she asked, dropping her towel onto a chair. We both shook our heads. I wanted her to go away. I didn't want her knowing I had broken a cardinal rule of the house.

"He's here, too?" Jason asked her, a little louder than I would have liked. My heart sank. My cover had been blown.

Katie gave me a hard look and walked to our side. "Keep your voice down, stupid! We're not supposed to talk about that. Jack, what are you doing? Keep your mouth shut or you're going to get everyone in trouble."

Jason sagged, face desperate. "But what am I supposed to do?

He's always hurting my mom and dad. I don't think we're going to make it. I can see it on my parents' faces. When he showed up, Dad tried to shoot him, but he missed. I can't stop thinking about that. About what would have happened if his aim had been a little better. Maybe all of this wouldn't have happened, you know? And Mom…she's a mess. She can barely get up in the morning. I'm surprised she's doing yoga right now. Of course…it wasn't her idea. She was forced to come. He didn't like her attitude and told her to get out of the house for a little bit." Jason looked into both our faces. "How is it here? Is he mean to you?"

Katie and I exchanged looks and my sister bit her lip before answering quietly, "Sometimes. He creeps me out and I keep hoping I'll wake up and he'll be gone. But so far, no luck. When he first arrived he was really nasty. But not so much anymore. Not for a while anyway. But he scares me…he scares me so bad. Sometimes I'll wake up in the middle of the night and he'll just be standing there, watching me. He won't move, won't say anything at all. He'll just stand over me, smiling, those eyes so bright in the darkness…I get nightmares all the time now."

Suddenly, we all jumped as the back door creaked open once again. My sister's mouth snapped shut so hard her teeth clacked.

"There you all are," Tommy said, stepping out onto the patio. "I've been looking for you."

Jason's eyes went wide and he swallowed hard in disbelief.

Tommy smiled at him, "Hello, Jason. Playing catch with Jack?"

Jason nodded, eyes still bugging out of his skull.

Tommy grinned. "That's wonderful. It's so good to see you kids having fun. But I need you to come over here for a second.

I need to ask you something very important before the ladies are done with their class."

He waved us over from across the pool and we sullenly obeyed, dragging our feet through the grass and onto the concrete. Tommy sat down on the edge of the pool, crossing his legs and patting the pavement next to him. We joined him and formed a circle, the three of us exchanging nervous looks.

Tommy folded his hands in front of him, the edge of the house casting shadows across the four of us. Despite the heat, Tommy showed no sign that it bothered him. The rest of us mopped sweat from our faces and I could feel the back of my shirt sticking to my skin. I tugged at it uncomfortably as we waited for Tommy to speak.

"I have something I need to ask you two," Tommy said calmly to Katie and me. "And I need you to be completely honest." My sister and I exchanged a worried look and shifted on the concrete.

Tommy reached behind his back and pulled something out of his waistband. He placed it on the ground in front of us and waited for a reaction.

It was a revolver.

Tommy folded his hands in front of him again, his tone never changing, "Do either of you know when or how your father got this?"

I bit my lip and quickly shook my head. "No, I've never seen it before. I didn't even know Dad had a gun."

Tommy looked at Katie. "And you?" Katie shook her head vigorously.

"You wouldn't lie to me, would you? We've talked about how bad it is to lie," Tommy pressed. "You're positive you've never seen this gun before?"

"We haven't," Katie urged, "we promise."

"So what you're telling me," Tommy said dangerously, "is that you have no idea what this is?"

"It's a gun," Jason said dumbly, eager to please.

Tommy snapped his head to Jason. "I know what it is, Jason. Your father certainly knows what it is, too." Jason quickly dropped his eyes.

"We don't know, I'm sorry," I said quietly. I didn't like the gun. It scared me.

Still sitting, Tommy dug into his pocket and pulled out a handful of bullets. He dumped them next to the pistol.

"I found these in the wheel. He loaded it and hid it in his closet. That's very, very dangerous. Especially with children in the house. What if one of you had found it? What if you had accidentally fired it? How tragic would that have been?"

We said nothing. I would never go hunting in my parents closet for anything. And even if I had, I certainly wouldn't have touched it. I wanted Tommy to put it away, to put it back where he had found it and just leave us alone.

"Has your father taught you about gun safety?" Tommy continued, leaning into the circle. "Has he explained how dangerous they are?"

"We know they're bad," Katie said bravely, "and we would never play with them. That's adult stuff."

"That's good," Tommy said, "that's very good. But since your father has neglected his duty to educate you, I feel that it's my responsibility to do so."

He reached down and picked up the gun, releasing the cylinder to reveal five empty chambers. He spun the wheel.

Clickclickclickclickclick...

Tommy reached down and picked up a single bullet and

placed it into one of the chambers. Then he spun the wheel again.

Clickclickclickclickclick...

I felt my throat tighten and I pulled at the back of my shirt, freeing it from my skin. Jason wiped sweat from his eyes and looked like he wanted to go home.

Tommy snapped the cylinder closed and cocked the hammer back. It was one of the scariest sounds I had ever heard.

Tommy handed it to Katie. "Put this to your head and pull the trigger."

Our eyes went wide and I saw my sister recoil from the pistol. She shook her head, "No, Tommy, I don't want to. You...you just put a bullet in there."

Tommy's eyes went dark. "How else is your father going to learn?"

"Please don't make her do this," I begged, my voice a hissing plea.

Tommy shoved the gun into Katie's hands. "Do it. There's only one bullet in the chamber. Your chances are pretty good."

Trembling, Katie took the gun. She looked at Jason and me, terrified. We just stared at her, hostages of the same misfortune. Surely Tommy didn't actually mean for her to go through with this. He would stop her before she pulled the trigger...he had to.

"Put it to your head like this," Tommy said, placing his fingers to his temple, "and pull the trigger."

"P-please," Katie cried, tears filling her eyes.

"It's going to be ok," Tommy smiled. "Now do it or I'm going to put four more in and have your brother test his luck."

The barrel of the gun shook as Katie placed it to her head. Sobbing now, she squeezed her eyes shut, fingers wrapping around the trigger. Tommy would stop her now...any second...he couldn't let her do this...

Click.

We all gasped as Katie pulled the trigger and dry-fired into her own skull. Immediately, she pushed the pistol back into Tommy's hands, crying opening. A bronco galloped across my chest as I exhaled, panting and squeezing my sister's hand.

"Good girl," Tommy smiled. "That's a good girl." He opened the cylinder and slid another bullet in next to the one already loaded. My eyes went wide. No, no, no, no, please no....

Clickclickclickclickclick...

Tommy flicked his wrist and the cylinder closed. He passed the gun to me. "Your turn, Jack. Around the circle we go."

"No!" Katie cried, protectively gripping my hand, almost pulling me into her lap. "No that's enough! Don't make him do it!"

Tommy urged me to take the pistol, his eyes dancing with mine. "Do you want your sister to go again, Jack? No? Then take the gun."

I swathed my face with the collar of my shirt and picked up the pistol. It was heavy in my hands, almost as heavy as my thundering heart. I turned it around in my hands, my sweaty fingers curling around the grip.

"Go on," Tommy said quietly, "just like your brave sister."

Slowly, I brought it to my head, prayer flowing through me like a river. This wasn't happening, this couldn't be happening.

Someone stop this, don't make me pull the trigger.

I begged Dad to come home from work and walk out to see this scene of horror. He would put a stop to it, I knew he would.

But no one came and I felt the cold lips of the barrel kiss my wet skin just above the ear. I closed my eyes and wondered if this would be the last time I did that. I could hear my sister whimpering next to me and Jason's labored breathing. We prayed in Sunday School and now I summoned every word we had ever recited as my finger coiled around the trigger.

Click.

"Oh, thank God," Katie cried, pulling the gun away from my head and pushing it into Tommy's hands. She pulled me into her arms and cradled me in her chest. "I love you, Jack, I love you so much. I'm sorry I can be mean sometimes, I don't mean to be, I'm going to be so, so nice to you all the time now I promise."

Tommy chuckled and pulled the cylinder back out. Another bullet went in.

Clickclickclickclickclickclick...

"My turn. Then it's your turn, Jason," Tommy said, watching the boy's face go white. "Don't worry, we're halfway through...hehehehe..."

He snapped the cylinder back and put the barrel to his head. We all watched him, breath catching in our throats. I could feel the tension building in my shoulders as Katie held me like a vice, her arms wrapped around me, my head against her shoulder.

Tommy pulled the trigger and the pistol exploded in his hands. Tommy's head whipped to the side as the bullet passed through his skull like a freight train. The three of us screamed in unison as Tommy slowly fell over, slumping lifelessly to the concrete. The air was tinged with gunsmoke and the echo rang in my ears like an alien scream. In the insanity of that moment, something came back to me like a rising monster from a swamp, a question that had been uttered to me over a year ago.

Tell me, Jackie…do you dream?

I snapped out of my shocked state as Katie jerked us both away from Tommy's motionless body, Jason scrambling to his feet and moaning. A smoking, black hole tunneled into Tommy's head but no blood gurgled from the wound.

I struggled from my sister's arms, blinking, eyes wide, unable to believe what I had just seen. He had just…had Tommy just killed himself? At first, I felt fear and confusion, but as the seconds ticked by, I realized that a massive weight was slowly leaving me. A weight I didn't even know I carried with me until just that moment. It was as if something had been standing on my chest and was just now stepping off. Tears bubbled in my eyes and I let out a gasp of disbelief.

"Hehehehe…"

No…no PLEASE, NO.

Slowly, like a corpse rising from the grave, Tommy sat up. He put a finger to the hole in his head and then smiled, staring up at us.

"Looks like I drew the short straw, huh?" He stood and picked up the pistol. "What rotten luck. I was really hoping it was going to be Jason."

Katie stepped back, pulling me with her, her eyes never leaving Tommy. "What are you…?"

Tommy just stared down at us, "Hehehehe…"

Suddenly, the back door burst open and Mom came running out looking confused and afraid. Sweat lined her shirt from her yoga class and her face dripped with concern. She appraised the four of us and then her eyes went to the gun in Tommy's hand.

"What are you doing?!" she cried, "and why do you have Mike's gun!? What are you doing to the children?!"

Tommy's face became a mask of nightmares and his voice dropped to a growl. "Mike's gun?"

Immediately, my mom realized her mistake and clamped her mouth shut. Tommy reached down and picked up a fourth bullet from the ground and slid it into the cylinder.

"Mike's gun?" he repeated. "So…you knew about this secret purchase. You've been keeping secrets from me…"

Mom took a step back, frightened, "No, Tommy, I—"

Tommy turned the pistol over in his hands. "And now you're lying to me. Looks like we have one more player, kids."

Clickclickclickclickclickclick….

"No, Tommy this is a huge misunderstand—" Mom cried, backing up further. "Please!"

Tommy raised the gun and pointed it directly at her face. "I'm not liking your chances, Penny."

"MOM!" Katie screamed, frozen. Jason had wet himself and was crying, unable to tear his eyes from the horrible scene unfolding before us. I balled my hands into fists, shaking from head to toe, fear ripping through me like a hot spear. Sweat poured down my flushed face and I said the only thing I could think of at that moment. A phrase that had been confided to me from the emptiness of my headphones.

"Six-six-three-five-eight-Rez!" I screamed, the nonsensical expression feeling like another language.

Instantly, Tommy's head whipped around and I saw his eyes grow wide with blinding shock. He stood there, mouth hanging slightly ajar, our eyes clashing. Then, something seeped into his face so dark I begged to look away. His eyes practically exploded with an anger so real I thought I would melt into the concrete.

"Where the fuck did you hear that?" Tommy hissed, trembling with barely controlled rage, spittle flying from his lips,

I retreated, whimpering.

Tommy dropped the gun and advanced on me, hands forming fists at his sides. "Who the fuck told you to say that?" He was now standing over me and I curled away from his looming shadow.

He suddenly grabbed me by the throat and lifted me off the ground. "WHERE THE FUCK DID YOU HEAR THAT JACK!?"

Mom screamed with concern and charged Tommy, batting at him as his hand tightened around my throat. Tommy backhanded her hard across the face and she went sprawling to the ground, scraping her hands and knees against the concrete.

Gasping, sputtering, I tried to release Tommy's grip from my throat, my head expanding as my oxygen was slowly cut off. I could feel the blood pumping in my ears and my face felt very hot all of the sudden.

Tommy leaned into me, his face inches from mine, his voice dropping to a vicious whisper. "Did he tell you to say that, Jack?"

"You're killing him!" Katie was screaming, running to my aid and drumming her small fists into Tommy's back. He ignored her, his eyes boring into my own as the world dimmed.

Inside, the phone began to ring.

Tommy's eyes flared and he immediately dropped me. I gasped and coughed, going to my knees and clutching my throat. Katie rushed to my side and cradled my head in her arms once again, crying and rubbing air back into my chest.

Tommy stormed to the back door and threw it open, the phone chirping from the kitchen. He marched out of view, but seconds later we heard him smash the receiver off the wall, his voice cracking with hysteric madness as he bellowed in a rage.

Mom crawled to her feet and scooped up the gun. She quickly shoved it into the waistband of her pants and covered it with her shirt. We crowded around her like frightened lambs, her arms wrapping around us protectively.

Tommy came back outside, fury blazing like the surface of the sun.

He pointed to Mom, voice burning like embers. "You go back downstairs and get everyone out of the house. Tell them whatever you have to, but you're done today." He glared at Jason. "Go home with your mom when she comes up. I'll deal with you later." Then his eyes fell on Katie and me. "As for you two…you're to spend the rest of the day in your rooms. There will be no dinner tonight. I need to have a few words with your father and it's not a conversation children need to hear. GO!"

We all dispersed in a frantic jumble of nervous confusion. Katie clutched my hand and dragged me inside, leaving Tommy and my mother alone. Jason ran into the house behind us and waited anxiously by the front door. My sister pulled me up the stairs and practically shoved me into my room.

"Just stay here and keep your door closed," she whispered. "I don't know what you said to Tommy, but I think it's going to be bad tonight." I looked at her pleadingly and she suddenly embraced me in a hug. "I love you, Jack. We're going to get through this." In that moment, my sister grew up before my eyes. I hugged her tightly and tried to suppress the bubble of emotion gurgling in my chest. Katie released me and went to her room across the hall, shutting my door as she went.

I turned around in my room, unsure what to do. I was a mess of nerves and my hands fidgeted at my sides. I shouldn't have said that phrase. What was I thinking? It had done nothing but enrage Tommy. Who knew what kind of punishment I'd receive later tonight? And what was he going to do to Dad?

I fell in a helpless heap on my bed, the afternoon sun still high in the sky. I felt like I would go stir crazy, the long hours before bed a marathon of fear. Downstairs, I heard my mom's yoga class dispersing. I had no idea what she had told them, but I was confident she had created some kind of story to cover up the commotion. She was good at that: creating a believable fiction to mask Tommy's presence in our lives.

Time was a cruel mistress and each tick of the clock was another lash across my fractured, tired mind. Eventually, I turned and spotted my headphones sitting on the nightstand. It had been months since I had heard anything out of them, despite their nightly use.

I picked them up. I had a feeling today would be different. Gently, I pushed them over my head and the earpieces slid into place. And then I waited. It didn't take long.

The slow creep of static came first, followed by the strained, calm voice.

"Jack?"

I felt my heart flutter, but I didn't respond.

"You can talk to me, Jack."

Still, I didn't respond, the eerie voice reverberating in my head like the source was standing in a vast empty space.

"I want you to know that I'm on your side. I'm going to need you one day."

Finally. My voice was barely a whisper as I said, "Who…are you?"

The static washed over me and the voice disappeared. I

waited, begged it to come back as the sun sank in the sky like a deflated balloon.

I stayed on the bed, staring at the wall, lost in my own confusion and fear. At some point, I heard my father come home from work. I expected to hear a confrontation, but the house remained quiet. Darkness fell and the moon and stars salted the heavens. I didn't bother turning on a light as my room was laced in shadow, the clock marching indifferently on.

I was convinced my father was dead. The silence held secrets I couldn't decipher and so my imagination took over. Tommy had slit Dad's throat as soon as he had come home from work. That had to be it. And what had my mother told those women? Surely they had all heard the gunshot…what lies had been spread to cover for that? Regardless of how believable a story they were fed, they would all go home with a separate interpretation. Except for Jason and his mom. They knew…and they would keep quiet.

My clock glowed in the black, the green digits informing me it was almost midnight. And still, I had not heard a thing from my parents or Tommy. I was exhausted, but my mind was too troubled to fall asleep. I turned on my side and stared at the door.

Just as my eyes drooped shut, I heard it open. Immediately I shot upright, a jolt of adrenaline knifing through me. I blinking in the darkness as a shape slipped inside my room and quietly shut the door again.

"Are you awake. Jack?"

I sighed with relief, "You scared me to death, Katie."

She padded over to my bed and looked down at me, her face like a phantom in the night. "I can't sleep…I'm too scared. Scoot over?"

I shuffled across the bed, opening the blankets for my sister. She gratefully crawled in next to me.

"Where's Mom and Dad?" I whispered in her ear, turning on my side to face her.

Katie pulled the blankets up to her chin. "I think they're in the basement."

I shivered. "What's he doing to them?"

"I don't know."

We lay there in silence for a long time, sleep eluding us. I tried to keep my imagination from running wild again, but it was hard when I had no outlet. I thought about the headphones and the voice again. I needed to tell someone.

"Hey, Katie?"

"Yeah?"

I gathered my thoughts, taking a deep breath. "This is going to sound crazy...but something weird has been happening to me."

"Yeah, no kidding," she said grimly. "There's a doll man holding us hostage."

I shook my head. "No, not that. Something else."

Her voice changed. "Oh?"

I scooted closer to her, lowering my voice. "You know how sometimes...sometimes the phone rings and Tommy gets mad? Like today?"

"What about it?"

"Well," I continued, "the guy who keeps calling...he's been talking to me through my headphones."

"What? What do you mean?"

"Sometimes...when I put on my headphones to go to sleep, I'll hear static. And then he talks to me. He was the one who told me to say that phrase today."

"Jack, what are you talking about?" Katie asked slowly.

"You know the guy on the phone!?" I said, frustrated, "the one who talks to Tommy? Remember when Tommy first showed up? And the phone rang?"

Katie nodded. "Yeah…yeah, I remember. But Jack…you and Tommy are the only two people who have spoken with him. I don't know who this man is or what he says to you. It didn't seem to matter, all things considered."

"Well, I'm telling you what he's saying," I pressed. "Sometimes it's weird stuff, like that phrase, and other times like tonight—"

"He talked to you tonight?" Katie interrupted.

"Yeah."

"What did he say to you?"

"Do you believe me?" I asked first.

"What did he say to you, Jack?"

I lowered my voice again. "He said that one day he might need me."

"Need you for what?"

"I don't know," I said miserably. "He…left…before I could ask. But do you believe me?"

Katie looked at me and then hugged me close. "Of course I believe you."

"What should we do?" I asked, my voice muffled against her arm.

Katie hugged me tighter. "We stay alive."

Chapter 3 —1997

Two years he had been with us and still showed no sign of leaving. I was beginning to think that this hell would last for the rest of my life. The sun rose and fell, each dawn bringing with it another portrayal of beauty that I would never be a part of. Nothing in my life felt beautiful. Nothing felt alive. Each sunrise was another shuddering breath of daylight that I was missing out on. My childhood was slipping away from me. Dreams of normality began to feel like fantasy. Every time I woke up, came home, or walked out of my room I was confronted by grinning madness.

There are pieces of that year that still remain a mystery to me. Like what did Tommy do to my parents in the basement that night? What did Mom do with the gun? Why were the following months spent in almost complete silence? I think that was the worst part. Mom and Dad stopped talking and Katie and I were left alone on an island of isolation, our minds and hearts surrounded by the dark waters of uncertainty. I like to think that my parents were doing it to stay out of trouble. That maybe being silent was better than risking Tommy's anger. But looking back, I think that they were breaking. And who could blame them? The stress of keeping our family afloat, the never-ending secrecy, the lies we all had to tell...I could feel the fibers of our family begin to fray.

Dad looked like he was coming down with a terminal illness by the time New Years rolled around. His skin was tight against his bones, his eyes ringed with dark circles that reminded me of a picture I had once seen of a black hole. And that's what our household had become. A black hole, sucking everything into it and giving nothing back. Each of us consumed the torment silently and as winter melted into spring once again, we had all but forgotten what the light looked like.

Katie was my constant during those long, cold months. She remained a pillar of strength at my side, despite the almost constant silence our house basked in. It was her eyes. They still burned with a hope that one day this would pass. I wanted to believe in that warmth. I wanted to believe in that dream, that this captivity was only temporary. But two years is a long time when there's no end in sight. I remember being in school and thinking to myself, *Why doesn't anyone do anything to help us? Can't they see how miserable I am?*

I think it was that winter that I began to lose faith in humanity. It was then that I came to the cruel realization that people *just don't give a shit.* Sure, they may ask if you're doing ok, but those words rang hollow in my skull like the clang of a cracking bell. I don't know what lies my teachers told themselves as I slowly shrank into myself, speaking less and less, grades dropping, an emptiness in my face. Sure, they poked and prodded, but it was only enough to ease their morality. When I would just shrug and tell them I was fine, they locked the questions away in a vault. They had done their civic duty. Who cares if another kid slips through the cracks? Another one would just take my place with his or her own problems. Why get invested in whatever was obviously troubling me? Why put yourself out there?

Summer arrived in a blast of heat and humidity. I don't really remember much about that time. I played with Jason occasionally, swam in the pool, ate hot dogs, and watched fireworks on the Fourth of July. On the outside, we were still a perfectly constructed American family, and that was just the way Tommy wanted it. Keep up appearances, keep a smile on your face, and do what you're told. I didn't know too much about what was happening in the rest of the neighborhood, but from the bits Jason told me, it was bad.

But how could Tommy be here...and also...there? It didn't make sense and no matter how hard I tried, I couldn't wrap my head around it. The nightly lessons continued, now a neat thirty minutes of instruction on how to behave and act. Listening to Tommy lecture us on love and goodwill towards all...it made me sick. I learned to hate those sessions, the four of us crammed on the couch, nodding our heads, eyes vacant, as Tommy paced in front of us, teaching, talking, guiding.

The voice in my headphones only spoke to me a few times over the course of the year, usually when I was asleep. I would stir, the tail end of his voice lingering in my ears like a bad taste in my mouth, followed by a wash of static. I tried not to listen to it, tried not to think about it. It scared me and I felt like I was under a spotlight, like it was directing Tommy's attention to me. Like he would know it had been speaking to me. Things were stirring beneath the veneer of normality my parents kept up.

When the leaves began to change, I could tell something was going to happen. The mood had subtly changed in the house, my parents suddenly sharper. The dark circles around my father's eyes remained, but there was something else swirling in the void now. Something cautious yet dangerous.

It was a windy night in October when I found out what.

I was asleep, lost in a horrific dream. I was sinking in a great body of water, the night sky starless above me. I was screaming, calling for help, as the inky depths swelled around me and pulled my body down into their jaws. In the distance I thought I could hear something…it sounded like a…a horn or whistle. It was blaring from far off, a desperate screech into the empty night.

And I knew that it was important. I knew that if I wanted to save myself from drowning then I needed to get to the source of that sound. The deep notes churned across the water and as I descended, eyes bulging, I knew it would be the last thing I would ever hear. Right before death took me, I looked down and screamed.

The ocean was filled with hundreds of lights, all of them white and blinking lazily. Something about them sent a bullet of terror ripping through my heart. I opened my mouth to scream and water rushed in, pressing down my throat like endless, wet silk.

The lights…they weren't supposed to be down here…this was wrong, this was all wrong.

I'm going to need you someday.

The voice rose around me like tendrils and I pushed myself away, clawing at the murky depths, knowing I was about to die.

"Jack!"

I jerked awake, my body coated in sweat. I sat up, gasping, head spinning as I tried to get my bearings. I sucked down air, the sensation of drowning still fresh on my tongue.

"Jack, are you awake?" a voice I recognized asked quietly, a hand gently shaking my shoulder.

I looked up into the pale face of my father, his eyes two black spots on a white sheet. I rubbed my hands over my cheeks, ridding myself of the nightmare, and nodded. My chin touched my headphones, now curled around my neck. The ear pads were slick with sweat and I thought I could hear static faintly buzzing through them.

"We're leaving, son, right now. Come on, let's go," Dad said, pulling the covers off me. I blinked back the cobwebs of slumber and ran my tongue across my teeth. *What had he just said?*

"Stay quiet," Dad urged, pulling me toward the door. "Mom and your sister are already in the car waiting for us. We don't have much time."

"We're…leaving?" I croaked, throat dry.

"Shh, keep your voice down. Yes, now come with me," Dad said, reaching my bedroom door with me in tow. He peeked out into the hallway and then softly led us to the stairs. The house was dark and eerily quiet. In my dazed state, I thought of the ocean depths I had been drowning in.

"But what about Tommy?" I whispered, following my father down the stairs.

We reached the bottom and Dad looked back at me. "I don't know where he is right now, but we're getting out of this house. For good." His words took a moment to sink in, the two of us slinking to the front door. Were we leaving? Were we leaving this prison? Were we getting away from Tommy? Something blossomed in my stomach and it was such a strange sensation that it took a second for me to identify what it was. Hope. Real, true hope. Dad was doing something about this hellish situation, taking back the reigns of fatherhood and leading us out of the desert like tumbleweeds in the night.

Dad opened the front door after taking a cautious look over his shoulder and then pushed me through. A cool breeze washed over my sticky skin like cold fabric and I breathed in the sensation with a sense of relief. Dad clicked the door closed behind us and we double-timed it to the family van parked in the driveway. I could see my mother's silhouette in the passenger's seat and practically felt her urgency cracking like electricity through the vehicle.

Dad opened the sliding door of the van and I scurried up into the captain's seat across from my sister. As Dad closed the door, Katie looked at me, her eyes huge in the dim shadows. I returned the stare, shock finally finding me and shaking my scattered mind.

We're really leaving.

I reached out and Katie immediately took my hand, bridging the gap between the two seats. As Dad pulled the driver's side door open and got in, I realized I was still in my pajamas, my bare feet sticking out in front of me. I had a sudden urge to run inside and get my shoes, a purely reactionary instinct. I looked at the dark face of our house, my eyes peeling apart every shadow, every corner, every window.

Where was Tommy?

Dad turned the van on and backed us out of the driveway. My mother remained silent, but I saw she was gripping the armrest so hard her nails had punctured the cloth. At the foot of the driveway, Dad hit the gas.

We were escaping.

"It's going to be ok, Penny," my dad said quietly, his voice not quite steady.

My mother looked over at him as we departed down the street. "But, Mike…if he catches us…"

"He's not," Dad said a little more firmly. "We've been over this a thousand times. We have a plan, we have the kids, and everyone is safe right now. I'm not staying another night in that house with that…that…" He trailed off and let the hum of the engine finish his sentence. Our street was empty and still, each house like a coffin daring anyone to look inside.

"Where are we going?" Katie asked as we turned down a connecting road, the full moon illuminating the night. It was the only witness to our act of desperation, a lunar face lighting the way, rooting for us, urging us to follow its soft rays.

"Far, far away," Dad said darkly from the front seat. "We'll stop at a motel once we've put some miles between us and the house. I don't know if he will—or can—follow us, but I don't want to risk it. Why don't you try and get some sleep? I'll wake you in a couple hours once we get to the motel."

I looked at the green numbers on the dashboard and saw it was a little after midnight. I turned in my seat to look out the back window. A runway of darkness stretched behind us and I shivered.

We were…escaping.

We fell into an uneasy silence, none of us daring to speak. We let Dad concentrate on driving, his knuckles white against the wheel, the headlights blazing a path to freedom in front of us. I recognized where we were, but after an hour of tense travel, I lost track and gave up trying.

The neighborhoods and country houses faded into the hills behind us. I pressed my face to the window, trying to decipher where we were. The moon illuminated acres of cornfields, their long stalks swaying in the October wind. Endless miles of farmland grew tight against the edges of the road.

My mother broke the silence first, her voice a strained whisper. "I still think we should go to the police, Mike..."

Dad shook his head, eyes trained on the road. "No, we talked about this. Even if they could help us, we both know they wouldn't find Tommy. He's far too clever for that. And then, after the investigation and follow-up, he would find us again. He would know what we had done and then he would come back. It might be days, it might be weeks, but Penny...we both know he'd come back. I can't live my life like that. I won't. My first priority is protecting this family as best I can and I think the smartest option is for us to slip quietly over the horizon without making a sound."

Mom reached out and squeezed my dad's arm. "Ok, Mike. I believe you. I trust you. I just want to feel...to feel safe, to feel protected, if only for a night..."

I felt a heaviness settle over my father and Mom quickly rubbed his arm apologetically. "I'm sorry, Mike...that wasn't fair. You know what I mean."

Dad slowly nodded, his voice pained. "I'm sorry it's taken this long for me to do something. Tommy...he's just...we couldn't..."

Mom reached up and stroked his face. "I know, Mike...I know...you don't have to say anything."

I felt Katie suddenly tap my shoulder and I looked over at her. Mom and Dad were still talking so she just pointed to my neck. I looked down, hands going to my throat, and I realized I still had my headphones with me.

Faintly, I heard static buzzing from them.

I looked up at Katie and shared a worried look. She tapped

her neck, shooting a look at Mom and Dad in the front. It had been months since we had had the conversation about the strange man who spoke to me. We hadn't discussed it since, but I always felt like my sister wanted to ask more about it. And now she heard the static, as well, and was urging me to put on the headphones and listen.

I didn't know if it was curiosity or fear that drove her, but I slowly obeyed, hands shaking slightly. A tightness settled around my throat as I slid them over my ears, the dark landscape blurring outside the window.

And then the voice.

"He's in the cornfields."

My heart sank into my stomach and my legs suddenly began to tingle. A wash of soft static and the earpieces went silent once again, the single warning an echo in my head. Quietly, I pulled the headphones off and forced myself to breathe. Katie stared at me expectantly, wringing her hands in her lap.

Well? Did anything happen?! Her eyes begged.

I turned away from her and forced myself to look out the window at the rows and rows of corn zipping by under the watchful gaze of the moon. I felt fear uncoil its fist in my stomach as my eyes danced across the darkness, every shadow and swaying stalk growing eyes, teeth, and malicious intent. He couldn't be out there…please…don't let him be out there…following us…

BANG!

We all jumped at the sudden noise as the car lurched across the road, my father gripping the wheel with both hands as a horrible thumping sound hammered beneath us.

"Oh no, are you kidding me…?" Dad whispered, slamming down on the brakes.

"What is it?! What's happening!?" Katie shrieked, sitting straight up in her seat.

The van came to a rolling stop along the side of the road, the stalks of corn mere feet from my window. Mom was staring at Dad, eyes bulging, jaw clenched.

"It's a flat," Dad said, forcing himself to breathe as he turned off the car.

I clutched my headphones with both hands, a gurgling paranoia emerging from the pit of my stomach. *No, no, no, no…*

"Dad," I croaked, "Dad we can't stop. We have to go."

Dad turned around, one hand on the back of my mother's headrest. "It's going to be ok. We have a spare in the back. Everyone just stay in the car while I change the tire. We'll be back on the road in five minutes."

"Dad!" I practically screamed. "Dad you can't go out there!"

My father mustered a look of assurance and tried to smile. "I'll be quick, Jack…just…just keep your eyes open, ok?"

I watched in horror as he unfastened his seatbelt and opened the car door. I pressed my face to the glass as he walked around to the back and popped the hatch. Now on my knees, completely turned around in my seat, I prayed silently under my breath. This was wrong, this was all wrong. This couldn't be a coincidence.

He was out there.

Dad pulled the jack and spare from the compartment beneath the trunk and set about changing the tire. The wind rustled through the corn and I stared at their thin bodies like they were skeletons about to come to life and snatch us away.

"Jack, what did he say?" Katie whispered, leaning close, her hand gripping my arm.

I swallowed hard and turned to my sister, the full moon reflecting in her eyes, "I think he's close…"

Katie just stared at me, her face a canvas of terror. Mom fiddled nervously in the front as we felt Dad begin to jack the car up. I turned again to the cornfields and ran my eyes over every shadow and flicker of movement.

The cool October air blew through the open trunk and I shivered, the road behind us a long ebony tongue. The clank of tools along with the shifting corn filled the night and formed an ensemble of tension that dried my mouth to dust. Crickets unseen chirped in the pale light, a familiar song that felt out of place and nauseating.

"Come on, Dad," I muttered, biting my lip. "Come on, come on, come on."

Suddenly, the headphones buzzed once again, just a dim chuckle of static. Immediately I snatched them from my neck and crammed them over my ears, heart gurgling up my throat.

"He's coming."

I whipped my gaze back to the wall of corn and a shudder ran through me. For just a second, I thought I saw two blue eyes shining at me from between the stalks. But the image vanished just as soon as it came and I was left shaking in my seat.

"Jack…" Katie begged, clawing at my shoulder.

I undid my seatbelt, sweat forming on my bro., "Mom, I'm going to help Dad. Tommy is here."

Mom looked back at me and I saw her face change like the seasons. "What do mean? Did you see him!?"

I crawled past Katie, fumbling for the handle. "I don't know, Mom, but I think he's out there in the corn. I can't explain it."

"Jack, no!" Mom cried, spinning and grabbing my hands away. "Your father can handle it, sit back down!"

"Mom, I need to help him! This is taking too long!" I practically cried, slumping back in my seat. I heard a grate of metal as Dad slid the flat off.

"He's almost finished," Mom pleaded. "We're almost out of here." But her face betrayed her, a sheen of sweat now budding under her eyes.

Dad slid the spare on and began cranking the bolts back in. I could hear him breathing heavily with hurried desperation, a mental clock ticking down in all of our heads.

Then the crickets went silent.

It was like someone had flipped a switch as the night went numb. The wind ruffled the corn and now it sounded like the whispers of impending terror.

"Oh no," I whimpered, shrinking into my seat, nose peeking just above the window to stare at the swaying field just behind my father's back.

"Mike, hurry!" Mom called, her voice cracking with panic.

Something was coming through the corn. I could feel it, a ribbon of darkness parting the moonlit stalks. But I blinked and realized it was just the wind again, the dancing husks almost mocking me with their midnight tango.

"Got it!" Dad yelled triumphantly, dropping the jack and throwing the flat into the trunk. He hurried to the driver's door, wiping his hands on his pants. With a sigh of relief, I watched him resume his position behind the wheel and start the car again.

"Just the worst luck," Dad said to himself, pulling the car back onto the road.

I took one last look at the spot in the corn where I thought I had seen something.

It remained absent, the corn continuing their indifferent

disco beneath the brilliant moon. I felt a weight leave my shoulders like someone had been crushing them with iron claws. I sat back in my seat as we accelerated and continued our journey, uninterrupted.

Miles of asphalt streamed behind us as we all sat in shaken silence. I was exhausted but dared not close my eyes. I listened intently for the static to return, but my headphones remained silent. Katie had pulled her feet up onto her seat and she sat with her arms wrapped around her knees. I shot her a comforting look, but only got misery in return. I scooted over and patted the empty space. Katie slid from her seat and took the spot next to me. I linked my arm around hers and placed my head on her shoulder. It felt better being close to her. It felt better for both of us. Mom looked back and smiled sadly.

The clock on the dash strode aggressively into the night. At three, I began to feel my eyes droop, my sister's shoulder warm and assuring. Just as I began to nod off, I felt Dad begin to slow. I lifted my head and saw the light of a motel ahead of us.

"I need to stop," Dad said quietly, "I can barely keep my eyes open."

Mom nodded and sat up in her seat, scrubbing her face, "Ok, honey."

The van crunched over loose gravel as Dad turned into the parking lot. Only one other car was in the lot, a dusty junker that sat by the office.

No one sleeps on this lonely road, I thought to myself. I looked around and saw that the motel was depressingly isolated, a long L-shaped building that sat like a monument in the dark country. A tall sign towered over the structure that read "America's Best Motel." As I scanned the run-down lot, I deciphered that the sign was surely lying.

Dad crept the van over to the office and parked, taking the keys from the ignition and pocketing them.

He sighed heavily. "Ok, I'll go get us a room. Wait here." We watched him get out and walk to the office where he disappeared inside. Katie was looking through the windows at the empty parking lot and barren road. She looked tense, and the same fear rippled through me as well.

"How are you two doing?" Mom said from the front seat.

"I'm scared..." Katie whispered, still scanning the road.

Mom reached behind her and squeezed her knee. "I am too, sweetie. Just a little longer now. You and Jack have been so brave. I'm so sorry..." She trailed off and we let her. We knew what she wanted to say.

"Mom," I said slowly, "I...I don't think we're safe here. There's something I have to tell you."

Before I could go on, Dad returned, bouncing a key in his hand. He pulled the door open and crawled in.

"Ok, we got a room. I think the manager was surprised to see me. Don't think they get many visitors out this way. Don't know how they stay in business."

"Well they certainly aren't losing money on the upkeep," Mom said taking in the shoddy, single story motel. Dad backed the van up and drove down to the end of the building where #16 was located, our room for the night.

Gratefully, we all climbed out of the van. I stretched, my headphones rising up over my chin. The night air was cool and I shivered, staring out at the cornfield across the road opposite our room. I didn't like that, but the crickets were back which made me feel slighter safer.

Since we didn't have any luggage, we followed Dad to the paint-chipped door where he fumbled with the lock. I looked down the long row of rooms toward the office. It looked miles away. Again, I shivered.

"Why'd he put us so far down?" Katie asked.

"He probably didn't want to deal with us," Dad said, jiggling the key. "Ah! Got it."

We pushed into the room and I cringed. The blue carpet was stained and reeked of cigarette smoke. The walls were yellow and peeling at the top. The two queen-sized beds looked like ancient relics from another time.

Dad closed the door behind us as Mom and Katie went to claim their separate beds. Without thinking, I went to the large window and stared out at the dark road and barrier of corn resting on the opposite side. The moon hung above the ears of corn like a pendulum frozen in time. I closed the curtains and turned away from it all.

Mom turned on the bedside lamp and Dad switched off the overhead. The grimy room was washed in a greasy yellow glow. To me, it looked like someone had smeared cheese all over the walls. I sighed and plopped myself down on the bed next to Katie. She was already digging into the covers.

"Come on, Jack," she said, pulling the comforter aside. "Let's let Dad rest."

Dad came over and smiled down at us as I took my spot next to my sister. "You two are the best kids a guy could ever ask for. Thank you for being so brave."

As I gratefully sank into the pillow, Dad pulled the covers up and tucked us in.

"You want to take those off?" he asked, pointing to my headphones.

"I think I'll keep them with me…just in case," I said, knowing the real reason would be lost to him.

Dad kissed my forehead. "Of course, buddy." He reached over me and stroked my sister's cheek, "Sleep well, angel. In the morning we'll get some breakfast and keep driving. Who knows, maybe we'll go to the beach?"

"Mike?" Mom called from her bed, "Did you lock the door?"

"Sure did. I think we'll be ok tonight. Let's all just get some much-deserved rest and we'll start fresh when the sun's up."

He crossed the room and practically collapsed next to Mom, exhaling a mountain of unspoken worry. I watched him close his eyes, his face a mask of uncertainty. I felt Katie clutch my hand beneath the covers as Mom turned off the light. The room plunged into darkness, the crack between the curtains allowing a sliver of curious moonlight into the room.

Soon, my ears filled with the sound of my sleeping family. The night's activities had exhausted us all, but for whatever reason, sleep eluded me. I stared up at the ceiling, a dim surface of blank space. I imagined faces growing from it, leering down at me with broken smiles. I shuddered and closed my eyes. Katie still held my hand, her gentle snores assuring in their own way. We were together and we were ok…we had made it out of the house…

The night dove deeper and still, I could not find peace. I stirred restlessly, almost begging my headphones to come to life and tell me we were safe. The last message rattled around my skull like a pebble in a tin can.

He's coming…

I turned and stared at the closed curtains. Something called me to them, one last look to calm my terrified mind. I didn't want to; I begged my mind to shut up and release me for a few hours. But the thought insisted, a finger poking at the back of my skull.

Finally, I gave in. I slowly pulled the covers away, making sure not to wake my sister. My feet reached for the floor and my heart began to race. This was stupid, we were miles away from the house. Why did I need to go look?

I glanced at Mom and Dad in their bed, wrapped together like the fibers of a rope. Mom had her back to me and I couldn't see my father's face, but from the sound of it, everyone was out cold.

Taking a deep breath, I tip-toed to the window.

Stop, don't look, please don't look.

Bracing myself, I reached out and gently pulled the curtain aside, peeking out into the night. Immediately, my heart skipped a beat and a scream rose in my throat like a volcano of horror.

Tommy stared at me from the edge of the cornfield, his eyes like twin pools of glowing blue ember.

And he was smiling.

His arms hung loosely at his sides, the wind rustling the corn at his back. He stood like a statue in the oppressive darkness, the moon casting shadows across his smooth face.

Our eyes met and I knew it was over.

The scream finally escaped my lips as Tommy crossed the road, headed right for us.

"He's here! He's coming!" I howled, falling backward, eyes bulging, voice a desperate crescendo of imminent fear.

The room erupted in chaos as my family awoke, scrambling from their beds, bleary-eyed and confused. My dad was the first to his feet, blinking in the darkness, his hair a tousled mess. He looked down at me and then at the door.

"What's going on Jack?!" he half yelled.

"TOMMY!" I screamed, shuffling backward on my rear.

Katie was sitting up in bed now, staring down at me with wide eyes and a fearful look. She looked at the closed curtains and then at Mom, her lip trembling.

"Mom?" she pleaded.

Mom shot from the bed and scooped up my sister, pulling her to her chest in a protective embrace. The two of them huddled in the corner of the room, dread pulsing from every pore.

Dad grabbed me and hauled me up, spinning to face him. "Where did you see him!?"

"He's crossing the road and headed right for us!" I yelled. "We have to do something! We have to—"

The front door exploded in a flurry of violence, the hinges giving way as Tommy booted the fragile barrier aside. Katie screamed as the door launched into the room and struck my father across the head. He cried out and went down, clutching his temple, leaving me to turn and face the intruder alone.

Tommy stood panting in the doorway, the moon at his back, his figure a dark silhouette. Except for his eyes. They locked with mine and I felt my bladder give way.

"I am so disappointed in all of you," Tommy said softly, his voice like gravel. Katie and Mom shrank into themselves, crying, as Dad groggily got to his feet, a trickle of blood running down his head.

Tommy marched to him and grabbed him by the throat. "As the head of this family, I really expect better judgment from you." Dad winced and reached out, but Tommy threw him into the dresser. Dad let out a grunt of pain as his ribs crunched into the stubborn wood, gasping and going to his knees.

Tommy's eyes fell on my mother and his lips tightened at the corners. "And you…the little bird whispering in his ear the whole time. I'm sure it was your idea to try and leave. Isn't that right, Penny?"

Mom shook her head, eyes filled with tears. "Please...please don't hurt us anymore."

Suddenly, Dad was up and had his arms around Tommy. Growling, he drove him backward, striking the far wall with a thud. Tommy seemed surprised as his head whipped back and connected with the hard surface, a jolt running through him. Dad plowed a fist into Tommy's gut, and then another followed by a knee. Tommy grunted as the strikes found their mark; my father was a relentless tornado of determination.

I stood, piss running down my leg, helpless and unsure. Dad seemed to have the upper hand, one arm locking across Tommy's throat, keeping him in place, his other fist striking hard and fast. Sweat stood out on my father's brow as he rained down blows, his face knotted with fierce aggression.

And then Tommy had enough.

I watched in horror as Tommy casually grabbed Dad by the shoulders and spun him with tremendous velocity. Dad's feet left the floor seconds before his entire body plowed into the wall, partially caving it in.

Still smiling, Tommy crossed the room as my dad collapsed with a pained rush of breath, plaster crumbling around him. I was pushed aside and I fell to the ground, tears running down my face. Tommy grabbed the dresser and lifted it effortlessly. He gave my father one hard look before throwing it at him. I heard, rather than saw, the impact. It was a sickly sound, a blend of thumping flesh and crunching wood.

"Stop it! PLEASE!" Mom screamed from the corner, paralyzed with fear. Katie's face was pale and her eyes were wide with shock. Dad gasped from beneath the dresser and weakly pushed it away. His nose was cut and blood ran from his mouth. His eyes rolled in their sockets and he seemed to be trying to figure out where he was.

Tommy left him and advanced on my mother who clutched Katie in her arms. Tommy ripped my sister away and pushed her to the floor next to me. He grabbed a fistful of my mother's hair and hauled her up to stand on her toes. Tommy viciously backhanded her across the face, the blow silencing her screams.

"Don't think you can go unpunished for this," he whispered into her face. Her eyes widened as a red mark began to grow across her cheek.

Tommy dragged her into the bathroom, the open door visible from my spot on the carpet. He threw my mom hard into the bathtub, her clawing hands pulling the shower curtain down with her. I heard her head strike the lip and a shocked cry followed. Tommy followed her in. He hauled my mother up and snatched the shower curtain with his free hand. Without pause, he wrapped it around her head, the vinyl stretching tight against her face.

"You stupid bitch," Tommy snarled, "did you really think you could leave?"

And then he smashed her head into the mirror above the sink, shattering it. The impact crunched through my mother, but because of the curtain, the glass left no marks. Tommy let her drop to the floor in a broken heap.

He came back into the room as my father regained his senses. Katie and I were now clutching each other, our backs to the wall, shaking as our parents suffered. I didn't know what to do or how to stop it all. I was convinced that Tommy was about to kill my father.

Instead, he squatted down next to him and wiped a trail of blood from his lip.

"Ready to go back home, Mike? Has your family had enough or should I start on the children?"

Dad fought for air, the blow from the dresser severely impairing him.

"What's that?" Tommy asked, putting a hand to his ear. "Speak up Mike or Jack is next."

Dad coughed violently and spit a wad of blood onto the floor, his voice weak, "S-sorry…we're…sorry."

A smile slowly grew on Tommy's face. It was like watching the cracks of hell itself begin to split.

He reached down and patted my father's head. "Of course you are. You didn't mean for any of this to happen. You just made a mistake. It's something we all do from time to time. But you know what, Mike? I believe in forgiveness, just like I've been teaching you in my evening lessons. I believe in second chances. Is that what you want? A second chance for this family?"

Dad just nodded, his eyes half-lidded in pain.

Tommy's smile widened. "That's good. That's very good. I want that, too."

He reached out and pulled my father to his feet, brushing debris off of his shirt. Dad slumped into Tommy's shoulder, weak and defeated.

"I got you," Tommy said softly. "Come on big guy, let's get you to the van. When we get home I'll take a look at your cuts and fix you up."

Home. The word splattered through me like a harpoon.

He was taking us back home. Back to our prison. I began to sob loudly, an uncontrolled release of hopeless misery. Katie wrapped her arms around me and tried to put on a brave face. Her eyes never left my motionless mother on the bathroom floor.

Tommy, one hand over my dad's shoulders, looked down at us. "I'll come back for her once I help your dad." He noticed my tears and lowered his voice. "Oh don't cry, Jack. It's going to be ok. Your mom and dad are just a little banged up. Nothing I can't fix. Dry those eyes, little man. You too, Katie. No more sadness."

As he took Dad outside, his voice echoed back to me like a vulture to a corpse.

"We're going to be a family again!"

I vomited onto the floor.

Chapter 4 —1998

Complete and utter hopelessness. I think that best describes how I felt returning to our house. We weren't just returning to our house, though…we were returning to the grind. The daily tension, Tommy's constant presence, the nightly lessons, the punishments…I thought we had reached the bottom of hell, but that year I realized we could dig a little deeper still.

Mom and Dad covered up their injuries with whatever lies they needed to shed. Dad went back to work and Mom continued teaching her classes. Katie and I were stuck somewhere in the middle. We felt like pawns in a much bigger game. Pieces the adults used to circle one another, daring the opponent to make a move. I wanted it all to end. I wanted to kill myself.

I stopped wearing the headphones at night. I didn't see the point anymore. They didn't offer any comfort because I already knew that monsters were real. And the voice…the voice frightened me. Even at that young age, I struggled with concepts much heavier than I had any right to. Where did it speak to me from? What was it? Who was it? Why me? Why didn't it reach out to anyone else? Was there even a reason? As the months rose and fell, I felt the heavy weight of depression sink over me like a blanket of wet snow.

We had been brought back. But for WHAT? That was a question that thundered in my head day in and day out. Why was Tommy doing this? He seemed to be convinced that he was shaping us into better people, but his actions and hostile nature conflicted with the messages he taught. Was he just insane? Would he ever leave?

Tommy murdered one of my neighbors that year. I didn't find out until much later. Someone from across the street…Mr. Wellers. I don't know what he did, but it must have been serious enough to warrant such a reaction from Tommy. I remember looking out my window on Christmas Eve and seeing Tommy stare at me from the Wellers' house. He smiled and waved. I shrunk away, confused, scared, and terrified. Because I knew Tommy was also across the hall in my sister's room with my mother at that very moment.

How could an entire neighborhood be afflicted with such suffering for so long…and yet no one noticed? No one said anything? The depths of human selfishness broadened for me that year and I loathed the human race even more. No one looked out for one another. No one cared about the troubles of their fellow man. The signs were there, the hollowness around our eyes was visible. But no one asked beyond skin deep curiosity. *Trouble at home? The parents must be fighting, best stay out of that.* It made me sick.

And so I waited for something to happen.

The spring of 1998 came early for our community. The weather warmed at an alarming rate over the span of a couple weeks and soon Dad was preparing the pool for another year. I don't know why he bothered. None of us went in it anymore. It wasn't that I hated swimming, but I found it harder and harder to extract enjoyment out of anything anymore.

Tommy seemed to notice the grim mood encircling our household and so he prodded my parents to throw a cookout for the whole neighborhood. He was convinced that would brighten the spirits of us miserable people. I wanted to laugh when I heard him suggest it. All we needed to be happy was for him to leave…or to die.

And I soon found out that everyone else was thinking the same thing.

I sat on my bed with Jason, the windows open, a warm breeze wafting through the room. The neighborhood families milled about downstairs, a gathering of uncertainty and apprehension. From the bed, I looked out my window and saw my dad prepping the grill with a cluster of other fathers, including Jason's dad, Mr. Murphy. They were speaking in low voices; the sun was taking a slow, diving plummet for the hills. The mothers and wives were downstairs in the kitchen preparing the side dishes and making small talk. I couldn't image what they were saying, but everyone felt the pressure that swirled around us like dark energy. This was Tommy's idea. Play the game and put on a happy face.

"What did he say to you? About the cookout?" I asked Jason who was propped up against the wall on my bed, hands on his lap. He looked miserable.

Jason sighed, "He just said we were all too gloomy lately and that your family was going to host a party."

"A party," I snorted, "As if…"

Jason ran his hands over his face. "I'm so tired Jack…all the time. I keep waking up and telling myself that today will be the last day…that I'll go downstairs and Tommy will be gone."

"Better keep that fantasy to yourself," I said quietly, eying my open door.

Jason lowered his voice, "Can I ask you something?"

"Sure."

Jason scooted closer, "Does…does he ever get into bed with you?"

I shook my head, "Tommy? No…why, does he do that to you?"

Jason shrugged uncomfortably. "Sometimes. It's been happening a lot lately. I can't stand it…he scares me so badly. I'll wake up in the middle of the night and feel him sliding in next to me. He never says anything, he just lays there. I don't even think he sleeps…" He trailed off.

"What does he do, Jason?" I pressed.

Jason rubbed his eyes miserably, "Sometimes he'll…he'll touch me. I feel disgusting and embarrassed even telling you this, but who else can I go to?"

I said nothing.

"It's never really that bad," Jason continued, his voice strained, "But one time he…he…"

"You can tell me," I said softly.

Jason began to tear up, "One time he reached down into my pajamas and…and he just…held it. He didn't move, didn't speak, he just lay there with his hand down my pants…God, I get sick just thinking about it, Jack."

My stomach rolled and I felt horrible for my friend. Tommy had never done anything like that to me. Suddenly I thought of my sister and my heart skipped a beat. Had he done something like that to Katie?

"Why would he do that?" Jason said, furiously scrubbing his face, wiping emotion away, "Why would he do that to me?"

"I don't know," I said quietly. "I don't know why he does anything."

"I'm so scared to go to sleep now," Jason said, his eyes blood-shot. "I'm afraid that when I do he's going to come in and do that again."

"Can I ask you something?" I said, feeling like I needed to move away from the subject. "Something you have to swear to keep quiet about?"

"Well I just told you something super humiliating so...yeah, go for it," Jason said miserably.

I checked the open door again before continuing. "Have you ever talked to someone...someone weird on the phone? Some-one who seems to know Tommy?

Jason just stared at me.

"Like a voice that tells you things about Tommy?" I said growing frustrated.

Jason shrugged, "No, I don't think so. I don't really answer the phone much at my house though."

"Have you ever heard anything through your headphones? Maybe a voice that says it wants to help you? Or is going to need you one day?"

"What are you talking about, Jack?"

I waved him off. "Oh never mind. It's nothing. I think I'm just going crazy."

"I think we all are," Jason muttered.

"Where are all the other kids?" I asked after some time.

"I think your mom sent them all down into the basement to play. Do you want to go down?"

"No."

"Do you want to go outside and throw the baseball?"

"Not really."

Jason folded his arms across his chest. "Yeah...me neither."

I looked out the window again at the men milling around the grill. "What do you think they're all talking about?"

"I don't know, Jack."

"Doesn't it make you mad?" I said slowly, "how no one has helped us?"

Jason just looked at me. "You mean…like the police or something?"

I waved my hand. "Anybody."

Jason looked at his hands. "What could they do? Jack, the way Tommy is…I don't know if it would matter. I feel like he'll leave only if he feels like it. There are things about him we know nothing about. If anyone else got involved, it would just make things worse for us in the long run."

I continued to watch the men outside. "Yeah…maybe you're right."

Jason crawled off the bed. "Come on, let's go outside. I don't want to be up here anymore."

"Fine."

We left my room and wandered down to the first floor. Katie shot me a look from her cutting board as we weaved between the bustling moms. Everyone looked like they just wanted to get this over with. They chatted amongst themselves, but it was a thinly disguised veil of cheerfulness.

Jason and I pushed past them and went outside. A couple of the fathers turned to appraise us, exchanging looks with one another, and then turned to my dad and whispered in his ear. He was scraping the gristle from the grill when he saw us.

He turned and came to me, placing a hand on my shoulder, his voice low, "Jack, why don't you and Jason go downstairs with the other kids?"

"I don't want to."

Dad looked hard into my face. "Please? I need you to go."

Jason and I swapped curious glances, "Why? What's going on?"

Dad's eyes shifted around nervously, "You don't want to be here for this."

"Be here for what?"

The storm door creaked open and all heads turned to the new arrival, my question hanging in the air like some self-fulfilling prophecy.

"I'm so glad everyone made it!" Tommy said cheerfully, strolling out to join the men. "This was such a good idea wasn't it?"

A few of the men murmured reluctant agreement, parting as Tommy strode between them over to Jason, Dad, and myself.

He beamed at the three of us, "Hi, gang! You boys helping get everything ready? That's mighty fine of you. All the other kids are downstairs playing and yet here you are with the men, chipping in like the good sons you are." He slapped my shoulder cheerfully, his high spirits written plainly across his face. "Really proud of you."

While he was talking, the rest of the men had slowly made a circle around us. Tommy looked up and grinned. "Aren't these boys great?" He ruffled my hair and it made my skin crawl. The men said nothing, arms cross, faces grim.

"What's going on here?" Tommy asked, twirling a finger at the enclosed circle.

Dad took me and Jason by the shoulders and pulled us back against himself, away from Tommy.

Tommy's eyes locked with my dad's. "What's going on here, Mike?"

Jason's dad, Mr. Murphy, stepped forward, "I think it's time you were out of our lives." His voice shook slightly, but his face was a mask of iron.

Tommy's smile fell. "Oh? Is that what this is about?"

The circle nodded, pressing in close.

Tommy looked down at his feet. "Are we really going to do this? Today of all days?"

Another one of the fathers spoke up. "You're a cancer to this neighborhood. All the terrible things you've done to us over the years…it ends today."

Tommy closed his eyes, his smile returning. "Hehehehe…"

"We're giving you one chance," my dad said darkly. "One chance to leave and never come back."

Tommy opened his eyes. "But I'm not ready to leave, Mike. The children still have things to learn. Things I need to show them."

Another dad, Mr. Thompson from two houses down, jabbed a finger at Tommy. "There ain't nothing you can teach our kids. You're a monster, a vicious, violent monster."

Tommy rolled his head to meet his stare. "Are you just saying that because of what I did to your wife two years ago? Come on…you knew the rules. Besides, she's finally talking again so what's the problem?"

"You son of a bitch," Mr. Thompson seethed. "you evil son of a bitch."

"Get him," Dad growled.

Immediately, the men sprang forward, grabbing Tommy. Jason and I were pushed out of the circle as the swarm fell upon their prey. Two of the men grabbed Tommy by the arms, another fell in from behind and wrapped Tommy in a headlock. The others grabbed his throat, his shirt, anything they could get their hands on.

Tommy said nothing, putting up no resistance at all. He was pushed back and shoved into a patio chair where eager bodies held him in place. Someone fetched a rope they had brought, pulling it from beneath the grill. Quickly, they looped it around Tommy, binding him to the chair. Through it all, Tommy just watched them, his face neutral and emotionless.

As he was secured, Dad hurriedly came over to Jason and me. "Go inside, kids."

I looked up at my father, eyes wide, "No…no I want to watch this."

"Jack—"

"Please, Dad," I urged, an almost desperate edge in my voice.

He looked at me and saw the need in my eyes. "Ok…ok just stay back though."

The cluster of men retreated away from Tommy, his torso completely wrapped with rope, molding him to the chair.

"Not such a tough bastard when there's eight of us," one of the dad's snarled.

"Doesn't feel so good does it?" another jeered, "feeling helpless? Powerless?"

Tommy's voice was completely monotone. "Don't think for a second this is the first time I've been in this position."

"Talk is easy," Mr. Murphy spat, "and we're done listening." He plowed a fist into Tommy's face, the smack of flesh sudden and unexpected. Tommy's head whipped back as the blow connected, an excited cheer rising from the men. They all stepped up and took turns slugging Tommy, releasing years of pent up fear and terror.

Through it all, Tommy didn't make a sound, each strike rocking his body, but he gave no reaction until they were finished.

"You done?" Tommy finally asked.

My dad stepped forward and leaned down into his face, "Not even close. George, get the charcoal."

One of the men retrieved a hefty bag by the grill and dragged it over to my father who took it and held it up for Tommy to see.

"You wanted a cookout right?"

Tommy eyed the charcoal. "Hehehehe..."

Dad lifted the bag and upended it into Tommy's lap. The pieces tumbled and piled like a tiny mountain on Tommy, leaving ashy streaks on his skin and clothes. Dad tossed the now empty bag aside and reached for the lighter fluid.

"I'm going to enjoy this," He said, his voice grave.

"Mike," Tommy said slowly, "I'm going to tell you this once. You don't want to do this. It's not going to end well for you."

"Shut up!" Dad yelled suddenly, his eyes ablaze. "I am DONE listening to your POISON!"

He squirted Tommy with the lighter fluid, coating his face, chest, legs, and the pile of charcoal on his lap. When the bottle was empty, he tossed it aside. The men stared down at their captive, now soaked, an excited air of anticipation filling the backyard.

They're going to burn him, I thought, *they're going to burn Tommy.* A cloud of sparkling energy hovered around me and I felt my fingers twitch at my side. The men were ending this hell, they were finally ending it. I looked to the back door and saw the wives huddled behind it, watching the scene through the screen with deadly satisfaction. I spotted Katie, her eyes wide and disbelieving.

My dad struck a match in front of Tommy, the other fathers forming a semi-circle around him.

"It's over, Tommy," Dad said.

Tommy's eyes met my father's. "Don't do this."

Dad dropped the match and immediately a roar of flame engulfed Tommy. The men stepped back as the intense heat flared, licking up the lighter fluid like sweet candy. The coals caught next and began to glow like tiny suns.

Tommy's face never changed as he burned, the ribbons of fire licking his skin. In fact, he didn't make a sound. The air began to fill with nauseous smoke as the men watched with looks of shocked fascination.

Tommy began to char and pieces of his skin started to slough off in greasy, yellow puddles. As his face began to slip from his skull, he turned and looked directly at me. Through the blaze, he spoke in a soft, calm voice.

"See you soon, Jack."

And then he threw his head back and began to laugh.

He laughed until there was nothing left of him, his body collapsing in the inferno. When the fire was put out a couple minutes later, it was as if Tommy had never existed.

Two days went by in dream-like disbelief. After the men cleaned up the ashes, they hesitantly went house to house throughout the neighborhood, searching for Tommy. But Tommy…was gone. Hesitant relief began to ebb through the community like a rising tide. Was this hell finally over? After they searched the houses, they did it a second time, hope growing. And still, Tommy was not there.

That night the families parted ways, each returning to a life they had nearly forgotten. We were all scared still, terrified even, but there was a distant sunrise now and it brought warmth we had grown numb to.

My family slept together in my parents' king-sized bed that night. We crowded into one another, a relieved, almost euphoric feeling of comfort sweeping across our tired minds. I slept better that night than I think I ever had.

The next day, Sunday, we all went to church. My father spent a lot of time on his knees that morning. When he finally joined us outside after the service, his eyes were bloodshot and tear-streaked. The congregation welcomed us back with loving acceptance, questions about where we had been the past couple years pouring down on us. I listened to my parents make excuses, but no one seemed to be listening. They were just glad we were back. A couple comments were made about our haggard state, but my mother gracefully smiled and patiently explained that things had been rough for us. People nodded and stuffed their questions back down their throats.

I remember watching that and feeling anger stir in my gut. Despite my good mood and relief, that ember of resentment still lurked and I felt a great heat beneath it. They had no idea what we had just been through. Not one of these smiling faces had reached out to us over the past couple years to ask where we had gone or why we had stopped coming to church. We were paper thin drawings that had been erased once we were out of sight.

I was silent during the drive home that morning.

That night we all watched a movie in the living room and Mom pulled out all the stops. Popcorn, soda, candy, and no bedtime. My sour mood had lessened by then and I rediscovered an emotion I hadn't felt in ages.

Happiness.

When I couldn't keep my eyes open any longer, Dad and Mom both tucked me in and told me they loved me very much. Without warning, I started to cry. They held me as I did, remaining silent except for gentle whispers of assurance. They knew. They felt it too.

Before they left, Dad asked me if I wanted my headphones. I hadn't thought about them in months and I paused a moment before nodding. He pulled them from the nightstand where I had stashed them away and slid them over my ears. Immediately, I felt a little better, like this was how it had always been. They no longer scared me but instead filled me with the comfort they had once provided. Tommy was gone and the voice would be as well. Maybe it had never been there at all. Maybe my terrified, broken, confused mind had conjured it as a means to cope.

Dad kissed my forehead as I snuggled down into my covers. He turned off the light and left, closing the door behind him. I sighed heavily…and easily slipped into a deep sleep.

It was around two that morning that I heard it.

A buzzing in my ears, so familiar that I jerked awake, the noise pulling me from the arms of slumber.

The static grew loud in my head and I clutched the covers, eyes going wide. No…no, no please not this. I didn't want this. This was supposed to be over.

Then the voice came, so soft and strange I felt goosebumps rise along my arms.

"What are you dreaming about, Jack?"

I breathed harder, heart sputtering like a man choking on a sip of water.

"You haven't forgotten about me have you?"

I shuddered, the voice an echo across the space between my ears. I ran my tongue over my lips and took a deep breath.

"You're supposed to be gone."

And for the first time, the voice responded: **"I never left, little Jack. You did."**

I wanted to turn on a light, sit up, and call out to my parents, but I lay paralyzed in my bed. I spoke to the voice again.

"Who…are you?"

A wave of static carried my question away and I thought I had lost him. But then, faintly, the voice returned.

"A friend, hopefully."

I pressed the headphones tight against my head, "What do you know about Tommy?"

Silent, a crackle of static, and then, "I know that he scares me beyond anything I have ever encountered."

"But is he gone!? Is Tommy gone?!" I begged.

The buzzing grew louder and in the distance, I thought I heard whistles or horns, like a tugboat calling woefully to the horizon.

"Don't leave me!" I cried, suddenly panicking.

Barely audible through the static, the voice reached for me, **"I'm so sorry, Jack."**

And then a screeching whistle filled my head and I threw the headphones off of me and onto the floor. My heart was galloping and I could barely breathe. I sat up, gasping and trembling. Tears filled my eyes and I looked down at my shaking hands.

"I don't understand," I croaked. "God help me…I just don't understand."

Sleep eluded me that night and I watched through bleary eyes as the sun rose hours later. I didn't talk to anyone that day about my nighttime conversation. Katie sensed something was wrong, but I refused to talk about it no matter how hard she pressed. I felt like it would bring the fear back to life. That it would dig up things I wanted to leave in the past. I wanted that chapter to be over. I wanted us to move on.

But it didn't.

We were at the dinner table that evening about to eat when a knock came at the door. Immediately, the four of us exchanged terrified looks. Hot food steamed between us and I saw Mom bite her lip.

"Everyone relax," Dad said, his voice not quite steady, "I'm sure it's just one of the neighbors. Just stay put while I get it, ok?"

He stood and walked to the front door. My pulse was roaring and I saw Katie gripping the table.

Taking a deep breath, Dad opened the door.

And a hauntingly familiar voice greeted him, "Hello, Mike. Did you miss me?"

I saw Dad freeze. Katie let out a whimper beside me and my mind reeled with terror. This couldn't be happening. Not again.

Tommy pushed into the house and closed the door behind him. A smile lit his eyes as he looked over my father at the three of us.

"Good to see you all again," he cooed.

Dad took a step back, fear cracking his strained voice. "How…how the hell…"

Tommy looked at him sideways, still smiling. "Surprised? Did you think you could cut me out of this family? Is that what you wanted?"

"We…we watched you burn," Dad whispered, his eyes bulging.

Tommy placed a hand on his shoulder. "Yes…that wasn't very nice was it? After everything I've taught you about love and acceptance…it worries me. Have you learned nothing these past few years? Have you even listened to what I've shared with you about family? About being a decent person?"

Dad stepped away from him, raising his hands. "Look, Tommy, we didn't have a choice…the things you did to us…"

Tommy jabbed a finger at him, his voice growing hostile. "You always have a choice. It's what separates the morality of the masses. There's a great divide in this terrible world…and Mike…you chose the wrong side."

"T-tommy—" Dad sputtered.

Without warning, Tommy lunged forward and grabbed him by the collar and said in a venomous hiss, "I warned you, Mike…I warned you." He looked up from my father. "Jack, turn on the stove. We're going to need it."

But I couldn't move. I couldn't even respond. A ripple of shock had me in its grip and refused to let go. How could this possibly be? How could this happen again?

"You…died…" I heard Katie whisper.

Tommy locked eyes with her. "No…I just left for a little while. This community still doesn't understand the position it's in, even after all these years. I wanted you to feel hope," his eyes narrowed, "and then I wanted to come back and take it away."

"Why?" Katie breathed, her lips trembling.

Tommy smiled, a sick display that turned my stomach. "Because when you break something it needs to know what it's losing in the process."

"You monster…" Mom said softly from her chair. Her face was deathly pale and tears formed in her eyes. "Why won't you just leave us alone?"

Tommy, still holding my father in his grip, chuckled, "Because there are things I still need to teach you." The smile suddenly dropped from his face and he turned back to my father. "But not tonight. Tonight we break."

Dad's eyes filled with terror. "Please…I'm begging you…"

Tommy ignored him. "Jack, the stove. NOW!"

I jumped, scrambling off my chair. I looked to Mom, but her gaze was filled with the looming menace. Not knowing what else to do, hoping to stave off any impending punishment, I did what Tommy asked and turned on the stove. The four electric elements began to glow a brilliant orange, their spiraling shape filling my head with a never-ending pattern. Pain…suffering…torment…

"What are you going to do to us?" Dad whispered.

Tommy slowly turned to stare at him, "I'm going to teach you to do what you're told."

"We'll do whatever you w—" Dad started but never had the chance to finish.

Tommy threw him like a rag doll across the room and into the kitchen where he slammed into the fridge with a heavy thud. Mom screamed, standing up, the familiar fear returning in an instant.

I began to cry, backing into the corner of the kitchen, lost in myself. This was going to be bad. I knew this time it was going to be very, very bad.

Dad gasped from the floor, clutching his side. Mom went to him, sobbing, hands running over his body. Tommy marched into the kitchen, his face a mask of rising rage. He circled the table and grabbed my mother by the back of the neck, hauling her to her feet.

"You called me a monster," he whispered into her ear. "Let me show you how that looks." He slammed her face into the countertop. Blood exploded from my mom's nose and she let out a shocked gasp. Tommy pulled her back up and her eyes rolled in her head. Without pause, Tommy opened the fridge door and stuck her head in.

"MOM!" Katie screeched.

Tommy didn't even look at her as he slammed the door into Mom's head. Once, twice, three times…each blow draining the strength and resilience from her. Blood began to run down the sides of the fridge and onto the floor. Tommy let her go and she collapsed in a heap, sucking in wet lungfuls of air.

"You make me sick," Tommy said dangerously, now circling my father. "What kind of example are you providing your children? What kind of people are you encouraging them to be?"

Dad rolled onto his back, hands raised defensively as Tommy stood over him, "I'm sorry, please, I've learned my lesson. I realize my mistake!"

"No, you haven't," Tommy growled. He planted a foot on my father's knee and reached down, grabbing his foot, "But you will." He pulled back and I heard Dad's knee snap as Tommy inverted it in its socket.

I slumped to the floor, tears pouring from my eyes as my father screamed like I had never heard him scream before. Mom was trying to get to her hands and knees, blood running freely from her mouth, ears, and nose. My dad's howls seemed to stir her from her dazed misery and she tried to crawl to him but went down.

Tommy crouched over my father and snarled into his face. "Tonight you're going to feel the consequences of what you've done. You're going to feel it in ways you've never felt."

He stood then and swept his hand across the table, scattering food and dishware across the floor. Plates and glasses crashed loudly around me as I wept, shuddering, praying for it all to be over.

And then he grabbed Katie by the throat.

"NO!" I screamed, eyes going wide, "NO TOMMY PLEASE!"

Tommy looked at me and I saw darkness in his eyes that I didn't know existed.

He picked Katie up with one hand and slammed her down on top of the table. My sister cried out in futile terror, clawing, scratching, pleading. "No, I'm sorry, we'll be good, Tommy. WE'LL BE GOOD!"

Somehow Dad managed to heave himself up, screaming, tears streaking from the corners of his eyes, his leg jutting away from his body at an unnatural angle. He grasped a chair for support, desperate to save his daughter.

"Leave her alone! This wasn't her fault, she has nothing to do with this!"

Tommy's eyes blazed. "I know it wasn't. It's your fault."

Dad jerked forward in an attempt to bat Tommy's grip from my sister, but Tommy knocked his hands aside and pushed him back to the floor.

"Just remember," Tommy snarled down at my parents, "that this is your doing."

He bent down and scooped up a knife that had clattered to the floor. Its blade gleamed as he retrieved it and I felt a tornado of horror and sickness overwhelm me.

Holding Katie by the throat, Tommy began to cut her leg off at the thigh.

Darkness danced in my vision as Katie's screams cracked through my skull like blows from a hammer. Blood spewed from the incision as Tommy viciously parted her flesh like it was warm butter. Red pooled around the table in puddles as Katie howled, thrashing with a pain I couldn't imagine.

Her cries stirred my parents and they desperately tried to stand and stop this nightmare. Mom managed to get one hand on the table, but Tommy kicked her back to the floor before severing the bone.

Her leg dropped wetly to the floor. The sound it made as it splashed into her own blood brought bile to the back of my throat. My eyes were bloodshot and blurry and I felt dizziness course through me. Snot bubbled from my nose and spittle leaked from my quivering lips as I stared at the piece of my sister that didn't belong to her anymore.

And then Tommy began to saw off the other leg.

"NO!" My father screamed, pounding the floor, tears of horror pouring out of him, "DEAR GOD, NOT MY BABY GIRL! PLEASE, TOMMY!"

Tommy's face was a mask of hatred and fury as he continued to travel the blade through Katie's gushing flesh.

My sister roared with agony, her voice a piercing, pathetic thing, "DADDY, MAKE HIM STOP! PLEASE, DADDYYYY PLEASSEEE!" And then she was lost again in the pain, her body jerking with violent spasms.

Thump.

Her other leg dropped to the floor, and her two stumps sent blood like a waterfall over the table and onto the soaked linoleum.

"Stop this," I whispered, going mad, "p-please…" I covered my ears as my sister continued to writhe. I felt like I was trapped in a snow globe slowly filling with blood, the puddles around the table growing towards me.

Dad was trying to stand again, his voice a vengeful mourn. "How could you!? HOW COULD YOU DO THIS!?"

Tommy stepped back and observed his work, finally releasing Katie. Her eyes rolled wildly in her head and it reminded me of a crazed beast. Spittle and foam formed around her mouth. She twisted away, trying to escape the searing pain. With a wet thud, she fell to the floor, surrounded by red stains of her own making.

I pulled my knees up to my chest, weeping as I watched my sister try to stand, her stumps squishing and sliding in the mess of gore. Screaming, she went down and reached for Mom.

"Help me! MOMMY, HELP ME! WHERE ARE MY LEGS!?"

Mom crawled under the table, the cloud of pain leaving her as her motherly instinct kicked back in. She almost made it to Katie before Tommy kicked the table over her, a leg striking her across the mouth.

"We aren't quite finished," Tommy snarled. He stepped through the blood and hauled Katie up by the hair like she was a piñata waiting for more punishment. She twirled and spun helplessly as Tommy marched her over to the stove.

"Despite how it looks," he said, now gripping her under her arms, her severed stumps churning the air, "I don't want you to die."

He lowered her bleeding wounds onto the red-hot elements, the flesh sizzling like grilled meat. I saw smoke rise from Katie as she arched her back and let out a bellowing squeal. Tommy held her in place, staring straight into her eyes, as her thighs cauterized.

A sickly smell filled the kitchen and I felt my stomach buckle beneath its foul vapors. Both my parents were screaming. The world shook and I trembled beneath a hammer of horrific disbelief.

When Tommy finally lifted Katie back up, I saw blackened strands of flesh stick to the stove and pull away. What remained of her legs looked like pieces of bloody coal, the flow of blood now an ashy residue. Mercifully, Katie's head slumped as she passed out from the pain.

He held her like a toddler, his composure changing. He rubbed her back gently and whispered in her ear, "Shhh…that's good. Go to sleep now; it's all over now. Tommy's done…we're all done."

"You demon!" Mom screamed from the floor, arms shaking as she tried to right herself. "How could you!? How could you!?"

Tommy just rocked Katie's motionless body, his voice calm, the fury leaving his face. "Hush, now…let the girl rest. She's earned it, wouldn't you say?"

"I'm going to kill you," Dad snarled, his eyes red and disbelieving. "Somehow I'm going to kill you."

Tommy stared down at him, some of the sharpness returning, "Mike…please don't tell me this lesson has been for nothing."

Dad just glared at him, drool and blood leaking from his mouth.

Tommy smiled."If I even think that you're plotting something, either of you, it'll be Jack on the table next. And I won't be so gentle next time."

He looked over at me huddled in the corner and winked. I shrank deeper into myself, my mind splintering and drifting up into the cosmos. I wasn't here…this wasn't happening…I would wake up soon, I knew I would. Katie's mangled body horrified me, a repulsion I felt the deepest shame for. Fresh tears found my eyes and I covered my face in shaken grief.

Tommy turned away from us all. "I'm going to put her to bed and look after her wounds. She's on thin ice right now."

As he reached the stairs he looked back. "Clean up the mess," his eyes darkened, "and think of a convincing story about what happened. It better be good."

We watched him take my sister upstairs, humming a soft lullaby as he went.

"Jack."

I couldn't move. I was a million miles above the kitchen, looking down on the grisly scene with paralyzing repulsion. I thought someone had said my name, but everything felt fuzzy, muffled, and out of sync.

"Jack!" Dad called again, pulling his body across the floor, blood seeping into his clothes. "JACK!"

I snapped my head up, not sure where I was, what was going on, or who this man calling my name was.

"Jack, talk to me, are you ok!?" Dad called, inching closer. His leg trailed behind him and I thought he looked like a bird with a broken wing.

"Honey, are you hurt!?" Mom asked, looking just as dazed as I felt.

Slowly, I shook my head.

There was just so much blood.

"You're going to have to help me, Jack," Dad was saying, worming closer. His shirt was soaked, a human mop absorbing the evidence of my sister's torture.

"D-dad?" I finally croaked.

"Yes, son," he croaked, "yes, son, I'm here."

"What…what are we going to do…?"

Dad started to cry suddenly. "We…we're going to do what he says…we're going to listen…oh God…oh my God…" His body shook. "Oh my God, what have I done…?"

Katie died the following morning.

Chapter 5 — 1999

Tommy intended to break us that night. And he did. He broke us so completely that I have a hard time remembering anything that happened that last year. I shrank into myself and spent my days in my head. I was hollow. Time was just a concept I didn't understand anymore. Depression and despair were just words I associated with my state of mind. I was learning to always expect the worst. I was learning how to hate life. Each day was a lesson in devastation. Each sunset was a page turned in a book that seemed endless.

My sister was dead.

Her absence shook the very foundation of my psyche. Her brutal death uprooted the last shadow of comfort I had been afforded. Her empty bed was now a sarcophagus, her barren sheets a shroud that draped longingly to the floor.

My parents ceased to speak after that dreadful night. Only when prompted by Tommy would they openly converse and that was after much prodding. They didn't look at each other, didn't look at me, didn't even seem to be alive. They shuffled about the house and tended to their individual lives like robots on a track. My father tried a couple times to console me during that winter, but we just ended up sitting on my bed in silence, struggling to find the words.

Of course, they covered up Katie's death. Tommy wouldn't have it any other way. Coming up with a believable story though…that was a challenge. My parents just wanted to bury her and be done with the grief, but Tommy wouldn't allow it. He knew a child couldn't just go missing without someone showing up to ask questions. My mind was so poisoned with resentment that I wondered if anyone actually would have inquired if we hadn't conjured a plan.

The mental destruction my parents went through arranging the fake car accident is something I can only speculate about. I can't fathom such a horror. My father took Katie's dead body, including her severed legs, and placed them in our van. He drove out a little ways into the country and smashed it into a telephone pole. Then he set the car on fire. After it burned a little, he called 911.

I remember seeing a news report later that night on TV about it. "Tragic car accident kills a young girl." She wasn't wearing her seatbelt and the force of the impact threw her into the windshield where the broken shards severed her legs. She died on the hood of the van, as the flames burned around her.

My mother caught me watching the report. Instead of turning off the TV though, she just went upstairs to her room and closed the door. My dad was in the hospital, as well, suffering from minor injuries.

I wanted to throw up.

Apparently, Dad told the police that a semi-truck had swerved into their lane, forcing them off the road. With bloodshot eyes, he told them he suspected the driver had fallen asleep.

I remember Tommy sitting next to me on the couch, watching, a slow smile edging up his face. At one point he patted my leg and muttered, "Good…he's doing good."

A couple days later, my parents got the funeral they wanted. My sister was buried at St. Michael's and my eyes remained dry through the whole thing. I watched the mourners with an almost vengeful hatred. Old ladies sobbing, parishioners weeping. But what…*the hell*…had they done to help? Where had they been when we so desperately needed someone to see us?

The reception was a garble of condolences and comforting hugs. A lady I vaguely recognized tried to hug me, her lip trembling, and I almost smashed my glass of water across her face. Instead, I stepped away from her and spent the rest of the wake sitting outside, hating everything with unholy venom.

After a couple months, the tide of time washed the whole ordeal away. My family faded from the public eye once again and we were labeled as a tragedy. I couldn't believe no one saw through the façade. I couldn't believe no one was asking questions.

I think the vacant stares of shell-shocked horror my parents wore helped sell the pain. Everyone bought the story because there actually was no pain to sell. It was real and it was engraved into every crease and pore of my parent's faces. How else could human beings look so…inhuman? How else could that far-off gaze find my parents' eyes?

We had become phantoms of our own existence.

As winter faded and the world tanned once again, I noticed something through the fog of misery. Something different. Something different about Tommy. At first, I didn't think much of it because it was such an ordinary thing, but after a couple times, I realized I had never seen him perform such an action before.

He was writing. Somehow he had procured a small household notebook and I would often catch him scribbling in it. Whenever he took notice of me watching him, he would quietly put it away and smile at me.

When the cool of spring heated to the blaze of summer, I was overcome with dangerous curiosity. I needed to know what he was scribing in that notebook. It ate away at me and for some reason. I thought it would hint at his plans for our family. Or maybe it would detail his departure. Or was he just plotting future lessons for my family, storing them away so he wouldn't forget? I didn't know and the burning desire to peek into those pages rose like an all-consuming maw in my tired head.

I was sitting in the living room when I got my chance.

Tommy was in the kitchen, watching my mother prepare dinner for when Dad got home. The notebook was in front of him, closed. He was tapping a pen against the cover, staring at the back of Mom's head. He hadn't said much that day and I noticed an almost annoyed aura hovering around him that afternoon. He didn't like the state of despair we had all fallen into. I noticed that it turned his cheerful mood sour. More than once he snapped at the three of us because of it. But we were so numb to pain at that point, we didn't care. Let him hurt us. Let his anger billow against us. We simply didn't care anymore.

"I'm going to go start the grill," Tommy said from the kitchen table. "Mike prefers his chicken like that. Who knows, maybe it'll be enough to get him to smile tonight."

My mother just nodded from the counter, continuing to season the raw chicken before her. Her hair hung in a tangled mess around her shoulders, his clothes wrinkled and in a state of disarray. Tommy stood up, shaking his head.

"My patience for your mopey attitude is growing very thin, Penny."

Mom half turned. "I'm sorry, Tommy. I'm just…just tired today."

Tommy snorted, "Well, snap out of it. You're infecting the rest of us with your long face. What do you have to be so miserable about anyway? Huh? You have a roof over your head, a beautiful son, and a loving husband." Tommy advanced on her. "Are you ungrateful? Is that it? Have you become bored with your life?"

Mom just sighed, her voice barely a whisper, "No, Tommy…I'm just tired."

Tommy reached her and spun her around, his voice brittle. "I heard you the first time. And I told you to snap out of it."

He slapped her across the face, bringing a gasp from my mother. I clenched my fists from the couch as my mom doubled over, rubbing her cheek. A tear escaped from the corner of her eye and she brushed it away.

"I want to see a smile when I come back in," Tommy warned, turning. Mom just nodded and watched him go to start the grill out back. The storm door creaked and when it snapped closed, Mom looked at me and turned away. I wanted to say something.

Instead, I slid off the couch and hurried over to the kitchen table. Tommy had left his book. Mom paid me no attention as I scooped it up and retreated, heart pounding. This was dangerous, so dangerous, but in that moment, I didn't care. I had to know. It was the only clue I could hope to gain. I pressed the notebook to my chest and quickly walked upstairs to my bedroom, listening for Tommy. I prayed he would stay outside.

I paused at the threshold of my room, training an ear for sound below. The steady chop of my mother's knife was all I heard. Quickly, I sprang for my bed and propped myself up against the headboard. I took a moment to steady my hands as I turned the small book over in them. Did I dare? Of course, I did.

Taking a deep breath, I slowly peeled the pages open. At first, I didn't understand what I was seeing. I turned to a fresh sheet. Again, my brow furrowed. What on earth? Heart tripping over itself, I proceeded to tear through the notebook, practically ripping the pages in the process.

It was all the same.

Every single page mirrored the last. It was one phrase repeated over and over again but then crossed out in angry, thick scrawl, two massive Xs connecting the corners of the page.

Six-six-three-five-eight-Rez.

My eyes widened as the memory flooded my confused mind. I knew these words…I had been given them by the voice in my headphones. I continued to soak in the chaotic scrawl, the lines and lines of crossed out nonsense. He must have written it hundreds of times, each page darkly X'ed out.

What did it *mean* though? How could this help me?

"What have you got there, Jack?"

My head whipped up at the voice and my heart sank into my stomach. Tommy leaned against the door frame, his arms casually crossed. A small smile tilted the corner of his mouth. His perfectly smooth skin gleamed in the sunlight from the window. His eyes sparked their luminous, terrible blue light and I slowly closed the book. I knew it was useless to try and hide it.

Tommy crossed the room and gently plucked the notebook from my hands. I stared into my lap, the first shades of fear darkening my heart. I waited, knowing that some punishment was bound to follow.

Instead, Tommy placed his hand beneath my chin and tilted my eyes to meet his. They were gentle and he almost looked compassionate. I didn't dare trust it.

"I understand your curiosity," Tommy said quietly, still holding my chin in his hand. "It's quite natural for boys your age to be…curious."

I waited, my chest rising and falling with anticipation.

"You've grown up so much since I arrived," Tommy continued. "You've learned so much. I'm very pleased with who you're becoming. You have a big heart, Jack, a very big heart. You care deeply for those around you. I can see it. But sometimes I see clouds hovering behind your eyes: dark, angry, resentful storm clouds."

I swallowed, hovering in his grip.

"But I believe in you," Tommy pressed, his voice almost a whisper. "I believe you are going to be a good man someday. This darkness you feel…let it go. You're about to enter your teenage years and that is the most exciting time in anyone's life. Don't let your bitterness ruin it." He traced his finger up my cheek now. "Instead, embrace the warmth you feel towards those you care about. Focus on that instead of the anger. Do you understand what I'm trying to tell you?"

Emotionless, I nodded.

Tommy smiled again. "Good, Jack. You're a good boy." His

fingers caressed down my nose and his thumb brushed my lips. "You always were my favorite."

Adrenaline spiked through my system as Tommy pressed his thumb into my mouth, guiding it across my tongue.

"Such a beautiful boy," Tommy breathed, swathing my mouth. Gingerly, he pulled his thumb out past my lips and stared down at me.

Holding eye contact, his licked my saliva from his skin, his tongue absorbing it in slow strokes. My stomach churned and the adrenaline I felt oozed into dangerous terror. Tommy lowered his thumb and crouched down by the bed, now at my level.

His voice was breathy and shallow, "I think you're ready for your final lesson."

His hands traveled across the covers and found my legs, his fingers mounting them and sliding up to rest around my thighs.

"T-Tommy..." I sputtered, trying to scoot away from his toxic touch.

Tommy gripped my thighs and pulled me to the edge of the bed. "Hush, Jackie...hush now."

My hands balled into the sheets as I was pulled toward Tommy. My face was inches from his now and I almost gagged as his breath blew warm across my skin. It smelled like rotting meat.

"Do you know what I'm talking about, Jack? About what I want you...to do?"

I squirmed, trying to escape his eyes that now burned with focused intensity, "Tommy, I...I don't want to do this...please..."

Tommy reached out and stroked my cheek. "It's ok to be

afraid. Everyone is their first time. But it's going to be ok. I'll be with you. I won't let anything bad happen to you."

Tears found my eyes and ran helplessly down my face. I knew what he wanted…I knew what he planned to do with me. It was an act so alien and adult, a foreign secret that kids only whispered and joked about when their parents weren't around. And it scared me *terribly.*

"Please don't make me," I whispered, sniffling.

Tommy reached out and wiped a tear from my face. "Shh, shh, shhhh. No tears, Jack." He leaned in and for a horrifying second, I thought he was going to kiss me. Instead, his voice found my ear. "I want you to go across to Jason's house. I'll be waiting for you."

He pulled away and looked into my eyes, making sure I understood. I nodded miserably, dragging a hand across my blubbering nose. Tommy stood and ruffled my hair.

"Go on, be quick about it."

Wordlessly, I slid from the bed and followed Tommy out of the room. He took my hand once we entered the hallway.

Together…we descended.

When we reached the ground floor, I desperately searched for my mom. She could stop this; she had to stop this. The fear that rolled through my stomach teased vomit in the back of my throat. I looked to the kitchen, a cry for help rising.

Tommy didn't give me the chance. He pulled me to the front door and opened it. Placing a hand on my shoulders he pushed me outside. The hot summer sun dripped from the sky like steaming glaze and I felt its heat coat my skin in a sickly film of sweat. I turned around, one last begging plea fluttering from my lips.

But Tommy just smiled and pointed across the street. "Go

on. I'll be waiting." And then he closed the door. Miserable, I turned and began to sob. I raised my hands to my face. Not this...please...please not this...

I looked up, vision slightly blurred...and saw a car crawling down the road towards the cul-de-sac where I stood. I didn't recognize the car which meant it wasn't someone from around here. For a second, hope sprang deep and true from the pit of misery I was wallowing in. They could help...they could help me! They had to!

As the car continued toward me, I ran to meet it. My feet padded through the grass of our front lawn and met the hot tar. I could see the driver now, a man about my dad's age, his window rolled down.

And he was waving me over to him.

Breathless, I hurried closer as he slowed, practically slamming into the side of the car as I reached it. My fingers gripped the edge of the lowered window, eyes bloodshot and pleading.

"P-please sir," I sputtered, "please, you have to help me!"

The man looked startled, my distraught appearance catching him off guard. His face was weathered and red, sweat rolling through his graying hair.

"Whoa, easy kid," he coaxed. "Relax, I'm just lost and I need some directions. Been driving around the countryside for hours now. I'm looking for Poplar Street. You know it?"

My grip tightened against his car. "W-what? No! But listen you have to help me, there's a man who's...he's going to..."

The driver shook his head. "What are you talking about, kid?"

"He's going to hurt me!" I managed to sputter, snot and fresh tears running down my face, mind reeling.

The man's voice turned serious. "Who is? Who's going to hurt you, son?"

And that's when the Murphy's front door opened. Tommy stepped outside, smiling and waving to the two of us, his voice calling across the lawn.

"Everything ok, Jack?"

"That's him!" I almost screamed, turning back to the driver, "That's the man!" My eyes were wide and streaked with terror, my lips barely able to form the words.

The driver turned, confused, to stare at Tommy and then back at me. I could see conflict rise behind his eyes and uncertainly roll through him like an evening storm.

"P-please…don't leave me," I wept, trembling.

Tommy stepped forward onto the front stoop. "What's wrong, Jack? Come on, dinner is getting cold!"

No…no stop it. Shut up shut up shut up—

The driver turned to Tommy and called through the open window, "This your boy, mister?"

Tommy gave an exaggerated nod. "Yeah, sure is. He's a good kid, but he gets a little emotional sometimes. I'm sorry about the trouble. Come on, Jack, let's go your mother is getting impatient!"

I spun to the man, vision dancing with specks of darkness. "That is not my father."

The man looked hard at me and then, to my horror, I saw a weary understanding wash through him. He leaned out the window and lowered his voice. "Look, kid, everyone hates their dad at one point or another. Just respect him as best you can and one day you'll realize he's just trying to do what's best for you."

"N-no!" I cried as the man started to pull away. "No don't leave me! PLEASE!"

"JACK!" Tommy yelled.

The car inched forward and then my grip was lost. Completely dumbfounded, I watched as the man spun around in the cul-de-sac and headed back down the street, throwing Tommy a wave which he returned.

The sun threw itself against my face as I stared at the shrinking car. Sweat rolled down my face in great, sloppy streaks. My heart was beating so fast I could hear it in my ears, a roar like a bloody current.

How...how could he just *leave* me...?

How could he not see what was going on...?

Why...why wouldn't someone *save me* from this hell?

I suddenly felt something surge inside of me and I balled my fists, the impending future looming over my head like a razor-sharp axe.

I screamed a terrified, horrific sound that blasted across the evening sky. I screamed and I screamed, shrinking down to the pavement and curling into a ball. Tears poured from my eyes like rivers of sorrow and I shook with disbelief and terror.

I began to scream even louder when Tommy scooped me up from the pavement and marched us into the Murphy's house, slamming the door closed behind him. The silence that greeted us seized my howls and stole them away into the soft nothingness.

"You shouldn't have done that," Tommy said quietly as I gasped against him, his grip firm around my waist and neck. "That was very, very dangerous, Jack. You should know better."

"Stop it," I begged, finding my breath. "Stop it, put me down, don't DO THIS, PLEASE, TOMMY!" I began to struggle against him, a last-ditch effort to stem the flow of reeking fear. Tommy just held me tighter as we ascended the stairs.

Toward the bedroom.

"Don't take me in there," I hissed, spittle flying from my lips. "Please don't take me in there!"

The door at the end of the hall stood like a gateway into another world. A world devoid of understanding. A world not meant for children. Tommy walked us closer.

I suddenly realized that the Murphys were nowhere to be seen. The house was silent, a somber, empty thing that filled the quiet with unknown secrets. Had Tommy killed them? Was Jason dead? Why were we alone here? Why wasn't anyone stopping the horrific act about to happen?

We reached the bedroom door and Tommy pushed it open. Together, we entered.

I turned in Tommy's grip to stare inside...and felt a rush of fear engulf me like a blanket of ice.

Mrs. Murphy, Jason's mom, lay naked and bound to the bed. Her arms and legs stretched to the bedposts where they were wrapped tightly with strong rope. Her skin was a mess of bruises and scabs, evidence of a lesson taught.

When she saw me, she closed her eyes and moaned.

"No...no, please...Tommy, please..."

Closing the door behind him, Tommy put me down. His hands clamped around my shoulders before I could move, rooting me in place. My heart was racing and I averted my eyes, embarrassed and terrified at Mrs. Murphy's nakedness.

She struggled against her bindings, voice pleading, "Tommy, you can't do this, he's just a child! PLEASE, TOMMY!"

But Tommy said nothing, instead pushing me forward toward the foot of the bed. I kept my eyes locked on the floor, face flushed. I had never seen a naked woman before. Not even a picture of one. The brief glance I had stolen confused and bewildered me. A trickle of sweat ran down my spine and I shivered.

"Look at her," Tommy said quietly.

But I didn't dare.

Tommy grabbed a fistful of hair and yanked my head up. "Look at her, Jack."

Eyes watering, I did as I was told. I wanted to recoil, the alien landscape before me a terror of unknown. I did my best to avert my eyes, but despite myself, they were continually drawn back to the naked form before me.

"It's time you became a man," Tommy whispered, releasing my hair.

"No, no, no, no…" Mrs. Murphy sobbed, twisting her head, trying to get away.

"Take off your clothes."

"Please…" I begged one last time.

"Take. Them. Off." Not a request, but a command.

Trembling, I slowly peeled off my shirt, feeling horrifically cold all of the sudden. Tommy took my shirt and pointed to my pants. Lip quivering, I reached down and pulled them off, feeling deeply ashamed and exposed. Tommy took them, as well, now nodding at my underwear. I wrapped my arms around myself praying silently that someone would burst in and stop this.

"Jack," Tommy said quietly, "your underwear."

Squeezing my eyes closed, tears spilling down my cheeks, I leaned down and pulled my underwear off. I quickly covered myself, a gale of embarrassment blowing through me. I had never been naked in front of a woman before, not even my mom.

I heard Tommy sigh behind me and then his hands were gently running down my back. "Such a good boy."

"Please let me go home," I wept, turning up to look at him with bloodshot, weary eyes.

Tommy smiled down at me and ran a hand through my hair. "There's nothing to be afraid of. Just a little while longer now. Be brave. Can you do that for me?"

I cast my eyes to the ground, the carpet a blurry mess.

"Climb up on the bed," Tommy said softly, pushing me forward, "go on."

I let out a sob as I clumsily collided with the wooden footboard. Hands shaking, I pulled myself up, and then onto the mattress. Now I stood in full view of Mrs. Murphy, her exposed body splayed out before me. Her eyes were closed and her lips shuddered with unheard pleas. I traveled my gaze across her nudity and felt a mixture of terror and disbelief.

"Lay down on top of her," Tommy instructed, "like you're going to take a nap."

Mrs. Murphy's eyes met mine, two watery brown pools of gentle compassion.

"It's ok, Jack," she said, voice cracking. "It's ok, go ahead. Don't be afraid."

But I stood paralyzed, limbs like stone, hands locked over my crotch. My mind was splintering and breaking apart, pieces floating away into a darkness where I dared not look. The room swam and I felt like I was dreaming.

Tommy came up behind me and his hands guided me down. Eyes glazed, mouth slightly agape, I allowed myself to be folded on top of Mrs. Murphy. Her skin was much softer than I thought it would be, like a warm silk sheet that contoured to my body.

"It's ok, it's ok, don't be scared," she whispered to me, crying, as our bodies met.

Tommy hovered over us like a winged demon, his voice soft and commanding. "You know what to do. Became the vessel this young man needs to cross that final threshold."

Wriggling against the ropes, Mrs. Murphy met my eyes again. I saw terror but also a motherly need to protect the young.

"I'm so sorry," she whispered, "Just close your eyes Jack and it'll be over soon. Just think about something else. Think about happy things, about when times were good."

Not exactly sure what was going to happen next, I did as I was told and closed my eyes. I felt myself shaking against the body beneath me, the strange horrific reality of my situation collapsing my mind.

The rest was a blur of nightmarish memory. Tommy's hands on my hips, movement beneath me, heat, sour air, and then a rush of unexpected pleasure. As soon as the moment passed, I felt a sickness rise in my throat and I shuddered violently. A tingling sensation twisted below my waist and I went ablaze with dizziness.

"You did so well," Mrs. Murphy openly cried, her face a mess of tears and shame. "It's all over now Jack, it's finished."

Tommy had retreated away from the bed and I saw him staring at us, his eyes wide.

"Amazing," he whispered, "just...amazing."

My stomach buckled suddenly and I leaned over the side of the bed, vomiting onto the floor. The sweat clinging to my skin acted as a lubricant and I slid off Mrs. Murphy, following the trail of vomit before I could catch myself. I splashed into it and bounced my head off the floor, bringing stars.

I lay there, gasping, reeking, and wished to die.

Darkness tip-toed closer and I begged to be embraced by it. My mind floated miles above my head and I felt like a stranger in my own body. I don't know how long I lay there, broken and empty, but at some point, Tommy picked me up.

I was slung over his shoulder and he began to walk. I bounced like a sack of meat and bones, drool leaking from my lips. My eyes were glazed and I was suddenly clueless as to where I was. My body felt spent and fatigued. My legs hurt. My head ached.

I was dimly aware of sunlight at some point and realized we had left the Murphy's house and were walking across the street back to mine. Somewhere in the chaos, I heard my mother screaming. Colors and warmth filtered across my face like shifting rainbows.

When I became aware again, I was in bed. I groggily looked at the window and saw it was night, a smattering of stars painting the sky with pencil dot beauty. I felt disgusting and worn down like a used eraser. I heard my parents somewhere below me, talking, arguing, and then falling into silence. When had Dad come home? Where was I again? I faded…

When morning came, my parents were hovering over my bed. Tommy stood in the corner of the room, smiling, eyes shining.

"He's different now, isn't he?" he said. "Can't you feel it?"

My parents just held me, silent tears running down their exhausted faces.

"I think…" Tommy said slowly, "I think I've taught him all I can. He's an incredible boy. One of the best I've come across.

There are great things in his future if you two continue to raise and nurture him like I have. I'll stick around until I'm sure things have settled, but Jack is no longer the little boy he once was. The rest is up to him. Do you understand what I'm saying?"

We had no idea what he was talking about but nodded just the same. We knew better.

"Well, then," Tommy said satisfied, "let the boy rest a little more. He's earned it."

I was already half asleep again as my parents departed the room, casting sorrowful glances over their shoulders. I didn't understand why they were so sad. Why were they crying for me? Did I look different now?

It wasn't until years later that I fully understood what had been done to me. What had been forced on me.

But something else happened that helped distract me from the pain of my recovery. Something my family couldn't quite believe.

You see…four months later, at the turn of the year, Tommy Taffy vanished from our lives.

There was no grand exit, no violent or fearful farewell. He was just…gone. We woke up like any other day, the dread of the grind before us…but Tommy was nowhere to be found. He had disappeared into the night. We didn't know why, didn't trust the hope it gave us. Tommy was a malicious monster and we had grown accustomed to his games and treachery. Why would he just leave us? Was it because he felt his job was done? Or was it because he had grown bored with us? Where did he go and would he come back? What had been the purpose of our five year torment? Why had we been forced to suffer for so long? Had it just been a game to him?

A full year passed before my broken family allowed hope back into our lives. At any moment, we fully expected Tommy to come knocking at our door, that horrific smile on his face…but he never did. Time marched on and we slowly began to heal the parts of us we still possessed. I wouldn't say we were ever happy again…but we were adapting to the absence of our captor.

But never fully.

How could we? There was one less member of our family now and her memory burned viciously in my mind.

Katie…I never stopped mourning for her.

As for Tommy Taffy and what became of him?

I prayed I would never have to answer that question.

But I have to…

Because he wasn't finished with me.

Six-Six-Three-Five-Eight-Rez

Chapter 6 —2017

I was drunk. Jesus Christ was I drunk. The bar floor felt like the deck of a ship and I swayed in the rhythm of imaginary waters. I blinked lazily, my eyelids like anchors. I ran a hand across my numb face and my fingers came away covered in drool. I needed to pull myself together. Ah, fuck it. Live a little. It was my birthday after all.

I raised my hands and pressed my way through the crowds of people, their conversation just white noise hanging above my head. Images blurred together like streaking paint and I burped offensively. Bile tickled the back of my throat and I tasted tequila. That made me want to vomit even harder. Where the hell was the bathroom?

Someone yelled at me as I pushed them aside, an angry voice in my ear. I just curled my hand into a fist but couldn't seem to find who had chastised me. I gave up the hunt and continued the trek to the bathroom. I knew I had to be quick; the girl I had been talking to would soon grow impatient in my absence.

I needed to have sex tonight. I needed it in the worst kind of way. The drinking had made me horny and I felt a lustful stirring beneath the ocean of alcohol sloshing in my gut. I blinked and thought I saw the men's room. Yes, there it was, that little stick man calling to me through the buzz. I shoved the door open, knocked into someone, felt beer splash at my feet, and then I was standing in front of the urinal. I quickly unbuttoned and emptied my bladder, sighing with almost euphoric relief. Didn't think I was going to make it.

As I shook myself, I felt a hand grab my shoulder and spin me around. A face lurched into my vision, a young, angry face. He was shouting at me. Something about spilling his beer. I decided he was much too close and told him so. This just seemed to infuriate him even more and he grabbed my shirt, spittle flying into my face.

Fuck this guy.

I headbutted him across the nose and that seemed to shut him up. He cried out, clutching his face, and ironically dropped the last of his beer onto the floor. The other patrons of the bathroom all cheered in drunken exaltation.

Before he could recover and launch a counter attack, which was sure to come, I grabbed him by the neck and slammed him back against the wall. I heard him cry out once again. I leaned in close, my voice a slurred hiss: "Don't fucking touch me again, pal."

And then I let him go when all the fight was drained out of him. That was good. I didn't know if I had the motor skills to engage in full-blown combat. As the man slouched to the floor, eyes wide, I giggled. It was a cruel thing to do, the humor stemming from some unseen joke. Or maybe I was just shit faced.

I left the bathroom and my fans and stumbled back to the bar. The music was loud. My head drummed with the beat, a nauseating electric wash of neon noise and adrenaline. Oh no, I had forgotten to throw up. Too late now. Had to get back to this girl, seal the deal, and then find a place to fuck her.

I picked the spot at the bar where I thought she had been and wormed my way through the sweaty, loud mass of young people. I suddenly wanted to leave very badly. My face felt flushed and I was beginning to feel seriously sick.

I found the girl. She was cute in a simple kind of way. Short brown hair, brown eyes, nice figure, and probably a goddamn freak in bed. She saw me and to my relief, she smiled. I felt her hand grasping mine and then her breath was in my ear.

"Didn't think you were coming back."

I smiled a crooked thing and leaned into her. "I want to get out of here, what do you say?"

She bit her lip. I wanted to bite her lip. I wanted to sink my teeth into them and tear them off. I squeezed my eyes shut. Focus.

"Right now? Where do you want to go?" she asked. I knew I had her hooked, I just needed to reel her in, make her feel safe like it would be ok to come home with me. I took a breath to steady my thundering head.

"Your place or mine. Though my place is just a couple blocks away from here; we could walk. Up to you, whatever you're more comfortable with."

Bravo old sport.

She looked around, maybe for her friends, and then asked, "Do you have roommates?"

Oh shit, what was the right answer here? If I told her the truth, if I told her no, then she might feel more isolated. I could tell she was the nervous type. But if I said yes then how would I explain the absence of anyone at my place?

"Yeah," I mumbled, "yeah I do. But they're gone for the weekend." I patted myself on the back.

Her eyes seemed to settle and a coy smile crept up her face. "Oh? So we'd be all alone?"

I spread my arms. "'Fraid so."

She smiled openly now and nodded. "Come on then, let's go."

Hell. Yes.

Without a moment's hesitation, I pulled her toward the exit, toward the world, away from this noise and distraction. If she did have friends here, I didn't want one of them stopping us. That was the absolute worst and I didn't think my sex drive could handle that tonight.

We burst from the bar, a cold autumn breeze stirring the hair from my date's shoulders. Well…she wasn't really my date. I suddenly realized I didn't remember her name. I felt like this was very important and if I couldn't recall it she would leave immediately.

But she broke the tension first, the two of us hurrying down the city street.

"What's your name again?" she giggled.

I exhaled. Perfect.

"Jack," I said casually, "and what's yours? I could barely hear anything in there."

She giggled, excited, thrilled, alive. "Lucy."

Ok, not my favorite name in the world, but it wasn't like I was going to marry her. Now wouldn't that be something? I felt like my parents would die of joy if I brought home a girl. The thought of my parents suddenly dampened my drunken good spirit. I hadn't talked to them in…months. I needed to call them. See how Mom was doing…

"Hey, you ok?" the girl—Lucy—asked.

I shoved thoughts of my parents aside and plastered a smile

on my face. "Couldn't be better. Come on, my place is just around the corner." Our feet echoed off the late night sidewalk, the glow of streetlights casting shadows before us like future versions of ourselves.

As we passed another crowded bar, the windows full of laughing, dancing, happy people, I turned to Lucy.

"You know it's my birthday today?"

This seemed to delight her. "No way, really? Happy birthday, Jack!" My name sounded alien coming from the lips of a stranger, especially when attached to such a familiar congratulations.

"Thanks." I grinned instead.

"Where are all your friends? Shouldn't they be out celebrating with you?"

We stepped around a very drunk man screaming into his phone before I answered, excuses fumbling on my tongue. "Uh, yeah, I guess they should be. They all had to work tonight though so we're going to celebrate tomorrow night."

"Couldn't wait until then?" Lucy asked with a wink.

"You only turn twenty-eight once," I said stupidly. It was true, though, my friends…friend…was working tonight and couldn't join me.

Jason. The only one who seemed to stick with me. I smiled into the night. Thank God for Jason. Without him…without him, I didn't know what my state of my mind would be these days.

We continued down the street and I pushed thoughts of the past behind me. Lucy was chatting excitedly about something but I wasn't really paying attention. Instead, I focused on digging my keys out of my pocket as we approached my building.

As I unlocked the front door, Lucy asked me a question that I only got the tail end of.

"Sorry, what was that?" I said, pushing the door open triumphantly.

"How long have you lived here?" she repeated.

I shrugged. "I dunno…couple years now."

This seemed to satisfy some lingering question and she nodded. I stood in the doorway, one hand outstretched to her.

"Well, you coming?"

She giggled and took my hand, and the two of us bound for the top floor where my apartment was. The wooden stairs creaked beneath our feet as we ascended and I imagined it was the cries of my invisible fans, cheering me on.

Lucy didn't disappoint. The sex was fantastic. But when you're drunk and horny, is it ever not? The two of us thrashed about on my bed, sweating, panting, hungrily grasping at one another. I was worried for a second about how much alcohol I had consumed and how that would affect me. Three minutes with Lucy though and I realized that wasn't going to be a problem. At some point she bit my shoulder so hard it drew blood. No one had done that before and it excited me.

After a rather wonderful climax, the two of us lay sweat-stained and panting on my bed. The dark apartment around us was still and silent. I didn't own very many things and in the quiet, I wondered if she had noticed. Of course, she had. Women were always keen on details like that. Especially when entering a stranger's house.

Lucy rolled over and placed her head on my bare chest. "Mmm, you wore me out."

Her cheek felt hot against my skin. Her hair was a tangle of sweaty tentacles splayed out across my body. I suddenly wanted to push her off me. Now that all lust had been drained, I felt like my social lighthouse had gone out.

"I think I'm bleeding," I said distantly.

She giggled, embarrassed. "Sorry about that."

"It's fine."

She raised her head to look at me. "It's fine?"

I shrugged. "Yeah, it's fine. Don't worry about it. What do you want me to say?"

Her brow furrowed and she smiled, "I don't know. That's just a funny thing to say I guess." Her voice lowered in what I guessed was an impression of me. "It's fine. Just a little bite. I'm used to this kind of thing. Girls bite me all the time." She chuckled and tapped the tip of my nose. "You big lady killer."

I knew she was just playing around, but I suddenly found her annoying. I sat up, pushing her off of me and groped in the darkness for my pack of cigarettes. I found them on the night-stand and quickly stuck one in my mouth.

"Hey, whoa, I'm just messing around," Lucy said propping herself up.

My fingers closed over my lighter and I brought the flame to life. "Ok."

Lucy sat up now. "Ok? What does that mean? Why are you getting all weird?"

I inhaled and squeezed the bridge of my nose between my fingers. "Maybe you should just go."

"What?"

I blew smoke out of my nose. "Maybe you should leave."

Lucy shook her head. "Are you fucking kidding me?"

"No."

She stared at me for a moment, wrestling with her anger and

pride before saying, "Is this just what you do? Fuck girls then kick them out? Am I just another notch on your headboard?"

I sucked on my cigarette. "I don't know."

"Go to hell," Lucy spat, springing up. "You were a lousy lay anyway."

"Ok."

She was snatching her clothes from the floor, stomping back into her jeans. "Asshole…such an asshole. Well, I hope you had a great birthday."

I leaned my head back, smoke wafting from my lips like angels rising to heaven. "I'm glad you bit me."

"Fuck you," she snarled, now mostly dressed. "Have a great life."

"Ok. You too."

She stood in the bedroom door for a moment, like she was waiting for me to stop her. When I didn't she threw me the middle finger, a small thing clothed in shadow, and stormed to the front door. I winced as she slammed it shut behind her. Then I heard her stomping down the stairs back to the street. Didn't she know people were trying to sleep?

I sighed heavily and rolled my cig across my lips from one corner to the other. I swung my feet to the floor and sat at the edge of my bed. I put my head in my hands, staring at my feet. The silence closed in and I felt it hovering over my shoulder. I was still pretty drunk, but the sex had cleared my head a little. I puffed out tendrils of squirming wraiths. Why had I kicked her out? Why the hell had I done that?

I closed my eyes, a weight pressing at my back. Stupid. So stupid. She hadn't deserved that. She was a nice girl. Why did I treat her like that? For half a second I thought about chasing after her, but the thought of rising exhausted me. Somewhere outside, a siren mourned woefully, a low pulsing cry that made me shiver. Why had I been such a bastard to her? The sudden emptiness of my apartment was a cruel reminder of my state of being. Wouldn't it have been nice to ebb away that loneliness for just a little while longer? But no…Jack's a lady killer. Slam 'em and see 'em off. What a player. What a cool guy.

"Goddamn it," I muttered, pressing my palms into my eyes. A long bridge of ash dangled from my cigarette. I felt something hitch in my chest and roll through me, a cloud of dark emotion. After a second I realized I was crying.

I inhaled heavily, wiping tears from my face, and sniffled miserably. Jesus, what was wrong with me?

"Pull yourself together, idiot," I whispered, my voice cracking. This made me even more depressed, actually hearing the sorrow on my voice. I gritted my teeth and covered my face with my hands, shoulders shaking as grief suddenly poured into me like an avalanche. I slumped to the floor, silent sobs wracking my naked body. The cold floorboards chilled my skin as I lay down, tears running down my face. My cigarette fell away, another casualty of bad choices.

After a little bit, I was able to regain control of myself. I ran my hand over my eyes and scrubbed my nose, gasping and blinking in the dark. I felt the waters of grief slowly pull away, back to the ocean I knew was there.

I stared beneath my bed, waiting to feel ok again. I noticed something in the dim space, an object shoved out of site. Tentatively, I reached out and pulled it towards me. It was a shoebox. When had I put this here? I dimly recalled some memory of it, but the passage of time dulled my recollection. I forced myself to sit up, pulling the box onto my lap. I groped for another cigarette and lit it before pulling the top off.

I stared down at the contents. My blood chilled to ice. It was my headphones. They sat alone in the box, a relic of a time I had worked so hard to put behind me. The sight of them sent a rocket of discomfort through me. How long had it been since I had seen these? And why had I kept them? I struggled to remember and vaguely caught wind of a memory. I had almost thrown them away when I moved out of the house, but some malicious force had told me to keep them. A reminder of what had happened all those years ago. A visual cue that the nightmares were real and not some conjuring of madness. Oh yes…I remembered now…all those long nights, alone, wrestling with the concept of my own sanity. Because what happened to me as a child…how could that possibly be real? The sickening fever dreams I had suffered, the tossing and turning, the cold sweats and screaming, awakening from night terrors to question the constitution of my own memory. Yes…it was all coming back now. It hadn't gone away, merely recessed to some horrible vault in my mind. And now that I was staring down at this proof, this testimony, I knew that it had all happened.

I knew that Tommy Taffy…was real.

I shoved the headphones back in the box and pushed it under the bed. My head was spinning and it wasn't just from the alcohol. I crawled to my feet and walked into the kitchen. I didn't bother turning on the lights. I found a bottle of vodka and poured some into a glass. I drained it and winced, stomach protesting. I poured another. I downed it just as quickly. Wiping my lips, gasping, I stumbled over to the couch in the living room. I felt like I was going to throw up. Instead, I leaned back and closed my eyes.

When I woke up the next morning, the sun was peeking curiously through the windows. My head ached like I had been struck with a hammer. My mouth tasted like sour poison. Giving my senses a moment to settle, I scraped my teeth along my tongue and then spit onto the floor. It didn't do much good. Rising, I moaned and then walked into the bedroom to retrieve my cigarettes. I smacked one from the battered pack and ate some smoke for breakfast.

I felt disjointed, out of sorts, and pretty sick. I looked at the clock and saw it was a little after nine. I didn't have to work today, but the thought of staying in was impossibly depressing. I checked my phone for notifications and saw I had received a text from Jason last night wishing me a happy birthday.

I stared numbly at my cell. I needed to call someone. I needed to talk to someone. I could feel a monster on my shoulder and knew isolation would only bring it into view. I couldn't deal with that today. Not again.

I dialed my father, barely aware of what I was doing. The line rang twice before he answered.

"Jack?"

His voice settled me ever so slightly.

"Hey, Dad," I said quietly.

Silence for a second and then, "How are you, son? It's been a while," a pause, "I miss you. Your mother, too."

I squeezed my eyes shut. "I'm ok. How are you? How's Mom?"

Manufactured optimism. "We're getting by. One day at a time. We're good, Jack...we're good."

"Are you free for breakfast?" I asked, prayed.

Relief now: "Yes, of course. I'm afraid your mother is out this morning, but I'd be happy to meet you in the city."

"I'd really like that," I breathed.

"You want to do Corner Cafe?"

"Sure, Dad."

"Sounds good. See you in an hour or so?"

"Perfect."

"Ok...see you soon."

"Thanks, Dad," I whispered, but he had already hung up. I set the phone down and sat at the edge of my bed. I smoked another cigarette and it made me feel disgusting. Groaning, I stood and went to the bathroom. I dared to look in the mirror and didn't like what I saw. I turned on the shower and as the water heated, I shaved and brushed my teeth.

Once I was showered and dressed, I felt a little better. A little more capable to face the day. As I pocketed my wallet and car keys, I thought about the box under the bed. I thought about the headphones.

I left my apartment, slamming the door behind me.

I spent the drive across the city in numb isolation. I turned on the radio for a couple seconds but quickly shut it off. I didn't want any noise today. The murmur of the streets was enough: impatient car horns, the rumble of engines, and the natural hum that floated above us all. My mind wandered to my parents and how they were getting along these days. They had moved out of my childhood house years ago, favoring someplace closer to civilization. My dad hadn't been quite ready to commit to the bustle of a full-blown city, but they were close enough now that we could meet up like this with minimal inconvenience. I was wordlessly relieved my mother wasn't going to be there, as shameful as that thought was. I loved my mom to death, but she had changed. Her warmth was vacant and a deep sorrow had crept into her eyes as the years went on. I pitied her, but not in a condescending way. I knew what she felt. I knew what she carried with her. I held the same memories, but unlike her, I had learned how to block most of them out.

Until recently. Over the past couple of months I had noticed my depression grew worse, the violent outbursts more frequent. I thought about the guy I had bloodied last night and gripped the steering wheel a little tighter. That was something I needed to reign in. I was aware of that, knew that, but sometimes it was just too…too present to contain.

I stopped at a gas station and picked up a couple more packs of cigarettes. I checked my watch. Still had plenty of time before Dad would be around. I decided to go directly to the cafe anyway. When I crossed the city, I found a parking spot and walked the couple blocks to the humble breakfast destination. I smoked as I went, observing the bustle of people around me. They all looked so distracted. So full of life and purpose. I envied them. And then I loathed them.

I reached the cafe and finished my cig, tossing the butt into a storm gutter. I went inside and ordered two coffees. The place smelled of pastries and sugar. A woman sat in the corner, clacking away on her laptop, completely absorbed in whatever she was typing. She was gorgeous. I had a brief flash of confidence and considered going over to talk to her. The feeling passed as my coffees were handed to me and I left to go sit outside and wait for my father. She probably didn't want to be bothered by someone like me. A depressed asshole.

I sat down at one of the small tables and leaned back in my chair, breathing deeply. I needed to calm down. To stop being so hard on myself. Instead, I smoked another cigarette. My lungs felt like craters of sunken ash and I suffered a flare of guilt. I could actually feel the cancer forming. Two more cigarettes and half a coffee later, I forgot all about my imaginary disease. Who cares.

A couple minutes later, Dad arrived. He looked good, if not tired and slightly worn. He was wearing a crisp button up and tan pants. His graying hair was trimmed close and combed to perfection. But it was his face that betrayed him. Hard lines and a grim jawline spoke of hardships best left to memory.

The cane, along with his heavy limp, stirred those memories.

He smiled when he saw me and I stood up, embracing him in a hug. We stayed like that for a moment, exchanging more than words could ever value. Finally, I pulled away and we sat down. I pushed his coffee across the table.

"Might not be boiling hot, but I got you one," I said.

Dad took a timid sip. "It's great, thank you." He appraised me, eyes soaking in my appearance with familiar precision. "You look good, Jack."

"Thanks, so do you. I like the new haircut."

He chuckled. "Your mother's idea."

"Of course. How is she?"

Dad played with his coffee cup for a few awkward seconds before replying. "She's…doing her best."

I felt my heart sink. "That bad, huh?"

His eyes met mine and I saw them shimmer briefly. "She's trying some new medication. The last stuff she was on…well…it wasn't helping. I think it made the depression worse. There was a week there where she didn't get out of bed."

"Christ…"

"But," Dad said, his voice now optimistic, "this new stuff seems to be working. At least as much as it can."

I traveled my lighter across my knuckles. "You said she was out today?"

Dad nodded and took another sip of coffee. "Yeah, she's actually horseback riding with a friend."

I smiled. "I'll be damned."

Dad returned the smile. "I know. Her friend convinced her to try it. And I'm happy for her. She needs to get out more."

I suddenly felt a buzzing in my pocket. Annoyed, I pulled my phone out and checked who the incoming call was from. My dad paused mid-sentence as he saw puzzlement filter through my face.

"Do you have to take that?" he asked.

"No, no, it's no one," I said, ignoring the call. Liz? What the hell did she want? I hadn't seen her in almost three years. Not since she had broken up with me. My mind itched with curiosity, but I blocked it out as best I could. I didn't need any more noise today. I needed to enjoy a quiet morning with my father.

I placed a fresh cigarette to my lips and felt a telltale buzz in my pocket. A voicemail. At least I could check that later and see what she wanted. Not a word in three years...and now she was calling me out of the blue.

Whatever.

I lit my cig and puffed a stream of smoke. Dad looked on disapprovingly but said nothing. I kind of loved him for that.

"How have you been, Dad?" I asked, washing down the nicotine with Colombian brew.

Dad shrugged and sighed, "I'm ok, I suppose. I spend so much time looking after your mom that I don't really have time to think about myself." He paused, eyes dropping. "I think it's probably better that way."

Silence expanded between us like darkness between stars.

"You getting along ok these days?" Dad finally asked.

I offered him a smile I no longer felt. "Yeah. Yeah, I'm good."

"If you need money or something—"

I raised a hand. "I'm ok, Dad. Thank you, though. I mean it."

My father bit his lip and suddenly had a hard time looking at me. "I know we don't see each other as much anymore, but…but I want you to know that I'm here for you." An edge of emotion rose in his throat. "Whatever you need buddy, just let me know."

I reached out across the table and took his hands in mine. "Thank you, Dad. You're a good man. I want you to know that. You're a good man."

Tears were threatening my father's eyes now as he shook his head, voice shaking, "Not as good as I should have been…"

"Dad…"

And now the tears were falling, his face flushed. "I've just been thinking about your sister a lot lately…"

I squeezed his hands tighter and struggled with a rising wave of grief. "I know, Dad…so have I."

My father exhaled a shaky breath between puckered lips and wiped his eyes. "I'm sorry, I didn't mean to burden you with this. It's just been really…" I saw him fighting with his emotions again, but they seemed to be winning. "It's just been really hard lately…"

I leaned across the table, our hands pressed together. "I love you, Dad."

He looked up at me with almost relieved shock and then he broke, a sob escaping between his teeth, "I love you, too, Jack. You're a good son."

"A good son gets his dad hot coffee," I chuckled, trying to shake the sorrow away. "And that lukewarm garbage you're sipping just ain't cutting it."

Mercifully, that shattered the bubble and my dad laughed,

wiping his face. "Yeah, what is this crap, anyway? Can we get some hot joe and some damn breakfast already? I'm starving, kid."

I laughed, standing, and helped him up. "Yeah, me too. Come on, old man, let's get some grub in that gut."

He took my arm and grasped for his cane.

And it broke my heart, just like it did every time.

Chapter 7

During the drive home I realized I felt a little better. My mood wasn't so dismal now. Spending time with Dad had certainly helped once the conversation had settled and we were chowing down on some good food. When we parted ways, I promised it wouldn't be so long until our next visit. I had missed him.

Now, back in the isolation of my car, I remembered that Liz had called. Thoughts of my former girlfriend came creeping back into the silence of my mind. We had dated for a couple months, about three years ago, and then she had ended it. It hadn't been a messy breakup, but it hurt nonetheless. Her reasons were understandable and unavoidable. She had claimed I wasn't emotionally there for her. As I pondered this, I realized she was probably right.

I pulled my phone out of my pocket, keeping one eye on the road, and checked the voicemail she had left. With more than a little curiosity, I put the phone to my ear.

Her voice was calm but edged with caution: "Hey, Jack. I'm sorry to be calling you like this. I know we haven't spoken in a long time and I wasn't even sure you'd still have the same number. There's something I need to talk to you about. I've been contemplating this for a long time and decided to just buckle down and call you. I'm sorry if this sounds weird, but I'd like to meet up with you. Are you still in the city? I hope you're doing well; I really mean that. I've thought about you from time to time. Anyway, sorry, just give me a call when you get a chance? Please?"

I lowered the phone. My fingers drummed against the steering wheel. Huh. What could this be about? She sounded like herself. Apologetically to the point. I expected some kind of emotional rise but was relieved to find none.

"Screw it," I mumbled.

I dialed her number and waited anxiously as the line rang. She answered almost instantly.

"Jack?"

"Hey," I said lamely, "what's up? I got your message."

"Yeah, sorry about that. I know it sounded kind of cryptic."

"You don't have to apologize."

"Um," she sounded unsure now like she hadn't expected me to actually call her, "I was wondering if we could meet up somewhere. Soon. I want to talk to you about something. It's important."

I felt uncertainty bleed into my head. "Jesus Liz, you sound so serious. Did someone die?"

"No, no, nothing like that," she laughed. "Everything is fine. I promise."

"What are you doing tonight?" I asked.

"Uh, nothing..."

I shifted the phone to my other ear. "I can swing by your place tonight if you'd like. I'm not doing anything later. Is that ok?"

"Yeah, that'd be great," she said. "I'll text you my address. I've moved since we last...well...since we broke up."

"You sure everything is ok?"

"I swear, Jack. You don't have anything to worry about."

"Cool. Send me that address and I'll be there around seven?"

"Perfect. Thank you so much. This means a lot to me."

"Yeah, no worries. See you tonight."

"Bye, Jack."

I exhaled and tossed the phone onto the passenger's seat. That had been relatively painless, though the conversation didn't exactly satiate my curiosity. Waiting wasn't exactly my strong suit.

I turned onto my street and stuffed a cigarette between my lips. I parked in my space and lit it, taking a moment to just breathe. Smoke filled the car as I contemplated my decision. Upon closer examination, I realized with some guilt that I wanted to fuck Liz tonight. Maybe that's what this was about? Maybe she missed me and wanted to reignite our relationship? What better way to do that than make up three years of lost time with hours of great sex? I chuckled to myself. Wishful thinking.

I opened the car door, venting smoke from my nose. The sounds of the city rose around me as I went to my apartment and climbed to my floor, ashing on the hardwood as I went.

I had a couple hours to kill before I left again. I felt useless and kind of pathetic, standing in my nearly empty apartment, trying to conjure some semblance of entertainment. I settled on the TV, like most of us do, and plopped myself down on the couch.

The day felt eternal as I chain-smoked and watched TV. There wasn't anything good on. Never was. But I dutifully watched it just the same, knowing that each minute I murdered was another minute closer to seeing Liz again. At some point, she sent me a text with her address. I looked it up and saw she was about thirty minutes outside the city now. I wondered why she had moved out? A job? A guy?

Jesus, I hadn't even thought of that. What if she had a boyfriend? Or even worse…what if she was married? I groaned, cursing myself. Please don't be married. A boyfriend I could work around, but a ring? No getting around that circle of gold.

As it got closer to seven, I began to pace. The TV droned on in the background but I was mostly ignoring it now. My mouth felt gross, a pained, smoke splattered ruin, but I continued to puff away. There was nothing else to do. I went to the fridge and dug out a beer. I drained it in three gulps and denied myself a second. I didn't want to start down that road right now. Not tonight. Maybe later depending on how things went with Liz.

When the analog clock was fully erect, I decided to take a shower and change clothes. I did this with hurried anticipation, a nagging urge poking at my imagination. I stepped out of the shower, dripping wet, and stared into the mirror for a moment. For the first time in ages, I wasn't repulsed.

I dressed and soon found myself speeding for Liz's place. I rolled down the windows as I reached the city limits, the comfortable breeze calming my nerves. I wanted to smoke but decided against it. I didn't want to show up reeking of cigs. She had never liked that, my smoking.

Rolling hills grew around me, a congregation of peace and stillness that paired beautifully with the setting sun. Colors ebbed from the distant horizon and the earth reflected it back with stunning simplicity. I found myself absorbed by it all, the purples and pinks, the smell of grass and hay, the wind ruffling my hair as I zoomed down the empty roads. I needed to get out here more. Maybe I would if Liz wanted to—

No, I had to stop thinking like that. This wasn't about that. And if it was then I had to play it cool. Eagerness is always a turn-off. Right? Fuck, I wanted a cigarette.

Finally, mercifully, I reached her road and turned down it. A distant patch of woods loomed in the distance and I headed for it, checking my phone. Yes, this was the right way. Did she own a house now? Wouldn't that be something?

Turns out, she did. I pulled into a driveway, feeling slightly surprised. It was a one-story house, modest, small, but simple in a good way. It was backed by the woods, a wall of swaying trees. A plot of endless grass stretched out before it, broken only by the slice of the road leading past it.

I looked around for neighboring houses but found none. A single resident in this vast expanse of beauty. It almost seemed a waste. Closing my car door, I walked up the driveway and felt my stomach tingling. Here we go. I ran a hand through my hair, smoothing it, and straightened my shirt.

Liz opened the door before I could even reach it. She stepped out onto the meager front stoop and smiled, giving me a little wave.

"Hey, stranger."

My heart did a little flip and I returned her wave. "Hey, yourself." She looked gorgeous. Her honey blonde hair spilled across her shoulders like summer silk. Her brown eyes sparkled in the sun, almost turning them yellow. She had stayed in great shape as well, her jeans and T-shirt hugging her frame in ways that made me lust for her on sight.

"You look fantastic," I said, approaching her. She smiled

apprehensively and hugged me when I reached her. I breathed in her scent and a world of memory returned with it.

"So do you," she said, pulling away, looking up at me.

"It's been a while," I said, shoving my hands in my pockets, suddenly awkward.

"I know," she said, slowly, but still smiling, "I'm glad you came. Come on, let's go inside. Do you want a beer?"

"Would love one. Please."

She looked at me for a moment like she was appraising me and then we went inside. The interior of the house was pleasant and simple. Earthy colors dominated the space, accompanied by simple furniture kept in an orderly fashion. The house was clean and well kept and smelled slightly of unseen candles.

I followed her into the kitchen, heart racing a little faster than I would have liked, and asked her, "How do you afford a place like this? If you don't mind me asking..."

She went to the fridge and pulled out a pair of beers. "I know this probably seems strange. What's a girl like me doing all the way out here?" She popped the tops off and handed me a chilled bottle. "My father helps out a little bit. You remember him right? Of course, you do. But I do pretty well on my own. I teach at the elementary school a couple miles away and it pays the bills. During the months I can't quite swing it, my dad is always quick with the checkbook. I'm not proud of it, but I've learned to live with his generosity."

"I like it," I said, sipping my beer, eyes roaming around the kitchen. "It's beautiful out here in the country. I don't leave the city much, but the drive out convinced me I should."

"It keeps me away from distractions," Liz said. "Keeps me focused on what's important."

"And what would that be?" I asked, flirting a little.

She gave me a nervous smile and took a long swig from her beer. Setting it down, she eyed me. "I'll show you."

Curious, I watched her leave the kitchen and disappear around the corner. I exhaled slowly and forced myself to relax. A mountain of possibility towered over my imagination and I tried to ignore its glorious summit. I drank more beer and waited.

A couple seconds later, Liz returned.

And in her arms, she held a child. A little boy.

My heart sank and time seemed to freeze. Of all the possible outcomes, this was not what I had expected. I kept my mouth closed and let the shock settle over me. A kid. Ok…wow…

The boy looked to be about two or three years old, his baby fat still clinging to his rosy cheeks. He smiled at me and a smattering of tiny teeth rose out of his innocent grin. His eyes were large and brown, shining with fresh life and intrigue. His hair was short and matched the color of his eyes. He pointed at me and said something I couldn't understand.

"I think he likes you," Liz said, blushing. "Say hi! Say 'Hi Jack'!"

The child buried his face in Liz's shoulder, clearly embarrassed. Liz laughed nervously.

"You look surprised," Liz said, hefting the boy, Mason, on her hip. "I know it's probably not what you were expecting. Sorry to spring this on you."

I searched for words, but couldn't seem to find any. Liz had a…a kid? I was having a terrible time trying to wrap my head around that, the sight of my former girlfriend bouncing a baby on her arm. Jesus.

"Jack?"

I blinked, shaking my head. "C-congrats!" I said weakly, "wow…I had no idea. That's great."

Liz lowered her eyes, "I know this is probably so weird for you."

"Naw, it's cool," I said, hoping the lie stuck. "I mean, I'm happy for you. He's a cute kid." I twiddled my fingers at Mason but he quickly shoved his face back into his mom's shirt.

Liz looked at me and there was a heaviness to her gaze.

I shifted uncomfortably, "What's that look for?"

"I wish there was a better way to do this…" she said quietly.

I ran my fingers around the neck of my beer, something turning in my stomach "What do you mean? What's going on?"

"Jack…" she started, her voice grave.

My eyes widened and I suddenly understood what this was all about. My knuckles whitened against the bottle and I felt the pit of my stomach give out. No, no, no, please don't say it, don't say those words…

"Jack…he's yours," Liz said softly.

I gripped the counter and clenched my jaw. A pattern of darkness swirled around the corners of my vision. Dizziness rocked me and I felt like a wrecking ball had connected with my chest. My throat went dry and I swallowed hard, my saliva slicing like razor blades.

"Jack…?" Liz asked, stepping forward, her face riddled with concern.

I raised my hand. "Don't…don't come near me."

Now her concern bloomed into worry. "I'm so sorry, I didn't know how to tell you."

I was shaking my head, unhinging my jaw. "What the hell is this all about…? Why are you telling me this?"

Liz's eyes went moist. "I'm sorry, I've been thinking about

this a lot lately and…and thought that if I were you…then…then I would want to know."

I jammed my finger onto the countertop, voice suddenly dark and confused. "That is not my kid."

Her eyes went wide. "Yes, Jack…yes it is. I got pregnant just a couple weeks before we broke up. I didn't even realize it until after the split. And at that point…I figured I'd deal with it on my own. You have no idea what I've gone through. What I suffered during the pregnancy."

I stepped towards her, teeth bared. "Oh don't talk to me about suffering, Liz."

Mason began to notice his mother's mood and I saw sadness paint his face. He stuck his bottom lip out and began to whimper. Christ…he did kind of look like me…

"Why are you acting like this?" Liz pleaded.

"Why!?" I yelled, fighting an onslaught of fear and impending responsibility, "WHY!? Because you fucking left me three years ago and then call me out of the blue to tell me I have a CHILD!"

"I'm sorry!" Liz cried again, a few tears escaping now. "I just wanted you to know! I thought you'd want to KNOW!"

I gripped my beer bottle and threw it against the wall, an explosion of anger and terror erupting in my mind like a land mine. "Jesus FUCK!"

Mason began to cry, a pathetic sobbing that stuttered my rage. Liz looked at him apologetically and stroked his face, trying to calm him.

"I can't believe you," I said, seething. "I can't believe you'd…you'd DO this…"

Liz looked up at me, her face flush and wet. "What are you talking about? What was I supposed to do?"

I threw my hands up. "Abort the fucking thing! Get rid of it! Goddamn it, Liz, I am NOT a father!"

"I'm not fucking asking you to be one!" Liz screamed suddenly. "I don't want anything from you, Jack! Jesus Christ, how could you say something like that?"

I shook my head, losing my mind. "Oh piss off!"

She clutched the crying child to her chest "I've thought about you these past three years. I've thought a lot about you. It's hard not to when I'm raising your—our—child! But you know what, Jack? I made the right choice. You were a terrible boyfriend and I'm horrified to think of you as a father. I was just trying to do the right thing. I don't want money, I don't want your help raising him, I simply wanted to do what was best. What was right."

"Well do you feel better now!?" I yelled, shaking with anger and growing fear. "Maybe if you had taken your goddamn birth control like I kept telling you to—"

"Stop it!" Liz screamed, trembling. Mason was wailing now, but Liz stepped toward me. "Just shut up! Clearly, this was a mistake and I regret ever calling you! So get out of here! I don't need you here, I don't want you here, we're doing just fine without YOU! So crawl back to the city and your pathetic life! Just forget about us and go back to living like the sad, selfish bastard you are!"

Ice filled my veins and a sudden calm washed through me.

I towered over Liz, voice crunching like gravel. "Careful."

Liz took a step back, obviously surprised by my sudden aggression. She held Mason to her chest and pointed to the door.

"Get out of my house! GO!"

I took one last look at them and then left, head full of fire and fury. I slammed the door behind me, the world rocking. The moon rose in the distance, fighting back the retreating sun, now just a sliver on the horizon. I stormed to my car, ears filling with the sounds of growing night.

"What the FUCK!?" I screamed, slamming my fist into the door. The shock was burning bright inside of me and I felt its sickening, terrifying warmth spread to all aspects of my life. A kid…I had a kid. Jesus CHRIST.

You're a father, I suddenly thought and had to steady myself against the car. I closed my eyes and inhaled. Slowly, I released the air from my lungs and forced myself to calm down. Sparks danced behind my eyelids and I willed them to leave. Instead of getting into my car, I slumped down in the driveway and leaned against it, staring at the front door.

How could this possibly happen?

I reached into my jacket and retrieved a much-needed cigarette. I lit it and sucked down the nicotine desperately. I felt like a revelation about the world had just been revealed to me, altering the course of my existence forever. In a way…that's exactly what had happened. I closed my eyes again and pressed my palms into them.

What the hell was I going to do…?

I looked up at the house again, trying to force pieces into place. The kid…Mason…he looked about the right age. He looked like me. Could he actually be mine? I took another drag and shook my head. Of course, he was. I could see it in his eyes. My eyes.

"Oh, shit…" I said miserably, rolling my head back to look at the sky. "Oh shit, I messed up…"

But why had Liz waited so long to call me? To tell me? I contemplated that for a moment and realized what an asshole I was. We had only dated for six months before she had broken up with me. Why would she tell me about the pregnancy? What reason would that serve? She had always been close to her parents; she didn't need me. Obviously, she didn't want me. And why would she? I had been a mess in those days, an angry, depressed maniac.

Yeah, you've really changed, I thought, suddenly growing depressed.

Jack…he's yours.

"Oh, God…" I whispered, covering my face, "oh my God, I'm such an asshole."

I had the sudden urge to go back inside but didn't dare. Not yet at least. Let her settle the baby. Let her anger ebb a little. I didn't know what I was going to say, but my knee-jerk reaction left me feeling sick. Christ, why was I such a dick? Why couldn't I just be rational about things like every other adult? Why did I have to be the exception, the black sheep, the royal fuck up? Why couldn't I just pull my shit together?

Hating myself, I smoked another cigarette. I imagined Liz inside, cursing me, trying to soothe her little boy. Our little boy. I waited a couple minutes, stubbed out my butt, and pulled myself up with a groan. I raised my eyes to the heavens and let out a long breath.

I walked back to the front door and gave it a timid knock. I could hear Mason inside still crying. I winced. I knocked again, louder this time. My heart jumped when Liz opened the door, her face a mess of tears and anger.

"What!?" she demanded, still soothing Mason who looked distraught and confused. I could relate.

"I-I'm sorry," I stammered, "I shouldn't have said those things. I'm a complete asshole and I want to apologize."

Liz shook her head. "I don't know what I expected."

"I know," I said sadly, "I really am sorry. This is just so…unexpected and scary for me. You think we can talk about it? I promise to behave now."

Liz stroked Mason's cheek and his sobs finally subsided. "Not tonight, Jack. I just can't. I need to settle Mason down and feed him. Maybe tomorrow. Right now I just want to be alone with my son."

I nodded understandingly. "Ok, yeah…tomorrow. Maybe it's best I take the night to digest this all anyway. Again, I didn't mean to be so aggressive." I looked at Mason, his eyes huge and tear streaked. "I'm sorry, kid. I didn't mean to scare you."

Liz looked hard at me and then sighed wearily. "Go home, Jack. We'll talk tomorrow. I'll call you."

"Ok," I said, backing away, "I really didn't mean for it to go like this…"

"I know," Liz said quietly. And as I turned to go, "And Jack? Thanks."

I gave her a half-cocked smile and simply nodded. She closed the door and I went to my car, breathing in the night air. All right, things were a little better now. I didn't feel like a complete asshole. I still hated myself, but it was a start.

The drive back to the city was a blur. My head was swirling with so many thoughts that I barely saw the road. First, the reality that I had a son. Then the fact that Liz was the mother. Next came the fear inching its way back. What the hell was I supposed to do in a situation like this? I had brought a life into this world…didn't that make me responsible for it? What would my dad do? I winced. Of course, I knew what he'd do. He'd raise it, love it, and take care of it to the best of his abilities. I thought about calling him, but the shame stopped me.

The need to talk this out with someone was overwhelming and so I dialed the only other person I knew would understand.

Jason picked up almost immediately.

"What's good, Jack? You still recovering from your birthday hangover?"

I adjusted the phone as I approached the city limits. "Yeah, something like that."

"Sorry I couldn't make it out last night. Work, you know?"

"It's fine," I said, brushing it aside. "Are you free tonight though? There's something I really need to talk to you about."

"Oh, you sound kinda serious. Everything ok? Did something happen?"

"You could say that."

"Well," Jason said loudly, "I'm leaving work now, so I could head over to your place if you wanted. You home?"

"I will be in a little bit."

"Cool. Sure, man, I'll be there with bells on."

"Thanks, Jason," I said, relieved.

"You bet man. See you soon."

I hung up and set my phone down. My rattled nerves had settled a little but I planted a cigarette between my lips anyway. The moon continued its brilliant ascension as night spread across the sky. I looked at it through the windshield, hanging between the growing buildings before me, hiding among a dense concrete jungle. I felt like hiding, too.

At some point, I became aware that my phone was ringing. I thought it would be Jason, but when I checked the caller ID I saw that it was coming from a blocked number. I set my cell down. I didn't need any more distractions tonight.

I picked up a twelve pack of beer before returning to my apartment, and when I did I found myself pacing in anticipation for Jason's arrival. My fingers twitched at my sides as I patrolled my living room, the overhead light casting shadows I followed across the floor.

Finally, I heard Jason ring from downstairs. I buzzed him in and soon we were sitting opposite one another, beer in hand. Having come directly from work, he was dressed in a crisp blue button up and black dress pants complete with shoes that were polished so brightly I almost had to look away.

"Aren't we fancy?" I joked, taking a swig of beer and reclining in my chair.

Jason chuckled. "You got to look the part, brother."

"How's work been?" I asked idly.

He shrugged, eyes roaming around my small apartment. "Can't complain. I told you I got a raise last month right? I couldn't believe it."

"Mr. Money Man," I said, a little envious.

"Puts me just over eighty thousand. Never in a million years did I think I'd be making that kind of money."

I snorted, "It's not that much…"

Jason laughed, "Sorry, I didn't realize I was talking to a king."

"Damn right," I smiled, "the king of poverty."

Jason rolled his eyes, grinning. "Oh shut up. You do just fine. You have a place to yourself in the city. What more could you ask for?"

I spread my arms. "How about some decent furniture?"

Jason appraised the chairs and then the couch. "I think the worn, dirty look is very hip."

I barked a laugh. "Oh blow me."

We settled, the small talk easing the tension in my shoulders. We conversed about life a little bit more, finishing our beers and popping fresh ones.

After about twenty minutes, Jason finally asked, "So you going to tell me what's going on? You sounded kinda rattled on the phone earlier."

"Yeah, that's one way to put it," I said slowly, suddenly dreading the impending conversation.

Jason leaned forward, clutching his beer with both hands. "So what's up?"

I took a long, steadying breath. "Liz called me."

Jason leaned back. "Oh boy, here we go."

I licked my lips. "Jason…she has a kid. A little boy. His name's Mason."

Jason cocked an eyebrow. "Ok…? So what?"

I closed my eyes. "Dude…he's mine."

Jason blinked, a thick silence clouding between us. I bit my lip and looked at my sweating bottle. I scratched at the label.

"Wow…" Jason finally said, "I mean…wow."

"I know," I said quietly. "I went and saw her. She lives just outside the city now. I thought I was going to get laid. I had no idea. When I saw the boy and she told me it was mine…I didn't exactly take the news well."

"Oh jeez, Jack, what did you do?"

I shrugged. "I said some things I wish I hadn't. Yelled. Made an ass of myself. I mean Christ though, she completely blindsided me."

Jason nodded understandingly. "Yeah, man, that's a lot to process."

"I calmed down a little bit after," I continued, "and she's going to call me tomorrow so we can talk."

"How did this happen?" Jason pried, still looking shocked.

I shrugged. "I don't know. Apparently, when she broke up

with me she was already pregnant, she just didn't know it yet. When she found out she kept me out of the picture."

"Until now."

"Yeah, until now. She said she thought I should know. She doesn't want any money, any support, nothing. She just wanted me to know. I guess her dad is helping out financially."

Jason drained the rest of his beer. "Wow, Jack…I don't even know what to say. What are you going to do?"

I shrugged miserably. "Hell if I know. Honestly, just knowing I have a son scares the shit out of me. God knows I'm not father material."

"Why not?" Jason asked softly.

I looked up at him. "Dude, do you really have to ask?"

Something settled behind his eyes and he suddenly looked very sad. "Yeah…I get it, buddy."

I placed my head in my hands. "Fuck, man, when I think about my dad and what fatherhood meant to him…I just…I can't even imagine…"

"It's ok," Jason said gently, "I get it. I was there too, remember?"

I closed my eyes behind my hands. "How could I forget?"

"Hey, erase all that. Put it out of your mind where it belongs. You're doing good now, you really are. We both are. Don't let this crush you. You said Liz was going to call you tomorrow, right? Why don't you sleep on it and tomorrow things will hopefully have settled a little bit."

"You're probably right," I mumbled.

Jason stood and came over to me. He placed a hand on my shoulder, "You're going to be ok, Jack. I promise. Don't kill yourself over this. I know you tend to sway from one extreme to the other at the drop of a hat, but please, for your own sake, find a middle ground and get some rest. You look exhausted."

I looked up at him."I've been exhausted for twenty-eight years."

Jason smiled. "You and me both, dude."

"You have to go?" I asked.

He nodded. "Yeah, early start tomorrow. But if you need to call me, please do. My schedule isn't too crazy the next couple days so if you need to blow off some steam or just talk this out, I'm here."

I stood up and hugged him. "Thanks, Jay. I really appreciate it."

He hugged me back. "Don't mention it. Next time just buy better beer." We separated and laughed. I saw him to the door and wished him a good night, closing it behind him. Turning to face my empty apartment, I sighed heavily.

Then my phone began to ring from where I had left it on the chair. I walked over and checked it. Again, the incoming call was from a blocked number. I ignored it. No more tonight.

I needed to sleep.

Chapter 8

I was in the bowels of some nightmare when I awoke. Something had pulled me from sleep. A noise. I groggily opened my eyes and saw that it was a little after three in the morning. I blinked in the darkness and a sound, that noise, pushed me further from slumber.

It was my phone. The screen was lit up and I turned over and picked it up from the nightstand. Someone was calling me.

I looked at the screen, squinting. Liz? Why was Liz calling me so late? I rolled onto my back, taking my phone with me, and answered, voice thick.

"H'lo?"

At first there was nothing. Then slowly, something rubbed over the speaker like she had placed the phone back in her pocket.

"Liz?" I asked, scrubbing my eyes.

The sound continued like muffled movement. Had she pocket dialed me? This late? I pressed the cell to my ear, listening. Did I hear voices? I jumped as something thudded on the other side and then a clatter followed.

The line went dead.

"What was that all about?" I mumbled to myself. I tried calling her back, but after half a ring it went to voicemail. I sat up in bed, now fully awake. I reached over to my nightstand and snatched up a cigarette. I brought it to life and blew smoke across the darkness of my bedroom. Had she called me by mistake? Something about the late hour made me feel uneasy. I tried calling her back a second time but got the same result. Had that been voices I heard? Not just one, but two?

I set my phone down next to me and worked on my cigarette. Sleep seemed miles away now. I didn't have to work tomorrow, but the thought of starting my day this early made me groan.

Suddenly, my phone lit up and I snatched it from the bed. It was a text message from Liz. I opened it and as my eyes scanned the text, my stomach turned to ice.

There's someone in my house.

I read it back four times in rapid succession, a sense of dread growing each time. My fingers quickly danced over the keys as I sent her a text back.

Are you in danger? Who is it?

I waited anxiously, fingers drumming against my leg. After a couple seconds, my cell lit up again. I opened the text and felt my throat tighten.

He says he knows you.

That feeling of dread began to heighten, a spire of fear rising on a horizon of terror. What the hell was going on? I licked my dry lips and sent her a reply.

Who is it? What do they want?

I finished my cigarette, eyes wide, staring off into the black as I waited for an answer. The spire on the horizon was starting to burn, a tower of flame and fear that I refused to look at.

Something in my mind begged me to shield my eyes, to turn away, because something horrible was growing from the fire.

I jolted, startled, as my phone began to ring. It was Liz. Hands shaking, I answered, placing the cell to my ear.

"Liz?" I whispered.

First there was nothing.

And then a voice—a familiar, haunting, horrible voice: "Hello, Jack."

My room seemed to dip and rock, a shaking, shattering nightmare. My eyes went wide and an icy, skeletal hand gripped my head and squeezed with urgent terror.

"Tommy?" I breathed, voice a quivering croak.

"Hehehehe..."

The call disconnected.

I sat trembling in the silence of my apartment. My heart was racing and a sickly sweat had broken out across my forehead. My chest felt like it would cave in at any second, a collapsed, broken shell.

No, my mind begged, *please no, no, no, let me wake up, please let me wake up.*

I squeezed my eyes shut and shuddered. The spire roared, an impossible heat consuming me. It towered before my mind, absorbing, charring, burning, and destroying every sense and strand of sanity I had worked so hard to rebuild.

"No," I cried, "Oh no, please not again..." I covered my face with my hands. I felt like I was trying to hold in my screaming thoughts, chaos and madness leaking into my face and spilling through my fingers.

"Jesus Christ, this can't be happening," I croaked, eyes bulging. What was I supposed to do? Just what the hell was I supposed to DO?!

Liz…oh my God…he was with Mason and Liz.

"NO!" I screamed suddenly, leaping from my bed, tears springing from my eyes. "No, no, NO, NOT AGAIN!"

I paced furiously in my room, pulling at my hair. "Fuck, fuck, FUCK. This isn't HAPPENING! FUCK!" My hand swept across the nightstand, knocking the lamp to the floor in a crash.

What do I do? What do I fucking DO!?

The vault of my mind had been opened and all the horror and monstrous memories were pouring back in like a toxic avalanche. They swarmed me, clawed at me, consumed me, overloading my mind with terrors I had long locked away.

I shrank to the floor, clutching myself, sweating, mumbling, my world completely shattered. I felt the pieces shred my mind as they dislodged and scattered like broken glass. I wanted to throw up, but my stomach had nothing to offer.

The phone began to ring once again. I jerked my head up, staring at my bed where my cell glowed urgently.

Don't answer it. Just don't answer it.

But I did. I scrambled over on my hands and knees and grabbed it from the sheets. I didn't even look at who was calling; my thumb slammed across the screen.

"Yes?" I asked shakily, fully expecting my head to be filled with that haunting laughter.

But instead, a soft static buzzed in my ear. My eyes went wide.

"It's starting again, Jack."

I dropped the phone onto the floor and scooted away from it, gasping and panting, soaked with sweat. This couldn't be real, this couldn't be happening again, it just couldn't. Propped up on my elbows and knees, I lowered my face to the floor and pressed my forehead against the wood, squeezing my eyes shut. Tears rolled down my face as I desperately tried to keep breathing. My phone was still lit up, the call ongoing. I could hear a voice, *that* voice, calling to me.

"Please," I whispered, drool stringing from my lips, "please make it stop."

I looked at my cell and slowly reached for it.

I placed it to my ear, voice strained. "This was supposed to be over."

"You need to help me."

"No," I whispered, "no I can't do this again..."

"Listen to me."

"I don't want to," I cried, "I don't want any of this. Please, just leave me alone, why can't you just leave me alone?"

"It's going to get worse, Jack. I need you. I can't bear it anymore."

I felt sick. Every part of me wanted to close my eyes and go to sleep, never to wake again. I wanted to be swallowed up by darkness and shield my face away from this returning hell.

But Tommy had Liz now.

Tommy had Mason.

I squeezed my hands into fists, the phone trembling against my ear. Jesus...oh Jesus...I couldn't let them do this alone. I couldn't abandon them with Tommy. Liz had no idea what she was dealing with, who Tommy was, or what he was capable of. My mind shook at the thought of confronting the nightmare from my childhood, but I couldn't shake the clinging responsibility I felt toward her and the child.

Because somehow, I knew that Tommy was my fault. That he was there because of me. And as much as I hated, screamed, begged myself to just turn away from it all, I found that I couldn't. She needed someone to help her. She needed someone to understand what was going to happen, what was probably happening right now. She needed someone to take notice and do something about it.

Just like I had needed someone to notice all those years ago.

Despite all my bad habits and depressed, angry mood swings, I refused to turn into one of those people I had grown to loathe as a child. An ignorant coward who turned a blind eye on what was really going on. I remembered the helplessness, the need for someone to say something, do something. The maddening hell of having to carry it all in silence.

"I won't be that person," I whispered into the phone, a trickle of sweat running down my face. "I have to go help her."

"Yes, but there's nothing you can do for her right now. We have to plan and navigate this situation with tremendous caution. If we're patient and work together, we can stop this."

"Oh fuck you," I spat. "Liz doesn't have time. God knows what that monster is doing to her right now. I can't sit here and wait."

"No, Jack, you can't go; that's exactly what he wants!"

"Who the hell are you?" I suddenly hissed into the phone. "Why the fuck should I listen to anything you say? You've been buzzing in my ear for years and I still have no idea if you're even real."

A pause. On the other end I heard a low whistle followed by what sounded like a horn. I furrowed my brow, holding the phone tightly against my head, listening intently.

Finally, quietly: **"My name is Rez."**

I felt the word sink into my mind, into my memory, a slow anchor that seemed to be wrapped with distant familiarity.

"Rez," I whispered, "I've heard that somewhere before. It was part of a pattern...a pattern of numbers you gave to me years ago."

Silence on the other end.

"Yeah," I continued, "I remember now...six-six-three-five-eight-Rez. That's what you told me. What does it mean? What are the numbers? Is that your full name?"

Then, in almost a whisper, the voice answered, **"No, Jack...that's his name."**

I felt the room waver and tilt as I blinked back dripping sweat from my eyes. "What are you talking about? I don't understand."

"Tommy Taffy is what he calls himself. But that is not the name that was given to him." A low horn sounded from the other side. **"It was not the name I gave him, Jack."**

"Wait a minute," I said, chest heaving, "Just hold on...I..." I felt my head scramble with confusion and questions, a pressing mass of chaos. "Just who the hell are you?"

"I told you...my name is Rez."

"Ok, Rez," I said slowly, "If you want my help then you need to help me. You need to help me right now. Because the clock is ticking and every second I stay here running my mouth is another second Liz is suffering. Suffering because of me. Because Tommy followed ME. Isn't that right, Rez?"

"I'm...I'm sorry, Jack. But you mustn't go. Not yet. In this state, there's nothing I can do to help you right now, but if you're patient, there is a way."

I brought my mouth closer to the speaker, voice a snarl. "I'm not going to wait. Liz doesn't have that kind of time and I'm not going to play twenty questions with you while Tommy fucking rapes her or worse. So unless you can help me right now, I'm going over there."

"Jack, please don't do this. You know Tommy; you know what he's capable of. You can't change anything right now!"

"Well I'm going to try," I growled.

I hung up.

I mopped sweat from my face and quickly got dressed, heart thundering. I felt like I was being crushed beneath a mountain of madness, an unearthly mass of unanswered questions. As I raced out of my apartment, I realized that right now none of it mattered. That could all wait. Right now I needed to get to Liz's and try and stop this.

And how the hell do you plan on doing that? I thought, jumping in my car, *what exactly is the big plan here?*

As I pulled out of my space and hit the gas, I realized that I didn't really have a plan. But I thought, almost knew, that if I went there and showed my face it could—might—stop some of the inevitable violence. If I could just get Tommy to focus on me, if I could relieve Liz's physical or mental torment for just a couple hours, then it would be worth it.

My cell began to ring urgently and I looked down at it. It was the blocked number. I ignored it. I knew who it was now and had no desire to continue our conversation. Not right now anyway.

This is insane. What are you doing, Jack?

I shook my head as the city zipped by. I knew it was insane, but I didn't care. Liz needed someone there who understood.

The ride over felt like the longest trip I had ever taken. As I approached her street, I gazed out at the vast fields resting on either side of the road. The moon glowed brightly across the knee high grass, a gentle wind rustling the blades. How could such peace hold such a terrible secret?

I roared down the street and spotted Liz's house. The lights were on, a gentle illumination backed by the dark trees that bordered her backyard. I slowed and pulled into the driveway, shutting off the engine. I sat there for a moment, staring at the front window. I couldn't see anything, but I knew what awaited me.

I rubbed my hands together, trying to calm my stomach. Fear begged me to just drive away, leave all this, but I opened the door instead, stepping out into the night. I looked out at the field across the street, acres of rolling grass dancing in the wind. "Come dance with us," the grass called.

I turned my back on it. I had a different devil to dance with tonight.

"Jesus Christ, am I really going in there?" I whispered to myself. I felt paralyzed in the driveway, nails of terror impaling my feet to the asphalt.

She needs help. She needs someone. She needs you.

I exhaled shakily and walked to the front door. My heart slammed into my chest and roared in my ears to flee. A dizziness washed over me as I mounted the front steps, a horrific icy feeling that extended down the length of my body. I had worked so hard to put all this behind me.

I knocked on the door.

Standing there, waiting, I felt like I was going to throw up.

I heard footsteps on the other side of the door and I braced myself, a monstrous wall of terror pressing in on me from all sides.

And then the door opened, a body filling the space.

"Hello Jack," Tommy said, smiling.

I took a step back, the sudden sight of him sending a whiplash response through my body. He looked exactly like he had all those years ago. His blond hair, his perfectly smooth, almost plastic skin, his smile that held no teeth, just a strip of faceless white. And his eyes…those penetrating, shockingly blue eyes…

"You look a little rattled," Tommy grinned, "is everything ok?"

I took another step back, trembling, not wanting to actually believe he was back.

"Would you like to come in?" Tommy asked, gesturing inside.

"No…Why…?" I finally whispered, the only thing I could conjure.

Tommy stepped out onto the front stoop with me and placed a hand on my shoulder. "Why? Because you need me, Jack. This broken family needs me. I'm here to put the pieces back together." He touched my cheek. "You…Liz…and your beautiful child."

I jerked away from his touch, sickened. "What have you done to her?"

Tommy stepped back into the doorway, "Hehehehe…"

"Goddamn it, have you hurt her?" I asked, terrified of the answer.

Tommy jerked his head behind him. "Why don't you come see for yourself."

No part of me wanted to enter that house. I didn't want to see what lay inside, didn't want to hear the door close behind me.

"Come on, Jack," Tommy said, taking my arm, "we have so much to talk about."

I felt myself pulled inside, a dreadful, drifting weight settling in my chest. I crossed the threshold and the door closed behind me. I felt like screaming.

Tommy led me into the kitchen, blood pumping in my ears. We rounded the corner and there was Liz. She was sitting at the table, face tear streaked and terrified. She seemed to be in massive discomfort, leaning heavily over the table, panting, each breath causing a shudder to run through her body.

Lying on the table was a small trowel covered in blood.

"Oh my God…Liz…" I whispered, eyes going wide.

Tommy grabbed my arm, stopping me from going to her. "Ah ah ah, take it easy. Why don't you just have a seat so we can all talk?"

I turned to him, face pale. "What did you do to her?"

"Please," Liz said weakly, "please Jack, just do what he says."

I looked at her and then at Tommy, torn, scared, and horribly unsure of myself.

Tommy smiled, "You should listen to her."

"Where's Mason?" I asked, standing my ground.

Tommy let me go and walked to the table. He picked up the trowel leaving droplets of blood in its wake. He turned it over in his hands and just stared at me, his eyes piercing through my skull.

"He's sleeping," Liz whispered, wincing, "in the back room."

"Yes," Tommy said, still examining the trowel, "you did good not to wake him, Liz. Just like I told you. You're good at listening. You're quick to follow the rules." He looked up at me. "Something Jack here could learn from."

"You bastard," I whispered, unmoving.

Tommy tapped the table by an empty chair. "Sit down. We need to talk. The three of us."

I looked at Liz and she nodded. I circled the table and sat down.

"Good, good," Tommy said, standing between the two of us, "that's better. This is how it should be."

"Why are you here?" I said softly. "Why can't you just leave me alone?"

Tommy shook his head, smiling slightly. "Let me ask you a question, Jack."

"I'd rather you didn't."

"What is the most important part of family?" Tommy plowed on.

I looked across at Liz, our eyes meeting and exchanging unknown conversation. She looked like she was in torturous pain. She gritted her teeth and her brows knitted with concentrated sensitivity, like every breath she took held the possibility to kill her.

"I feel like you're not paying attention," Tommy said quietly, placing his hands on the table and leaning toward me. "Maybe I should show you how much Liz likes the trowel. What do you think?"

I snapped my eyes to his. "I'm listening, Tommy. I'm here."

Tommy smiled. "Good, good. Now…the most important part of family. Any guesses?"

I just shook my head. I was too scared to play his games right now.

Tommy sighed, "Well that's disappointing, considering." He rounded the table and stood behind me, placing his hands on my shoulders. "The most important thing is that no matter what, you stick together. Through thick and thin, the good and the bad, you stick with your family. You support them, you love them, and you try your best to be an example."

His hands tightened on my shoulder. "Would you say you've done that, Jack?"

"Tommy—"

His fingers dug into my collarbone, "Would you say you've done that?"

I winced, closing my eyes, "I—I don't know."

Tommy released me, now gently rubbing where he had been gripping. "I know this is scary for you. It's ok. I realize you were just made aware of your son's existence so I won't fault you for being absent the first three years of his life." Tommy leaned over me and whispered in my ear, "But that's going to change now, isn't it?"

Liz was crying, her head on the table and I just stared at her, fear and unease rolling through me like summer rain.

Tommy brought his lips closer to my ear, his voice barely a whisper. "You're going to be a father to your son, aren't you? Isn't that what you want? Don't you think that's best for him? A boy needs a father, Jack."

I cracked my jaw open, daring to speak. "Is that what you want, Tommy? If I stay, will you leave them alone? Will you leave me alone?"

I flinched as Tommy slowly rubbed his lip against my ear. "Is that what you want, Jack? Do you want me to leave?"

"More than anything," I whispered.

Tommy's hand found the back of my neck and traveled down across my chest. "It hurts when you say things like that. Don't you know I'm here to help? After all we've been through, haven't you learned that yet?"

I closed my eyes, trying to ignore his touch. "B-but you haven't helped anyone. You destroyed my family." I opened my eyes, now bloodshot, voice hoarse, "and you killed my sister."

Tommy suddenly pulled away and walked back to his place

at the table, "Ah, yes...Katie. I've thought a lot about her over the years. Such a sweet girl."

I clenched my fists, a swell of emotion rising in me. "Why, Tommy...? I've wondered for so long...why the hell did you do that...? She didn't do anything wrong. She followed all the rules."

Tommy smiled sadly at me, his eyes big and blue. "Sometimes the only way to understand a loving hand is to first experience an angry fist."

I suddenly slammed my hands down on the table, causing Liz to jump painfully.

"Goddamn it, that's not good enough! What the hell does that mean?!" Tears were beginning to form in my eyes. "Why did you do all those horrible things to us?! What were we supposed to learn!? What the FUCK did it all mean!?"

Tommy's face suddenly looked vacant, his voice emotionless. "Did you learn nothing, Jack? Think back on all of my teachings, my lessons. You remember those, don't you? Haven't those stuck with you over the years? Haven't they formed and shaped you into who you are today? Don't you think that now, because of me, you're a better person?"

"What are you TALKING about!?" I screamed, eyes running. "I'm a fucking MESS! We all are! Mom's depressed, Dad is just a shell of a man now, and none of us know what it all MEANT! Why did Katie DIE!? WHY DID YOU KILL HER, GODDAMN IT!? WHAT WAS I SUPPOSED TO LEARN FROM THAT!?"

Tommy's eyes suddenly went dark, but the smile remained plastered to his face like a cancer. "Oh, I expected more from you, Jack. I really did. Perhaps you're still just a child. A confused, scared little boy."

I threw my hands up, crying openly now. "I'm a disaster! My life is a mess! I'm so…so fucking sad all the time and I have this…this temper that just makes me want to…to fucking hurt people sometimes and I can feel it getting worse! I can feel it growing in the back of my mind and I have to smoke and drink and numb myself just so I can fall asleep and not see your fucking face! So I can stop hearing Katie screaming as you cut her legs off!" I wiped my nose, shaking, losing myself. "So you tell me, Tommy! You FUCKING tell me if you helped make me a better person! Because from where I'm standing…? From where I'm standing, you ruined me. You ruined my whole family." My voice lowered to a venomous, heavy whisper. "You fucking killed me years ago."

Tommy's face had grown as dark as his eyes, a dimming, haunting look that ate his smile away. He stood there looking at me as something massive and dangerous boiled beneath the surface. We stayed staring at one another, my face a mess of anguish and misery. I felt such fear and hatred coursing through me that I thought I would drown in it.

"We're not going to talk about this anymore," Tommy said finally, his voice so low I barely heard it.

"Fuck you, Tommy," I cried, feeling doors opening that I had locked years ago. "You have no idea what you're doing, do you? DO YOU?!"

Tommy stepped toward me, dripping with violence, and I knew I should stop, but couldn't.

"I don't know what the hell you are," I hissed through tears, "but whatever you think you're here for…whatever you think you're doing…you're *fucking it up*." I raised my eyes to meet his. "Isn't that right, six-six-three-five-eight-Rez?"

Tommy reached for my throat but froze as the phrase left my

mouth. His eyes went wide and I saw absolute shock electrify his body.

"He's been talking to you again, hasn't he?" Tommy whispered, a rising, mountainous anger in his voice.

"Tommy," I said, standing, leaning across the table, "what the fuck are you?"

For a moment, just a moment, I saw something like uncertainty flutter across his face. But in an instant it was gone, replaced by a fury so hot I could feel its heat from where I stood. I had a second to react, but even that wasn't enough. Tommy grabbed me by the throat and lifted me, his grip like a vice. I sputtered and coughed, clawing for air, but Tommy didn't allow me any. In one powerful motion he slammed me down across the table, face first. Liz screamed and almost fell backwards as my cheek crunched into the spot she had been leaning a second ago. She looked horribly scared and overwhelmingly confused; her eyes were wet and bloodshot.

Tommy held me against the table, planting an arm across my shoulders, nailing me in place. He leaned down, his voice hot in my ear.

"I told you once to never, ever, say that again."

I struggled to get air into my lungs, squirming and twisting on the table, but I found that I couldn't move. Blood trickled from my nose and I tasted it on my gums.

Tommy dug his arm deeper into my back. "What's it going to take for you to listen to me, Jack? You tell me. What do I need to do to Liz to get you to behave?"

From my spot, I saw Liz recoil into herself, struggling to stand, but gave up as pain bolted through her. She was crying, her eyes huge and afraid.

"Don't hurt her," I gasped, wincing, "she has nothing to do with this. This is between me and you."

And then Tommy chuckled and I felt a shiver run through me.

"Oh no, Jack," Tommy hissed, "this isn't about you anymore. It's about your son. Let this be my first lesson to you as a new father. You don't matter anymore. That sleeping boy in the other room? That's what matters and he's the reason you're going to stay and help raise him. Together—the three of us—we are going to make sure he's raised right. And if you refuse, I will break this woman in front of you in ways you couldn't possibly imagine. Do I make myself perfectly clear?"

Slowly, painfully, I nodded. There was nothing else to do. Endless emotions roared through me like a current and I fought against all of them. Tommy was spiraling down a violent hole I was all too familiar with. All that mattered right now was keeping Liz and Mason safe. Whatever came next, I'd confront when I needed to. I wasn't going to let this monster have the satisfaction of inflicting more pain on them while I watched.

"I understand," I said finally, "you don't have to hurt anyone. I'll do what you want."

"Will you, Jack?" Tommy asked dangerously. I nodded, feeling blood streak against my face. After a moment, Tommy let me up. I slid from the table and stood, knees shaking. I wiped my face and took a deep breath. Liz had her face in her hands, shaking, and I placed a hand on her shoulder.

"You're going to sleep here tonight," Tommy said, squaring me up from across the table. "You're going to do your duty and be with the mother of your child."

"Fine," I breathed, "that's fine, Tommy."

He pointed down the hall. "Take her to her room and go to

bed with her. I don't want to hear a sound for the rest of the night."

I raised my hand, "Yeah, but Mason—"

"Is sleeping and will be fine," Tommy finished. His eyes flared. "Now do what I tell you."

"Come on," I said quietly to Liz, taking her arm. As she went to stand she let out a cry and fell to her knees onto the floor. I looked at the chair she had been sitting in, and to my horror, I discovered why.

The seat was covered in blood.

"Oh my God..." I whispered, stunned, repulsed. I looked up at Tommy, face white. Tommy just stared back at me and then slowly, horribly, he smiled.

I knelt down next to Liz, gently scooping her up in my arms, "It's ok, shh shh, it's ok, Liz. I got you. Come on, let's get you in bed." She whimpered into my chest, hand wrapped around my neck. I felt my arms grow wet beneath her. I tried not to think about what happened before I had arrived tonight.

Leaving Tommy, I walked us into the bedroom across the hall from Mason's room. Without bothering to turn on the the light, I lay Liz down on the bed. She bit her lip, and even in the darkness, I saw what horrible pain she was in. I felt a heaviness settle around my shoulders as a thought swam into my stunned mind.

This is your fault.

I went to the door and closed it, leaving it open just a crack in case Mason began to cry.

And what the hell are you going to do if he does? What do you know about kids?

I ran a hand over my exhausted face and went back to the bed. I crawled in next to Liz. Immediately, she rolled on her side and placed her head on my chest. I wrapped an arm around her, feeling like the devil. What had I brought into this poor woman's life?

"Jack," she whispered after some time, her voice strained, "what the hell is going on?"

Silence expanded in the air above our heads, and then I said, "I wish I knew, Liz."

Her breath hitched in her chest as she shifted closer into me. "What is he? What does he want?"

I placed my lips in her hair and a comforting hand on her back. "He wants to teach us how to be good people. He wants to raise Mason with us."

"But why? Where did he come from?"

"I don't know...but I think I know who to ask."

"Please don't leave me," Liz whispered. "Whatever happens, please don't leave me here with him."

I said nothing, knowing I had no control over what I would be allowed to do. I empathized with Liz so completely that I felt my heart breaking. At one point I had been exactly where she was now. Confused, terrified, and feeling very, very alone.

"Just do what he says for now," I said quietly, the room dark and still. "And whatever you do, don't call the police. Don't try to escape. Don't tell anyone about what's going on here. If you do, I can't protect you."

Liz was silent for a moment, then sadly: "He's going to kill me isn't he?"

I stroked her arm. "Not if I can help it. Stay patient and stay complacent."

Liz turned her tear streaked face up to mine. "What are you going to do, Jack?"

I dropped my voice low, terribly low: "I'm going to kill that motherfucker."

From the kitchen, I heard a low, haunting chuckle.

"Hehehehe…"

Chapter 9

I didn't sleep much that night. At some point I think I dozed off, the stress and mental exhaustion finally overwhelming me. I remember waking just before dawn to see Tommy staring at me through the crack in the door, his eyes illuminating the sliver of darkness. When our eyes met, he smiled and faded back into the black. I didn't fall back asleep. Instead, I stayed in bed, staring at the ceiling and holding Liz. Thankfully she was still out, breathing heavily against my chest. It was a strange feeling. She was familiar to me and yet different. The passage of time had faded the ease of our relationship, brief as it had been. Even though we had been in this very position many times, it felt intrusive now, like I didn't have the right to hold her.

She needs you right now, I thought, listening for signs of Tommy in the house. *She just needs you to be here with her.*

But did she really? She had raised Mason by herself for three years, worked a job, and seemed to be doing quite well for herself, all things considered. What the hell did I bring to the table? I had done nothing but cause trouble for her since our reunion. How could I screw up her life so completely in such a short time?

That's just what you do.

I closed my eyes. I was tired, dreadfully so, but I knew the world of dreams had departed for the night. Liz stirred against me and I smiled sadly down at her sleeping face. I wanted to protect her from the hell I knew was coming.

She doesn't need protection. She needs me to fix my mistakes. She needs me to grow up and deal with Tommy. Because I know what happens now...I've already been through it once and I'm not going through another five years of it.

I needed to find a way to kill Tommy Taffy once and for all.

As the sun peeked through the windows, I gently slid Liz from my arms onto a pillow and crept out of the room. The house was quiet, as was the countryside beyond the walls. I padded down the hallway and into the kitchen, feeling a headache coming on. I needed a cigarette.

I froze as I entered the kitchen, heart fluttering.

Tommy sat at the table, smiling. "Good morning, Jack. Did you sleep well?"

"I just need some water," I mumbled, going to the cabinet to retrieve a glass.

"It feels right, doesn't it?" Tommy asked from behind me, "being here? Sleeping with the mother of your child?"

I said nothing, instead filling the glass from the sink and tipping it to my mouth. I gasped as I drank, grateful for the relief.

"Did you fuck her, Jack?" Tommy asked quietly, his voice coy and prying.

I turned around to face him, setting the glass down, "Of course not. What kind of animal would I be if I tried to pull some shit like that?"

Tommy grinned and spread his hands. "I was just curious...you made it very clear last night what a mess you are."

"I need to go get some things from my apartment," I said,

looking at the floor. "I mean, if you want me to stay here, then I'm going to need my things."

Tommy eyed me curiously. "Well aren't you compliant this morning."

I looked up at him. "I've watched you die twice now. And yet here you sit. What choice do I have?"

Tommy chuckled. "Very well, Jack. Go and get your things. I don't think I have to remind you what happens if you try and pull anything stupid."

"I learned that lesson a long time ago," I muttered.

"Just don't forget it," Tommy said, standing, "or it won't be you who has to pay."

I fished my keys out of my pocket. "If Liz wakes, please tell her I'll be back this afternoon. She's going to be scared."

Tommy came and stood in front of me, his face a shadow over mine. "She has nothing to fear. Not unless you do something rash. And don't worry about Mason, either. I'll take care of him while you're gone. I understand that a father can't be there for his child all the time."

I shrugged away from him, unease coiling in my stomach. I didn't like the way he had been looking at me, his eyes pouring into mine like he was searching my thoughts. Right now, I couldn't afford that. Not with what I planned to do.

I went to the door but stopped as Tommy called to me.

"Oh, and while you're out, get some groceries. There isn't much here and I want us to hunker down for a while. So we can all acclimate to one another."

"Sure, Tommy," I said, emotionless.

I opened the door and left, feeling his eyes on the back of my neck.

As soon as I reached my car and departed, I pulled out my

phone. My heart was racing and I could feel a mental clock ticking precious seconds away. I pulled up my father's number and dialed it.

I felt a surge of frustration as it went to voicemail. Keeping one hand on the wheel, I spoke urgently into the phone.

"Dad, it's me. I need your help," I paused, the fields rolling past the window. "He's back, Dad. He's back and he's got me again. I need you. Please. Call me. I don't know if I can do this without you."

I hung up and then dialed Jason. Thankfully, he answered.

"Jack? What's up, buddy?"

"Oh thank God," I groaned, "Jason, something terrible has happened."

A pause. "What's going on?"

My voice was strained and painful, knowing what I was about to bring back into my friend's life. "Jason, I need you to listen very carefully to me."

"Jeez, man, you're scaring me…"

I braced myself. "Tommy's back."

Silence.

"Jason, did you hear what I said? He's back and he has Liz and Mason."

Jason's voice was soft and horrified. "Oh no…"

"Please," I begged, "I need your help. I can't do this again, not alone. You have to help me. I won't let them suffer like we did. I won't do it. I *can't*."

"Jack…how…how the hell…damn it…Jack, what are we supposed to do though? What can we do? We both know what he's capable of. We both know what he does…what he will do if we deny him. Shit….oh shit, man…"

"I know," I urged, "but I think something is different this time. I think I know someone who can help us."

"Who?!"

"I don't have time right now to explain," I pressed, "but when the time comes, I think I'm going to need you to help me."

A pause.

"Jason?"

"I thought we were done with him," Jason said distantly. "I thought we had moved on and were leaving all this behind."

"So did I. I'm so sorry for even asking this of you."

"Don't apologize. This isn't your fault. Of course I'll help you. Jack…I want to kill that bastard. I want to watch him die. The things he did to us…the things he put us through…" his voice was changing, growing violent, hateful. "I want to put a bullet through his eye and know that this time he won't get back up. Where is he, Jack? Where the hell is he?"

I told him he was at Liz's house and gave him the address but then quickly added, "Don't do anything stupid. Wait to hear from me."

"I want him dead."

"I know, so do I, but we both know he'll come back unless we do something different."

Jason's voice was laced with inpatient anger. "We were just kids, Jack. We didn't know how to kill. Things are different now. We can fight back."

"And we will," I stressed, "but we have to be smart about it."

"Sure."

"Jason…"

"I get it, Jack."

"Ok," I said, breathing a sigh of hesitant relief, "just…just wait until I call you, ok? I can't promise when that'll be, but just sit tight, all right?"

"I don't know how long I can wait, Jack…just knowing he's out there…hurting more people…"

"I'll call you," I said firmly.

"Right."

I hung up, feeling things begin to settle in place. I hated myself for involving Jason, but I needed him. I also needed my father. I checked my phone and impatiently prayed he'd hurry up and call me back.

I entered the city and pulled into a small grocery store. Groceries first, then my apartment. I hurried inside and began throwing things in a cart. As I did, I realized I needed to get Mason something to eat as well. What the hell did kids eat? He was three, did he need special food? Frustrated, I grabbed a couple jars of applesauce and animal crackers. It would have to do.

Cigarettes. I needed cigarettes.

I went to the checkout and began tossing things onto the conveyor, feeling anxious and impatient. I tapped my fingers against my leg as I watched the teenaged boy working the cash register slowly start to ring up my items. Behind him was a glass case full of cigarettes.

I pointed to them. "Hey kid, can I get a couple packs please?"

Without even looking up, he responded in a monotone voice. "Nope."

I felt irritation spike through me. "Why not?"

He rang up the applesauce, "Don't have the key, dude."

I gritted my teeth, "Well who does?"

"The manager."

"Well can you call him over?"

"He's busy."

I felt a primal rage ignite through me. I slammed my hand down over his, stopping him from ringing up the next item. My voice was grated coals through burning fire.

"Call. Him. Over."

The kid looked up at me. "Hey, man, you can't do that. That's assault."

I gripped his hand in mine, pulling his face inches from my snarling teeth. "I will fucking murder you where you stand if you don't get me some goddamn, motherfucking cigarettes right fucking now. Do you understand, you little cunt?"

The kid's eyes went wide and he just stared at me in complete shock.

I let him go. "Call him over. *Now.*"

Swallowing hard, the kid fumbled with the phone and called the manager over. When he arrived, the kid kept his mouth shut and I was granted my cigarettes. I paid for everything and left, leaving the cashier in a state of terror.

As soon as I got into the parking lot, I tore open a pack and hungrily lit a smoke. Nicotine flooded my system as I inhaled and the world felt slightly less dark. I loaded the bags into my car and peeled out of the lot, heading for my apartment. I smoked four cigarettes on the way over.

When I arrived, I threw the car in park and rushed upstairs. I burst through the door and rushed into the bedroom where I began stuffing things into a duffel bag. Satisfied, I tossed it next to my bed and dropped to my hands and knees.

The headphones.

I reached under the bed and pulled out the box where I had stashed them in. I tore off the top and pulled them out, ramming them over my head. I pressed the speakers to my ears, voice a trembling plea.

"Are you there? Rez?"

I waited in silence, a trickle of sweat running down my face. My mouth tasted like ash and I was terribly thirsty. I closed my eyes and forced myself to breathe.

"Rez?"

A trickle of static entered my head and then the voice said, **"I'm here, Jack."**

"Oh thank Christ," I whispered, "I need your help."

"I know you do. You shouldn't have gone over there. That was a mistake. It's going to make things much, much harder now."

"I couldn't just leave them," I argued, "Liz has nothing to do with this."

"She does now."

"Goddamn it, are you going to help me or chastise me!?" I yelled.

"Of course I'm going to help you. Remember, years ago, when I told you that one day I would need you? Well…that day is almost here."

"That day is today," I growled. "I'm sick and tired of standing by while Tommy does whatever he wants. We have to stop him and I think you know how."

"It's not as simple as that, Jack."

"WHY NOT!?" I roared, "why won't you just help me!?" I adjusted the headphones over my head, "Where are you? I want to meet you. We need to formulate a plan and I need some answers."

Static was followed by a series of low horns far off in the distance. **"Jack…I'm afraid."**

I blinked, stunned. "You're…afraid!?"

"I knew this time would eventually come, but now that the moment is upon me…I…I don't even know where to start."

"You have to give me something," I snarled. "Where are you!?

"Let me ask you something. Do you believe the universe is infinite?"

I shook my head. "What!? What does that have to do with anything?!"

"It's going to help you understand exactly what we're dealing with."

I fumbled, dumbfounded, "Yeah…yeah sure, the universe is infinite, so what!?"

A chirp of static as Rez sighed heavily, **"No Jack…you're wrong. There is an end to the cosmos. A…a surface, a plane that separates the universe from the realities beyond."**

"What the fuck are you talking about?" I cried.

Rez continued, **"The expanse of space is massive and cold. Its dark fingers stretch further than your mind could possibly comprehend. But there is an end to it. And at that end, at the very corners of the universe, lies The Barrier."**

"The Barrier?" I asked, incredulous.

"Yes," Rez continued, **"it is a band, a ring, that encircles the walls of this existence. It is a dangerous thing full of metal and wire and wailing engines. It is as enormous as it is mysterious. I don't know where it came from or what cosmic nightmare built it. But it divides the world you know from the planes of existence not meant to be seen. It protects you and all of humanity from the horrors beyond. It separates this universe from those of greater darkness and evil."**

"Rez…" I said, mind spinning, "I don't understand...this...this Barrier...if our reality ends at its walls...what exactly is on the other side?

Static buzzed in my ears and then was cleared by a distant whistle.

"I dare not speak of that place," Rez whispered,

"I don't understand," I struggled.

"And for your sake, I pray you never will," Rez said quietly.

I adjusted the headphones, trying my best to piece together the jigsaw of information. "Rez...how do you know all this? About this Barrier?"

A long pause...and then:

"Because that is where I came from."

My eyes went wide and I slumped against the bed. Impossible. None of this could be true, it just couldn't. It was too fantastical, too insane. A barrier encircling the universe? A monstrous, pulsing creation of dark machinery? How? How could that possibly be true?"

"Jack?"

"What the hell are you?" I whispered.

"There is no possible way I could describe to you the intricacies of my existence, Jack. It has taken me eons just to figure out how to communicate with you."

I sat up, sweat running down my face. "Try."

Rez exhaled heavily, a chatter of static in my ears, **"Almost forever ago, I became aware of my existence. I don't know how I came to be; I only know that I suddenly I gained a consciousness of some kind. As I awoke, I realized that I was pulling myself out of the mouth of some horrific machine. After freeing myself, I remember standing on the precipice of The Barrier and staring down into the vastness of space. And I fell in love with it. It enthralled me. The possibilities**

it held, the magic it must possess. I wanted to dive into it, fill myself with it, discover and experience everything it had to offer. And so I began to walk among the stars, searching for life. Searching for someone like me. I don't know why I exist. Perhaps I am some anomaly birthed from The Barrier, a mistake or misfired pulse of life. Regardless, I rose from that dark, mechanical plane and found myself filled with curiosity.

And so I began to search, Jack. I spent entire lifetimes wandering the coldness of space, fighting despair and hopelessness. I was convinced that I was alone in this existence. Was I some cruel creation of the same forces that made The Barrier? Was that it? Was I entertainment to fill a lifeless reality? Or was my original thesis correct? Was I an anomaly of The Barrier? I didn't know and that drove me ever onward."

"Jesus Christ," I whispered. "This is madness."

"I too, once, thought I was mad," Rez continued, **"but when I stumbled upon Earth…when I discovered life and other beings…oh, Jack…your language doesn't possess the words necessary to express my relief and overwhelming joy. Finally, after endless ages, I had found something that made me feel not quite so alone."**

I felt dizzy, waves of disbelief crashing into my skull. "How can I believe any of this? Just what the hell are you exactly? Some kinda of…of alien?"

"There are no aliens, Jack," Rez said softly. **"I have traveled the expanse of the cosmos. There is only you…and me."**

"I just…this is impossible," I whispered, "How can this be true? How can I accept this without losing my mind? And if it is true, how can you possibly be talking to me right now?"

"That wasn't easy," Rez said quietly. **"No matter how hard I tried, I just could not figure out your language. Any of them. There were too many and I became lost in the different dialects and variations. You're a complicated people."**

"So…how?"

"Your technology. That was something I understood and I began to figure out ways in which to use it so that I could communicate with you. But even now as we speak, what you are hearing is not my voice. What you are hearing is what the wires in your headphones are transmitting and translating. If we were to stand face to face, I'm not even sure you would know I am talking. Just the concept of speech was something I had to learn."

I ran my hands over my face, feeling like my mind would explode. "Ok…ok, say I buy into all this…where does Tommy fit into the picture? What the fuck is he!? How do we stop him!?"

Suddenly a screeching blast rocketed through my skull and I cried out, wincing. The blast faded and static crunched through my ears, followed by far-off horns.

"Jesus CHRIST!" I yelled, holding my head in my hands, "what *was* that!?"

"Oh no…" Rez whispered, **"Jack, you need to get back to Liz's house right now."**

An alarm suddenly went off in my head, a terrifying, pressing urgency. "What happened?! What's going on!?"

"There's no time! GO!"

"Wait, I need to know—"

"We'll finish this conversation later, Jack, NOW GO!"

Cursing, panicking, I pulled the headphones off my ears and

stuffed them into the duffel bag. The panic in Rez's voice scared the hell out of me and I fled my apartment.

I threw my bag into the car and roared out of the city. My stomach bubbled with fear and I drummed my fingers against the steering wheel as the busy streets bled into streaking countryside. *What the hell was going on? How was I supposed to accept any of this? And how the hell could it help me kill Tommy?* Questions bombarded my mind as the road blurred beneath me. *What was happening at Liz's house? Why had Rez been so insistent I go back?*

When I finally reached Liz's street, I discovered why.

Jason's car was parked in the driveway.

Chapter 10

I abandoned my car now parked next to Jason's and ran for the front door. I felt sickness infect my stomach and spread throughout my body as I sprinted up the stoop and practically ripped the door open. I knew that whatever I was about to walk into wasn't going to be good. I stepped inside and stopped, pulse racing.

Tommy was seated in a kitchen chair directly in front of me like he had been waiting for my arrival. He had one leg crossed over the other and a smile twisted his lips to reveal that alien strip of white that aligned his gums. He didn't move when I entered, just stared at me in silence, grinning. Behind him I saw Liz in the kitchen, crying and holding Mason. He was looking at her, repeating "Mom? Mom? Ok? Ok?" over and over again in his toddler dialect.

"Where's Jason?" I whispered as the door slammed shut at my back.

Tommy slowly closed his eyes. "Oh, Jack…you just couldn't help yourself, could you?"

"Where's Jason!?" I yelled. Mason jumped in his mother's arms and began to whimper.

Without looking, Tommy pointed into the living room on my left. I turned. Fireplace, couch, TV, recliner…but no Jason.

"What is this?" I asked cautiously.

"Don't you see him?" Tommy asked, finally standing. "He's right there."

I looked again but still didn't see him.

"What the hell is going on…?"

And then I heard my friend, his voice pained and muffled.

"Jack?! Jack, help me! PLEASE!"

My eyes went wide and I looked at Tommy, a shudder running through me. Tommy just smiled wider, his eyes flaring with color.

"Jesus Christ," I whispered.

He's in the chimney.

Tommy chuckled. "It was a tight fit, but I got him in. Don't think he's doing very well, though. I heard a couple bones snap when I stuffed him up there." He ran his hands together. "I hope they didn't puncture anything important."

I raced into the living room and dropped to my knees by the fireplace. Blood dripped from above and splattered onto a pile of wood that had been prepared in the hearth. I craned my head into the space above and looked up. A dark mass squirmed in the chimney and I heard Jason try to shift around.

His voice was hysterical. "Jack, get me out of here, please! PLEASE!"

"Oh my God," I cried, desperately trying to reach him. My fingers brushed against the bottom of his shoe, but that was as far as I could stretch. I felt wet warmth trickle onto my face and I spit it away, pushing my arm in as far as I possibly could.

"Try to scoot down a little bit, I can't reach you!" I yelled, panic and horror overwhelming me.

"I CAN'T!" Jason howled, "it hurts! It fucking hurts! I think my shoulders are broken! Oh God, Jack, don't let me die in here; *please* don't let me die in here!"

I pulled myself out, panting and searching for something to snag him with. I twisted around, wiping my friend's blood off my face. I needed something, *anything.* Jason's cries dug deep into my mind like screaming termites.

As I turned around, I came face to face with the barrel of a pistol. I froze, blood draining from my face. I slowly looked up the barrel and saw Tommy smiling down at me. He pressed the gun against my forehead.

"Jason brought a present. What do you think?" Tommy asked quietly.

I said nothing. I didn't dare.

Tommy kept the gun against my skin, its metal kiss cold and foreboding. "I think he wanted to kill me. Now…that's not very nice, is it? He should know better. He of *all* people should know better. Maybe he forgot about our little game all those years ago. You remember, don't you, Jack?"

Slowly, I nodded. Of course I remembered. I had watched Tommy put a bullet through his own skull and then get back up like it was nothing. What the hell had Jason been thinking?

Tommy stayed immobile. "Was this your idea? Did you tell him to do this?"

"Of course not, Tommy. I know the rules."

My eyes shifted past the gun and I saw Liz and Mason watching us from the entrance way. Mason looked scared and worried.

"Gun," he said, the world meaningless on his lips.

Tommy looked over his shoulder and laughed. "That's right Mason! It's a gun! Would you like to hold it?"

Liz took a step back, eyes going wide. Tommy lowered the pistol from my head and walked to Liz. She held Mason tighter against herself.

"Tommy..." she begged.

Tommy suddenly brought the gun up and pressed it against the side of her head. She let out a whimper and closed her eyes.

"TOMMY!" I screamed, still on my knees. At my back, Jason howled as his mangled bones shifted against the hard brick.

Tommy looked at me, digging the gun into her head. "Something wrong, Jack?"

"Please..." I croaked, "this isn't her fault. I'm the one who called Jason. I just had to talk to someone. I didn't know he would come over here. I'm sorry!"

Tommy lowered the gun and held it casually at his side. "Did...did you lie to me, Jack?"

I said nothing. Jason wept in the chimney, blood dripping onto the firewood at my back.

Tommy ran a hand over his eyes. "Oh, man...what a situation this is, huh? What am I supposed to do? What kind of example are you setting for your son? What's he supposed to think?"

"I didn't know this was going to happen," I said carefully.

Tommy nodded understandingly, "Of course, of course. How could you? You're not in control of your friend. He's not your responsibility. But regardless, he did come charging in here like a wild animal. You should have seen him. I didn't know Jason had it in him. He certainly has changed from the scared little boy we knew, huh, Jack?"

"We're all scared right now," I reasoned, "and confused and hurting. Let's just take a breath and make this right, ok?"

Tommy seemed to think it over, but slowly, he shook his

head. "No…no, I can't do that. You see, if Mason thinks lying is ok, that it can go unpunished, well…how am I supposed to live with that? How can you, as his father? That's just not good parenting."

"I'm sorry," I hissed. "Please."

Tommy strode toward me. "I'm afraid that's just not good enough."

I went to stand, adrenaline surging through me, but Tommy clocked me on the side of the head with the butt of the pistol. I moaned and fell on my side, my world ringing. Stars exploded across my vision and I felt my face hit the floor. The room swam, an inverted view of pandemonium. I blinked sluggishly as I watched Tommy retrieve something from the floor.

Oh no…

I heard Jason scream for mercy, but it fell upon deaf ears.

Tommy lit a match.

"Tommy, please, NO!" Liz screamed. Mason wept, a distant sound to my battered senses.

Tommy looked over at me, his face shifting in my altered vision. "This is your fault."

He tossed the match into the fireplace and I watched the wood ignite with a fiery passion.

"Jason!" I screamed, crawling on my hands and knees. My skull pulsed with pain and I couldn't seem to get the room to stop rocking.

Jason screamed as the long tongues of flame reached him. The house trembled beneath his cries and Tommy smiled through it all.

I scrambled to the fireplace, desperately trying to clear the logs from under Jason, but Tommy kicked me away. I collapsed in a heap, gasping for air, and listened as my friend burned alive. I gritted my teeth and pounded on the floor, struggling to get up. Tears ran down my face and a sickly smell entered the room.

Liz retreated back into the kitchen, shaken, horrified, and lost in herself. Tommy turned to watch me as Jason's sputtering, panting pleas now grew feeble and thin…until they stopped.

I looked up at Tommy with tear-stained eyes, breath blasting between clenched teeth. "You monster. You *fucking* monster."

I jumped as Jason's charred body dropped from the chimney, collapsing in a heap on top of the blazing wood. All his muscle had melted away, allowing room for him to slide back down. His body curled and turned to ash, the disturbing sight reflecting in my watery eyes.

"You've caused quite the mess," Tommy said darkly, a smile plastered to his face like a paper cut-out, "and I'm afraid this isn't the end of my lesson."

"Haven't you done enough!?" I screamed, finally crawling to my hands and knees, the air returning to my lungs.

Tommy left me and went into the kitchen.

As soon as he was out of sight, Liz began to scream.

"No!" I howled, "STOP IT!" Panting, sweat sticking to my skin, I pulled myself across the floor. Everything was spinning out of control, a terrible nightmare brought to life with violent, stark clarity. Mason was weeping as I got to one knee and pulled myself up along the wall. I grasped the corner of the molding and turned into the kitchen.

Mason was standing helplessly by the table, crying, face flushed, his little body shaking with fear. Tommy was dragging Liz by the hair down the hall toward the bedroom, her hands wrapped around his in an attempt to free herself.

As Tommy pulled her into the bedroom, he called to me over his shoulder, "Could you watch your son for a little bit?"

And then he disappeared with Liz and the door slammed shut so hard the hinges shook.

"Leave her alone!" I screamed, "Goddamn it! LEAVE HER ALONE!"

I heaved myself to Mason and scooped him up in my arms, holding the little one to me as he sobbed, confused and scared. From the bedroom, Liz began to howl and beg.

I stood up, stroking Mason's back, my own tears mixing with his as we stared down the hall together, helpless to the wrath and shocking violence of our captor. My eyes fell upon the table and I saw that Tommy had left the pistol. For a split second, I thought about going to the bedroom and blasting Tommy away, but I knew it would only make things much worse in the long run.

With Tommy, it could always get worse.

I huddled Mason into me and turned back to the living room, crying, hating myself, as Liz's howls peaked in strenuous agony.

"Shhh," I sobbed, staring down into Mason's teary eyes, "Shhh, please don't cry, please..." I kissed him on the head, the first time I ever kissed my son, and suddenly felt tremendous guilt. I walked him around the room, heart thundering, mind breaking, as the punishment continued down at the end of the hall. I was powerless, a pawn in Tommy's sadistic world. Fighting back would bring harsher Hell upon us. It would engrave more emotional scars onto Mason's already bleeding psyche.

I collapsed onto the couch, Jason's smoldering bones smoking in the fireplace. Mason sniffled and rested his head against my chest. I felt my shirt dampen under his tears. I stroked his head and wished I was dead.

"I'm so sorry," I whispered to Mason, "I didn't mean for this to happen…"

Suddenly my phone buzzed in my pocket. It snapped me out of my horrified, manic state and I quickly dug it out, heart thumping.

It was Dad.

The slightest sliver of hope rose from the misery, a faint light at the end of a very long, dark tunnel. If anyone could help me, it was him.

I quickly answered, wiping my eyes with my free hand. "Hello? Dad?!"

"Hi, Jack."

I blinked. "Mom?"

"There's something I need to tell you," she said. Her voice was distant and emotionless.

"Mom, where's Dad!? I need to talk to him!"

My mother's voice was barely a whisper as she said, "Your father killed himself an hour ago. I'm at the hospital."

The phone slid down my face as my body went rigid. My hand hung empty in the air and a haunting darkness rushed in on me. I felt vomit rise in the back of my throat as a blast of cold disbelief rocketed through me. I stared off into nothing, motionless.

Impossible.

Mason reached down for my phone, my mother's muffled voice still talking from the other end. Numb, freezing, and dead, I took the cell from his tiny hands and hung up. I couldn't breathe, couldn't speak, couldn't seem to sort anything out. Hell rushed in on me and I burned in its icy currents.

You did this.

This is your fault.

Why did you call him…

Dead…killed himself…

Dad…

Daddy…

I don't know how long I sat there holding Mason as the world spun around me. At some point, Mason slid from my lap and sat on the floor, watching me, whimpering. The sun outside dipped behind the hills and a purple haze grew from the darkening horizon beyond the windows.

As the last of the light faded from the sky, I heard the bedroom door open. Completely empty of any emotion, I turned my head and saw Tommy watching me from the hall.

"Something wrong, Jack?" he asked, grinning. Blood stained his hands up to his elbows. I just shook my head.

No…nothing was wrong.

"Oh, wonderful," Tommy said. "Hey, did you happen to pick up those groceries earlier? Are they still in your car?"

The way he stood there talking about food so casually while covered in blood made me clutch my head. This was a dream…surely…this was a dream.

Wake up, Jack.

Dad's dead…

Dad killed himself.

Dad…is…

…dead.

Please wake up.

Jack?

"Jack?"

"They're still in the car," I whispered, looking up.

"Good, good," Tommy said, nodding approvingly, "I'm going to go get them. You don't look like you're in any state to move right now. Tough night…I get it."

I watched him walk to the front door and step out into the night. This had to end…this needed to end…I could feel myself breaking, dying, collapsing into myself as the walls of insanity pressed closer and closer.

Liz. I needed to go to her. What had he done? What had he taken from her this time?

I picked up Mason and placed him on the couch. He looked up at me and I handed him my phone to play with. Taking a deep breath, I walked into the kitchen.

And there was Liz.

She was leaning against the kitchen table, tears pouring from her bloodshot eyes. Her mouth was twisted into a silent cry. Her legs were covered in blood, her knees shaking with the effort just to stand.

And she had the barrel of the pistol pressed against her temple.

My eyes went wide and her name escaped my lips in a hurried plea, "Liz!"

"I can't," she croaked, "I can't anymore. Take care of Mason."

Liz shot herself in the head.

A scream rose in my throat as I lunged forward, "NO! NO, NO, PLEASE, LIZ!" Her body hit the floor and blood poured from the hole in her skull. I fell next to her, holding her, begging, weeping, crying. I lifted her against me, taking her face in my hands.

"Oh no, please don't leave me!" I sobbed, shaking her,."Wake up, please, I'm sorry. I'm so fucking sorry, PLEASE!"

Blood gushed over my hands as I stared down into her lifeless eyes.

"FUCK!" I screamed, squeezing my eyes shut, shoulders shaking with grief. "FUCK FUCK FUCK!"

Mason, face full of worried concern, walked into the kitchen. As his eyes fell upon his mother, he broke down. He ran to her, his little legs carrying him with terrified urgency. He slumped next to me, his chubby fingers running over his dead mother's face.

"Ma?" he cried, eyes wide. "Ma? Ma? Wake up! Wake up! It's not time for sleep!"

"Jesus Christ," I cried, "Oh Jesus Christ, stop this…" I reached out and pulled Mason away, his hands already dripping with blood. "Go back into the living room!" I ordered, vision blurring, voice cracking,

"Please, go back into the living room, Mason!"

But he just stared at Liz, his eyes wide and disbelieving. He kept looking at me and then back at her, confused, scared, and unsure.

"What happened here?"

I turned at the voice and saw Tommy standing in the doorway with bags of groceries in hand. He looked hard at me, his eyes sparking and spitting blue.

"Jack?" Tommy asked calmly, "Did you do this?"

"You motherfucker," I snarled, a sudden white-hot fury exploding in my chest, "YOU MOTHERFUCKER!"

Screaming with primal rage and roaring anger, I grabbed the gun from Liz's motionless hand and charged Tommy. I plowed into him with all the force I had and we went tumbling out the door and down the front steps.

I heard him grunt as his head struck the concrete and the weight of my body came crashing down on top of him.

"YOU GODLESS FUCKING MONSTER!" I bellowed, fire and spit blasting from my lungs. "HOW COULD YOU DO THIS TO HER!?"

Lost in a hurricane of violence, I smashed my face into Tommy's, crunching my forehead into his eyes. I heard him exhale as the blow connected.

Without pausing, I shoved the pistol into his mouth. I pulled the trigger once, twice, and didn't stop until the clip went dry.

Tommy's head rocked back with every explosion, a jolt shuddering through his body. Time seemed to slow and spin around us, the deafening report of the pistol ringing in my ears.

I looked down at my victim, panting as gun smoke filtered the air above us.

"Hehehehe..."

An icicle formed along my spine.

Tommy looked up at me, smiling, his eyes clear and shining brightly. "Are you done, Jack?"

I scrambled off him, suddenly terrified. He wasn't dead. *Of course* he wasn't dead. I got to my hands and knees and then stood in the night, backing away from him.

Tommy crawled to his feet and rubbed his jaw. "Get your bag from the trunk and go inside, Jack. Take Mason and go into the bedroom. I'll deal with you later. These groceries need to be put away before they go bad." He looked at my stunned face and blue flared from his eyes. "Unless there's anything else you wanted to say?"

I shook my head, panting, suddenly very afraid. I forced myself to move. I retrieved my bag of clothes from the car and hurried inside. I picked up Mason and practically ran for the bedroom.

"Shit, shit, oh shit…" I whispered, a sinking weight lowering deep onto my gut.

I closed the bedroom door and locked it. I tossed my bag onto the bed and then crawled up next to it.

"What have I done…?" I cried into the dark room. Mason's little hands groped for me and I held him close. He rested his head on my shoulder and I could hear him crying quietly.

"It's over," I said miserably, sobbing.

Chapter 11

I didn't sleep that night. I stretched out on the bed, bloodshot eyes staring up at the blank ceiling. Tears rolled down my cheeks and I cried silently. Mason was curled up next to me, nestled gently into my arm. His little chest rose and fell with slumber I could only fantasize about.

Jason was dead.

Liz was dead.

And Dad…oh Christ…

No matter how much I tried to escape the misery, it just seemed to fall heavier upon me as the night went on. I couldn't shake Jason's screams as he burned alive nor the look on Liz's face seconds before she shot herself in the head. The blood…there had been so much blood…everywhere, on everything…

My mother kept calling me, completely unaware of the situation I was trapped in. Or did she know? Had my father said something to her, given her a clue before his abrupt death? No…not death…suicide. I closed my eyes, dripping with grief. I thought back on our conversation in the city at the cafe. I should have known then that he couldn't handle any more. I knew he carried Katie's death around with him in ways I could only imagine. It was the wrinkles on his face, the twist of his lips, the sadness buried so deep behind his eyes.

And I had called him and asked for help, knowing the symptoms were there. I squeezed my fists together and hated myself in the most depraved ways. So much loss…how was anyone supposed to bear it all?

I looked down at Mason and felt a rise in my chest. Would he even remember his mother? How drastically had his young life been altered tonight? What was I supposed to do with him? What were we supposed to do now?

Jason's howls re-entered my fractured, exhausted mind and I exhaled shakily. My friend—my only friend—gone. Taken away in a violent, horrific act. And again…I hated myself. I had brought him back into this nightmare, extended my hand and he had taken it, following me back into the darkness of our childhood.

"This can't go on…" I whispered, bleary-eyed and alone. I could feel the isolation, the emptiness of my situation swirling around me like a blizzard of helpless fear.

I checked the door from my place on the bed. It remained closed and locked from the inside. I could hear Tommy moving throughout the house…opening doors…shifting furniture…dragging…something…across the floor. Deep into the night, the house went silent and I wondered if he had left. But where would he go? Was he simply sitting in the kitchen, waiting for me to open the door?

He's letting me digest all this, I thought, *if he really wanted to, he would come in.*

That did nothing to comfort me, knowing that I was still caught in Tommy's web, his plan…whatever the fuck that was.

At four, Mason stirred at my side. I gently scooted his head up on my shoulder and stared down into his peaceful face. So innocent. I couldn't even imagine the horror his young mind was trying to make of all this. What would he remember? What would stand out? The gunshot? His mother's lifeless eyes staring back up at him? The blood staining his hands?

I started to cry again, unable to stop myself.

"Dad's here," I whispered. "Dad's here little man…I won't leave you again…I promise." I gently kissed the top of his head and felt something change inside of me. It was a warmth, a loving warmth that slowly spread across my chest. This little person was depending on me. He needed me in the most basic of ways. I was now completely and solely in charge of his care, safety, and upbringing.

The thought terrified me. But it also gave me strength. I had to be someone. I had to be a father. *His* father. I didn't know how, but looking into his peaceful face, I felt myself hardening. I would be whatever he needed me to be. And I would take care of him to the best of my ability. We were going to get out of this nightmare. Together.

Suddenly, I felt the door handle rattle. I stiffened at the sound and I went on full alert, head whipping toward the door.

Tommy's muffled voice came to me from the other side. "Still need some time, Jack?" A pause, waiting, then: "I understand. Take as much time as you need. I'll be here when you're ready."

My heart pounded in the darkness. *Don't come in…please don't come in here…*

"I'm leaving you some food by the door. Mason is going to get hungry and he's going to need to eat. Again, I understand if you don't want to come out for a little while. We've all had a traumatic experience tonight."

Leave me alone...please...

"I've taken the necessary precautions with the bodies," Tommy continued from the other side of the door. "We won't have to worry about the police snooping around if it comes to that." A pause. "You're welcome." And then he was leaving, back down the hall.

I needed to do something. I needed to take advantage of this silence.

I needed to talk to Rez.

I carefully slid Mason from my arm, knelt by the bed, and unzipped my duffel bag. Quietly, I dug out the headphones and held them up.

"Please be there," I whispered.

I went to the far corner of the room and sat down on the floor, opposite the door. Slowly, I lowered the headphones over my ears.

"Rez?"

The familiar buzz of static was almost instant.

"Jack...I'm so sorry."

I sat for a moment, letting that sink in.

"Rez...we have to end this. Please...help me..."

Rez's voice was soft. **"I'm almost ready, Jack. If you can just make it through the day then I think tonight is the night."**

"What are we waiting for?" I whispered, voice weak and impatient.

"Because, Jack, I need to come to you. I need to be there. And that is going to take a tremendous amount of energy. The energy I have been absorbing from the cosmos for decades now. I've been preparing for this day for years, dating back to that first phone call I made to you."

"I don't understand," I said, trying to piece things together.

"What is it exactly you have to do? Why do you have to be here with me?"

Rez's voice became heavy, almost tragic. **"Because, Jack...the only way to kill Tommy Taffy...the only hope we have of stopping him...is if he watches me die."**

My eyes grew wide. "What...?"

"In order for you to understand exactly what it is you're going to have to do...you need to understand what Tommy is."

I waited, the night frozen around me, "Yes..."

Rez gathered himself and then spoke, his voice careful and deliberate. **"Tommy Taffy is a dream."**

I squinted in the darkness and pressed the headphones tight against my head. "A...dream?"

"Yes...he's my dream."

"Rez," I whispered, "I don't understand."

"When I found Earth and began watching you, watching the way humanity behaved, interacted, cared, and loved for one another...I was fascinated. I studied the way you worked, the way you lived, the way you formed relationships and developed bonds.

And Jack...I wanted that. I wanted that so badly. I had spent eons in isolation wondering if there was anything out there. You humans...you showed me a world I had been searching for my whole existence and I lusted after that. So...I began to dream. At first, it was harmless fantasy, an otherworldly desire that helped ease my loneliness. But the more I watched, the more I craved. I wanted to be one of you. I wanted to speak with you. I wanted to know what it was like to laugh, to have a friend, to fall in love. It became an obsession, a driving urge that I couldn't ignore any longer."

"Jesus, Rez," I breathed, eyes wide in the dark of the room.

"And so…I began to dream. Not like you humans do…no…this was something different. Something more powerful. Something real. I channeled what I saw into energy and life. I wanted to create a vessel in which I could finally descend to you. But such a massive creation is not conjured so easily. I spent centuries trying to form a perfect host and failed hundreds and hundreds of times."

Rez paused, and then whispered, **"To be more exact, I failed sixty-sixty thousand three hundred and fifty-seven times."**

I blinked and then felt an onslaught of dizziness. "Oh my god…six-six-three-five-eight…"

"Yes, Jack…he was my last dream. The one that worked."

I exhaled shakily, mind collapsing.

"But I made a mistake. a horrible, terrible mistake. With each failed attempt, I thought I was discarding the previous effort, the previous dream, and focusing my energy on a new creation. But…that wasn't the case."

"I don't understand," I murmured.

"Jack…the reason Tommy acts the way he does is because I was layering my dreams on top of one another. Instead of starting fresh, I was compounding my creations, unaware of what I was doing. And with each attempt, with each dream cycle I channeled, I would change and tweak little things that I had learned about you. About life on Earth."

"So…?" I breathed, trying to wrap my head around everything.

"So, when the final dream emerged from my consciousness, it held the previous sixty-six thousand three hundred and fifty-seven versions of itself as well."

"Wait a second," I stammered, pulse roaring, "does that mean..."

"Yes, Jack...if Tommy realized it, he could create sixty-six thousand three hundred and fifty-eight versions of himself here on Earth."

I slumped against the wall, face growing pale. "Oh my God..."

"When the final dream was birthed, I grew very, very tired. I floated in a state of...well, I believe you would describe it as sleep. When I awoke, the dream had vanished. Panicked, I thought I had lost it, absorbed into the universe. But when I turned my gaze back to Earth...I saw him. I saw him in your neighborhoods, in your homes...I saw him with your children. The dream had abandoned me."

"Rez...I...Jesus Christ."

Rez continued, **"When I saw what he was doing...how he behaved...I was terrified. It was wrong—so, so wrong. What I didn't understand, what I didn't realize during the final dream, the one that birthed Tommy...was that in its perfection, I had made him not merely a vessel but a living, breathing entity. One that mirrored humanity almost immaculately. But there were flaws—and not just with his physical appearance.**

During the early days of my dreaming, I didn't understand humanity. You were so...violent and cruel to one another. The wars...the slaughter...the genocide. I thought maybe that was just part of your existence. And so I dreamed versions of Tommy that replicated that behavior. Hundreds of them."

Sweat ran down my face in streaks and I licked it from my lips. "And those versions compounded into the final cycle."

"Yes. A flaw in my design. A terrible, murderous flaw."

I sat up and checked to make sure Mason was still asleep before asking in a hushed voice, "Is that why he is the way he is?"

"Yes. But he has all the qualities of a good person in him, as well. You see, in my later attempts, I began to see the good rise out of the hearts of humans. My viewpoint began to change and alter, as did my dreams. Tommy has the capacity to love, to teach, and care for others. But those good characteristics are buried beneath countless versions bred with violence. He is constantly at war with himself, fighting internally with which version he is. He's completely unaware that such a battle is taking place, but surely you've seen it."

I rested my head against the wall, closing my eyes, and focused on breathing.

The lessons…the constant insistence that we need to be good people…

…Katie's death…

"Rez," I said quietly, "there's something I still don't understand."

"What is it, Jack?"

"Why families? Why does he…infect our homes? Why does he stay with us? Why is he so infatuated with children?"

"I'm afraid that stems from my own curiosity. You see, when I first started watching Earth from the shadows of space, it was the concept of family that intrigued me the most. How two people could fall in love, bond with one another, and then create life. I wanted that more than anything. And that became the base of my dream. To raise versions of myself, to teach them, to love them, to show them

how to love in the ways you humans do. It was so perfect, so beautiful, that I became lost in the dream."

"And it became the base of your desire," I said quietly.

"It did. But that fantasy clouded when it came into contact with the previous versions I had envisioned. It wasn't until Tommy left me that I realized my terrible mistake. The clarity of what I wished was lost beneath the weight of it all. Love...parenting...sex. They became warped and malicious, twisted ideas that became entangled with one another.

Tommy sees sex as a rite of passage. A doorway into adulthood. He sees it as the end of his work, a compilation of all that has come before. His mind is a grave of dead concepts I thought I had buried. When the child he has worked to raise passes that threshold...he leaves to find another family. At least...that version of him does. I don't know if he is aware of the extent of his reach just yet. And that is why we need to stop this now. Before his reach grows. Before he starts to invade not just one neighborhood at a time...but two...or three...or perhaps an entire city."

"Christ," I hissed.

"All he wants is to be a part of your family. He wants to be one of you. He wants to raise you and teach you. He wants to shuttle you into adulthood through one final, disgusting act of sexual depravity. Then, and only then, will he see his purpose fulfilled."

"But Rez...he came back," I whispered. "If what you're saying is true, why is he BACK?"

Static buzzed in my ear and then Rez continued, **"Because he leeches himself to a family. A bloodline. He wants to see the fruit of his labor. He wants to see the children he raised into adulthood. He wants to see what kind of fathers and**

mothers they have become. He wants to compare himself to them."

"Why...?"

"Because he wants to be the best he can possibly be, just like I dreamed him. And in his eyes, because of the layers I stacked upon his creation...he truly thinks he is. There's nothing simple about the way he thinks, Jack. Even during the most chaotic situations, Tommy has calculated every result. He is the most rationally insane being I have ever witnessed."

"So why me...why has he taken such a special interest in ME? Why didn't he kill ME instead of my sister? Doesn't that go against his...his fucked up parental code?"

"No, Jack...and again, this comes from my own flaws. When I dreamed up Tommy, I modeled him after the male sex. They were simpler, easier to understand than females. That lack of understanding bled into Tommy. He can't relate to women in ways a sane human should. He sees them as...expendable. If he enters a family and there are children of both sexes, he will always turn his attention on the male more than the female. And that's because he relates to them. He feels a bond with them and that young boy because of the focus of his desires. Everyone else is collateral, if it comes to that. And only if he thinks, in his warped, violent mind, that in some way he can imprint some lesson or balance into the boy's life."

"This is absolute...insanity," I said, closing my eyes.

"Tommy Taffy is a being composed of constantly shifting ideals and values. A consistent clash of logic and shocking violence. He is a multi-layered nightmare birthed from a

desperate desire to be one of you…and to be part of a family."

"Rez," I muttered, "I don't know what to say…I don't know what to think…"

A long pause of wavering static filled my head as Rez sighed, **"I'm so sorry, Jack. I didn't mean for any of this to happen…you must believe me."**

I snorted, feeling the walls of my mind strain beneath the influx of information, "I don't know what to believe…" I ran my hands over my face and sighed. "Can I ask you something else?"

"Of course."

"Why me…? Surely there are other versions of Tommy out there right now, terrorizing homes…so why did you pick me to talk to?"

"Because, Jack…you were the one who answered the phone."

I sat up, shaking my head. "You hadn't tried to contact anyone else until then?"

"No…you were the first. Jack, you have to understand…I was terrified of what I had done to you. To all of you. To everyone who suffered under Tommy's oppression. It took all the courage I had to call that day. But even then, I wasn't ready. I tried to talk to Tommy…to convince him to stop. Do you remember?"

My mind soared back and I nodded. "Yes…I remember."

"When I realized that Tommy wasn't going to stop, I knew I had to do something. I knew I needed to reach out to someone. Someone who could one day help me stop Tommy."

"And I was the one who answered the phone," I whispered.

"Yes, Jack. It was you. A child…an innocent child. It was

at that moment that I began to gather my energy and prepare myself to eventually come down and confront the monster I had created. But I knew in order to stop him, to kill Tommy, I was going to need another. And there you were…lying in bed with those headphones on…"

I said nothing, Rez's voice ringing in my ears. Seconds ticked away in my head like bombshells.

"Jack?"

"I'm here…"

Rez fell back into silence, allowing me to contemplate everything. It was an overwhelming tidal wave of impossibility, and yet…what choice did I have but to believe him? I pictured Tommy smiling at me, his eyes glowing…knowing…

"Rez," I whispered, "Tell me how to stop him. Tell me how to kill him."

Static buzzed in the distance and I heard a low whistle, masked by a solemn horn.

"There are two ways to get rid of Tommy. One option is to sever the family and end the bloodline. To extinguish the focus of his intent."

"You're not talking about—"

"Yes, Jack. You could kill Mason. Without him, Tommy has no purpose here. There is no child to be reared, no parent to compare himself with."

"That's not happening," I said angrily. "How could you even suggest something like that?"

"I'm sorry. I'm merely presenting you with what I know. I've seen it done before…a pair of twins, in fact…"

"Stop," I hissed, "I don't want to hear this. What's the second option?"

"The second option is the one I have been preparing myself for. To erase Tommy entirely from existence."

"We can't let him continue," I said quietly. "We can't let him do this to any more families, Rez."

"I know. And I am prepared to do what I need to in order for that to happen. It grieves me to think it has come to this. That I have failed so completely in my dream. I know Tommy is a monster. I know he won't stop. And yet, even so…I can't help but feel utterly defeated that it must end this way. I so hoped he would change…that eventually, he would become the creation I intended. I am connected to him in the most intimate of ways. I even named him after myself."

"Rez…" I warned.

"You don't have to worry about me changing my mind, Jack. I'm ready to do what I must."

I sat up and saw light now peeking in through the windows, a low simmer of oozing dark purple against the horizon. "What exactly is going to happen? How do we stop him? How do we end this?"

"I will come to you tonight. I will stand with you before Tommy."

"And then what?"

"And then you will kill me."

I leaned forward, voice hoarse. "What?!"

"I can't do it myself, Jack. When it comes down to it, I've realized that I am a coward. I'm going to need you to do it. I need you to do it in front of Tommy. I need him to see me die before his eyes."

"God, Rez, why?" I asked. "Isn't there another way?"

"None that I know of. I am the dreamer, Jack. I am his source of life. My prayer is that when I go, he will, too. But

that is a very slight hope. Regardless of what happens, without me he will be forced to channel himself into a singularity. His grip on this reality has become strong over the years and I believe he possesses enough of my energy to remain even after I die. But Jack, he will be reduced to one. One final being. An echo of my dream. A shadow on your world. Smoke without flame. And it will be up to you to eliminate his final breath."

I ran my hands through my hair, shaking my head. "I can't…Rez, I can't do it. He's too strong…he'll kill me."

"Not if I'm dead. If I'm dead then Tommy will become severely weakened. It is in that moment that you must strike. You cannot hesitate and you must not doubt yourself. You can do this, Jack. You have to. You're the only one left."

"Jesus," I hissed, closing my eyes, "how has it come to this…"

"Are you with me, Jack?"

I opened my eyes as the sunlight crept into the room. I looked over at the bed, at Mason sleeping soundly. I thought of Liz, of Jason…

…of Dad.

Katie.

"I'm with you, Rez."

Rez sighed gratefully. **"Then we shall do it tonight. I must go now. This has taken a lot of energy out of me and I need to make sure I'm prepared to break through tonight. To descend. I will be ready when the time is right. Until then…stay safe, Jack."**

"Sure…"

And then my headphones went silent. I slowly pulled them off and wiped sweat from my ears. I rested my head against the wall and stared at the ceiling. Could I really do this? Did

I have a choice? I looked again at Mason on the bed. No…I didn't have a choice.

I stood up and crawled into bed next to him. I leaned down and gently kissed his cheek. It was warm and soft and I smiled sadly.

"We're going to make it through this," I whispered to him, "I promise you."

And then I closed my eyes and finally…mercifully…I slept.

Chapter 12

I awoke as something brushed against my face. I turned over, trying to swat it away. A second later, the same something was tapping my cheek. Groaning, I forced my eyes open, shielding them from the blinding sun that now hung high in the window.

Mason sat next to me, his finger poised for another poke.

I ran my hands over my face and forced myself into alertness.

"What's up, little man?" I asked, voice groggy.

Mason put a finger in his mouth, "Where's Ma?"

I sighed heavily, the reality of our position flooding back with crushing weight. "She's…not here right now," I said cautiously.

Mason pouted and then changed the subject. "I'm hu-u-ungry."

I sat up in bed and looked at the clock. It was already 6 PM. My head felt thick and a numb kind of hollowness sat in my chest.

"Shit," I mumbled, getting up, "I'm sorry, buddy. I bet you're starving. Have you been trying to wake me up?"

Mason nodded, wide-eyed.

I stood and went to the door. I pressed my ear to it and listened. I gave it a full thirty seconds before I was satisfied. I didn't hear Tommy which was both a relief and incredibly concerning. Where was he? What was he doing?

Cautiously, I unlocked the door and peeked out. Nothing. I looked down and saw a box of animal crackers. I quickly snatched them and closed the door again. I turned around and offered them to Mason. A smile lit up his face.

I sat down next to him and opened the package. As soon as I did he plucked the box from my hands and began jamming crackers into his mouth. Crumbs flew as his small teeth chomped down with a vengeance.

"Easy, kid, easy," I said wearily, "slow down or you're going to choke, ok?"

Mason scrunched his face up at me and stubbornly continued his conquest. I sat back against the headboard and pulled him to my side. Content, he leaned against me, plucking little animals from the box. About halfway through he suddenly stopped and held one up to me.

"Want one?" he asked, his voice curious and pure.

I smiled, taking it. "Sure. Thanks." Satisfied that he had done his due diligence, he turned back to the box and proceeded to demolish the rest.

"How long have you been up?" I asked, brushing crumbs from his shirt.

Mason just looked up at me and blinked.

We sat like that for a while, Mason's stomach poking out from under his shirt. When he was finished eating he placed his small hands on his belly, almost proudly. He seemed content to just stay by my side, resting comfortably against my arm.

As evening came, I noticed the sky changing outside. Clouds

began to form in front of the sinking sun. An hour later and the clouds turned dark and angry. In the distance, I heard the rumble of thunder. An urgent wind had developed and I listened as it passed through the long grass outside. The room grew dim and I felt Mason sinking next to me. I looked down and saw he was fighting to stay awake. I pulled his shirt down over his little belly and watched him drift off. It was…soothing.

When full dark entered the room, I scooted off the bed and lowered Mason's head onto a pillow. After a second, I pulled a blanket over him and ran a hand through his hair.

"I think it's time," I whispered down to him. "I promise I'll end this and get you out of here."

Rain began to tap against the window panes as I stooped to retrieve my headphones. In minutes, the rain began to throw itself against the house. The walls moaned beneath the developing gale and I shuddered.

I went to the door and listened for Tommy. When I didn't hear anything, I slid the headphones on.

"Where is he, Rez?"

"He's outside," Rez answered almost immediately. **"I think he knows."**

Quietly, I opened the door and peeked out into the hallway. The house was dark and the storm grew around it. Lightning flashed and ignited my surroundings. In that moment I saw Tommy Taffy hiding in every corner, watching me. I ran a hand over my face. My imagination was on high alert and I shook the images away.

I crept down the hall and into the kitchen. Rain lashed against the windows, a drumming, insistent sound. Thunder groaned outside and I felt the blasts echo in my head. I went to the counter and began rummaging through the drawers.

I needed a weapon.

In the second drawer, I found a large steak knife. I picked it up and felt a little better. The blade gleamed as lighting sparked the sky and lit the windows. I kept searching, hands fumbling in the dark. In the last drawer, I found a scattering of household tools. I pushed aside a couple of wrenches and found what I had been hoping for.

A hammer. I picked it up and slid it into my waistband behind my back. More thunder boomed overhead and I turned to the front door.

"He's waiting for us."

I nodded, the headphones resounding with the weight of what I was about to attempt. What we were about to do. I walked to the door, each step heavy with dread and looming fear. Could we really do this? Could we kill Tommy Taffy? Could we destroy six-six-three-five-eight-Rez…forever? Images rose in my mind, memories of my childhood. My head became a picture book for every terrible thing Tommy had put us through, every scream, cry, and drop of blood…

"Focus, Jack."

"I am," I muttered, brushing my disturbed thoughts aside.

I opened the door and let the night in. Rain crashed to the earth in heavy sheets and the wind whipped past me, carrying the gale with it. I stepped out onto the front stoop, heart racing. In seconds my hair hung down in my eyes, soaked and dripping.

"Where is he?" I whispered.

"In the field across the street. He's watching us."

Goosebumps formed along my arms. I squinted in the darkness, knife gripped firmly in my hand. I stepped down onto the front lawn, rain lashing against my skin. I didn't see him...Christ, I didn't see him...

My nerves bunched and screamed with frantic adrenaline, like at any moment Tommy would come roaring out of the night, hands reaching for my throat.

"I don't see him!" I hissed desperately, trying to control my panicked mind.

"Across the street, in the tall grass. Wait for the lightning."

My fingers tingled at my sides and my legs felt weak and heavy. I blew moisture from my lips as I squinted against the onslaught of rain. Come on, come on...

Lightning ignited the world.

My heart skipped a beat and I felt my throat close in terror.

Tommy was standing thirty yards away, facing me, eyes glowing a brilliant blue. He was immobile, the grass reaching his waist, rain pelting him as he waited in the night.

And he was smiling.

"Shit," I said shakily, willpower waning.

Tommy began to slowly walk toward me, that horrific smile frozen on his lips. Thunder growled and I took a step back.

"Rez, where are you?" I asked urgently.

Muffled static echoed in my ears.

I swallowed hard, "Rez?!"

A faint whisper, **"I'm coming."**

Tommy was twenty yards away now, his fingers running over the top of the grass. A roar of thunder shook the earth and I wiped rainwater from my face, knife shaking in my hand.

"Has it really come to this, Jack?" Tommy called, his voice rising with the storm. He was getting closer. I backed up, my heels hitting the front stoop.

"Rez!" I cried, pressing the headphones against my head.

"Is this really what you want!?" Tommy called, his voice harsh on the wind.

I exhaled rain from my lips and readied myself. My heart echoed like the thunder in the sky. My clothes stuck to me soaked through. My hair hung in strands across my face. The hammer dug into my back and the knife handle was slick in my hand.

"Where are you, Rez?!" I asked through clenched teeth, "REZ!?"

And then his voice came to me, clear and unbroken: **"Look to the sky."**

I turned my eyes to the heavens and felt the blood drain from my face, "Holy shit..."

Tommy stopped walking and turned, noticing the change.

A corner of the sky had ignited a luminous, pulsing blue tear that pushed the ebony night away. From the center of the light came an incandescent streak of cobalt fire that pulsed like the sun. It rocketed toward us at an incredible speed, trailing sapphire smoke in its wake. It grew in my vision, a cannonball heading directly for us. The sky shook as an earsplitting blast cracked the storm clouds, a devastating, shrill whistle that echoed into a skull-crunching bellow, like a low horn calling down to us from the night.

I stood paralyzed as the roaring trail of cyan fire hit the earth between Tommy and myself, a missile of raw power that shuddered through the ground, causing me to stumble.

Blue smoke enveloped the impact and my ears rang from the collision.

And then, slowly, Rez emerged from the glow.

My blood turned to ice as I gazed upon him.

He stood nine feet tall, an imposing tower of alien design.

He was humanoid in shape, his arms and legs extending from a torso composed of the darkest black. Wrapping his figure were coils of squirming wire and cable, a metallic, living machine that pulsed with intricate, meticulous purpose. Hundreds of gears protruded from the lines of complexity that engulfed his body like pieces of an engine carefully assembled into human form.

His limbs ended in rounded caps like logs of iron and steel. Running up his back was a long, neon tube of electric blue fluid wrapped in a translucent casing. Upon his shoulders sat a cage, a square block of grated metal. Through the bars, I saw his head, a large, circular nest of contorted, moving machinery. His eyes were massive and round, two spotlights of dazzling blue, the light cold and brilliant. Stretching from his mouth was a long cable that snaked between the bars of the cage and connected to the neon tube along his spine.

"Hello, six-six-three-five-eight," I heard Rez say through my headphones.

He was standing directly between Tommy and me, a titan of glowing power. As he spoke, I saw something exhume from his eyes, a small cloud of blue smoke. As his words filled my ears, I saw the strange cloud pulse with light.

That's how he communicates, I thought in awe.

A bolt of lightning extended across the sky and I saw Tommy's eyes grow wide. He took a step back, shock etched across his face.

"Rez…" he breathed, his smile vanishing.

"It's over, six-six-three-five-eight," Rez said, my headphones buzzing, that eerie cloud of pulsing light emanating from his eyes. "It's time for you to leave."

Tommy's hands curled into fists. "Never."

"You weren't meant for this earth," Rez said, pointing at Tommy. As he moved, his form groaned beneath a symphony of whistles and horns. "You're a mistake, a terrible, horrible mistake. A dream in a world that can no longer host you."

Tommy's eyes flared in the night, a reflection of his creator's. "I'm not going anywhere."

"That's not for you to decide, six-six-three-five-eight."

"STOP CALLING ME THAT!" Tommy roared suddenly, his body quivering with rage.

"But that is your name. That is what you are. Just a number at the end of a long line of mistakes."

"Leave me!" Tommy yelled, "go back to your lonely wanderings, Rez! I belong here, I was MADE to be here!"

"No," Rez echoed, a chorus of creaking horns, "you don't belong here. You don't belong anywhere. It's time for the dream to die."

Rez turned his head, a chirping of soft whistles and hums as he did so. "Are you ready, Jack?"

The hand holding the knife was shaking uncontrollably, but I nodded.

"Take your blade and slice open the casing on my back."

Tommy took a step forward, suddenly on edge. "What are you doing!?"

"Jack! Do it now!" Rez yelled in my ears.

Rain slapped my skin with cold fingers and I blinked back dripping moisture. My limbs felt frozen, impaled in place. I knew what I needed to do, screamed for my body to obey, but the sight of Rez shook me to the bone.

"Don't think, just do it!" Rez screamed.

Tommy began to run toward Rez, understanding illuminating his face. His jaw was clenched and I saw a terrible anger in his eyes, a dark hatred.

"JACK!"

I jerked into a sprint, rediscovering my ability to move again. Rez was standing with his back to me and I honed in on the glowing tube of neon blue that ran up his spine. Thunder crashed overhead, my breath blew wet, and my lungs heaved with urgency. My feet splashed across the soaked earth and I brought my knife up. Rez towered before me.

I reached him seconds before Tommy and as I plunged the blade down into Rez, I saw something like fear ripple across Tommy's face, a blast of disbelieving shock.

The knife punctured the long tube and electric blue liquid sprayed from the incision, coating my face. I screamed, terrified, shaking, and ran the blade down the length of Rez's back, opening up the entirety of the casing. The glowing liquid gushed down his body and the night trembled as Rez howled, a cacophony of deafening horns and shrieking whistles. He fell to his knees and I saw the light from his eyes flutter and blink.

Tommy skid to a halt before us, quivering beneath the rain. "NO!"

I stepped away from Rez, dropping the knife. My hands were soaked in Rez's fluids and I watched as the blue ooze poured out of him.

Rez gasped in my headphones, his voice weak, "Finish this, Jack."

"I'm sorry," I gasped and swayed. "I'm so sorry…"

Rez sputtered violently, his body going into spasms, machinery failing, wires and cables smoking.

"I'm going to miss you," Rez whispered, fading. "I always

considered you…a friend…my only…friend…in this whole universe…this cold…dark…cosmos…"

"WHAT DID YOU DO!?" Tommy shrieked, losing himself as a burning, furious light entered his eyes.

With the last of his strength, Rez looked up at Tommy and whispered, "Ending the dream…"

And then the light vanished from his eyes and he slumped forward, dead.

A sudden force of energy exploded around us, a cyclone of rain and wind, a torrential, unrelenting pulse that blinded me in a detonation of sound and insistent violence. The night trembled beneath the pressure, an expanding bubble of rising change.

Tommy clutched his head and began to scream. My ears were momentarily deafened as a final horn erupted from Rez, the dying release of a desperate being. The world shook and I raised my hands to shield my eyes from the stinging rain and wind. Through the chaos I saw Tommy bent over, hands like claws around his skull, howling as his figure began to shimmer. I blinked and wiped my eyes, hair whipping across my face. This was it, the moment I had been waiting for. I stooped down and retrieved my knife, hardening myself.

Kill him.

As I approached, the storm raging around us, I saw Tommy's image begin to blink and shift. Suddenly there were three of him, then seven, all screaming and holding their heads. In the same instant, they were gone, leaving just one, and I raised my knife into the sky, poised for the murderous blow.

"You deserve so much worse," I whispered, staring at the writhing figure before me, "but this will have to do, you malicious bastard."

I brought the blade down, a streak of cold steel in the blackness of night. A split second before the tip punctured Tommy's head, everything changed.

The wind died instantly.

Silence swarmed my ears like the world had been put on mute.

My arm froze, locked in place.

And Tommy was looking directly at me, whole, unwavering and smiling.

I struggled to free my arm from his grip, eyes going wide with horror, "No…"

Tommy stood, his hand like iron around my wrist. "Hehehehe…"

And then all sound rushed back down around me like a nuclear warhead. And with the noise came a towering, crushing, overwhelming fear. A dread birthed from the darkest hells. A mountain of impossibility and power that I knew would destroy me.

And that mountain was Tommy Taffy.

His eyes roared with life and he leaned into me, voice light but deadly. "Oh, Jack…you shouldn't have done that."

Before I could respond, Tommy lifted and threw me through the air with tremendous force. I went soaring, a missile in the night, a scream caught in my throat. I slammed my eyes shut and covered my head just as I exploded through the front window of the house. A dozen teeth sliced me as glass shattered and rained across my body. In the next instant, my breath was crushed from my lungs as I slammed into the far wall. I dropped to the floor and gasped, my body spiking with shock and excruciating pain. I clawed at the ground, wheezing, eyes bulging as every point in my body howled with agony. Stars danced before my eyes and a dizziness coursed through my head like an angry wind.

The first thought to puncture through the pain was, *Oh shit...*

Rain blew into the living room; the window was a black hole filled with glistening fangs. I frantically tried to regain my senses, desperately tried to rebuild my broken, panicked mind. Moaning, I placed my hands under me and pushed myself up, turning to stare out into the night.

I saw Tommy smiling from the field, his eyes two pinpricks of shining blue across a midnight canvas.

He started to walk toward the house, a bolt of lightning illuminating his figure with haunting clarity.

Get up, GET UP! My mind screamed. Blood oozed from between my tattered clothes as I managed to stand, slumping heavily against the wall. I shakily wiped my face, drool stringing from my lips. I sucked in thick lungfuls of air, my beaten body in sharp protest. I lazily searched the ground for my knife but the rain and darkness swallowed it from sight.

Hide! HIDE!

I turned and half fell, catching myself at the last second. Glass clinked beneath my feet and the dark house creaked beneath the storm. Thunder rolled overhead and I knew I had precious seconds before Tommy was upon me again.

I limped into the hallway, heart racing, mind crippled with pain. Had Rez's death meant nothing? Had Tommy even been affected?

Gritting my teeth, I hobbled down the hallway and slid into the bathroom, pressing myself against the wall. I closed my eyes and tried to catch my breath, lungs burning. The image...that image I had seen...the flash of multiple Tommies, all mirrored and in pain as Rez exhaled his final breath…that had to mean something…had he truly been reduced to a singularity? One final version clinging to this reality in a last ditch effort to reclaim his place among us?

I heard the front door explode inward as Tommy booted it open. If he found me like this, weaponless and hurt, I was dead. I knew this. I needed something…*anything*…some kind of advantage or edge…

I hugged the wall tighter and felt something digging into my back. Confused, delirious, I suddenly remembered the hammer. I quickly reached behind me and pulled it from my waistband, relieved it miraculously hadn't been lost in the violence.

I heard a floorboard creak and I held my breath. Tommy's voice cooed to me from the hallway.

"Come on out, Jack…" he whispered. "We need to make this right."

He was getting closer to the bathroom door and I gripped the hammer, knuckles white against the handle. I needed to cripple him somehow…I needed the shadows…I needed the darkness…

Suddenly, Tommy's footsteps ceased.

I strained in the black, trying to pick up any sound at all, but all I heard was my pulse roaring in my ears. It blasted through my skull and I felt panic squirming through my chest. Where had he gone? Where the *hell* had he gone!?

I pressed my ear against the wall, blood staining the wood, and closed my eyes. Faintly, ever so faintly, I could hear something…rubbing…against the other side. My eyes snapped open.

He's up against the wall, just like you are.

Swallowing hard, I stepped back. I hefted the hammer in my hand and placed the other against the door frame.

It's now or never...DO IT!

I clenched my teeth and swung my body out into the hallway, hammer rocketing toward where I suspected Tommy's head was.

As I rotated in the dark, Tommy came into view, like a predator caught in a beam of light. I saw his eyes go wide a split second before the hammer crunched into his forehead. The blow traveled up my arm and I stumbled back and was rewarded as Tommy screamed. He stumbled forward, one hand swatting blindly at me, the other pressed against his head.

A fire howled through me.

I could hurt him.

I swung the hammer a second time and caught him underneath the jaw. He grunted in shocked pain and fell against the wall. His eyes rolled wildly in his head and I stepped into another attack. This time I took him in the stomach, the impact doubling him over as the wind was forced from his lungs. My own body shook in protest, but I had given in to the adrenaline.

I slammed my knee into his face as hard as I could. He gasped in pain, his hands groping for me as I advanced. I grabbed him by the throat and stood him up against the wall. He was contorted with surprised, horrible pain. Our eyes met and I snarled, twisting the hammer in my hand.

Surging with a sudden, boiling hatred, I swung at his face and buried the hammer's teeth into his eye. Roaring, holding his head in place, I gutted his socket. His eyeball erupted and gushed from the cavity, a vomiting mess of white puss and squirting yellow.

Tommy screamed so loudly it made my head hurt. He shoved me back hard and I thudded against the opposite wall. He clutched his ruined eye, hands shaking, desperately trying to stem the flow of searing agony.

I burned with righteous fury as I watched him, readying myself for another assault.

"That's what pain feels like," I growled, my voice like raging coals.

I stepped forward raising the hammer again but froze as Tommy's head whipped up, his good eye radiating light.

And it blazed with the deepest, darkest rage I had ever seen.

Before I knew it, Tommy had me by the throat, pinning me against the wall. He gripped one hand over mine, staying another blow from the hammer. Grunting, I tried to push him away but the hallway shook as Tommy brought his forehead smashing into my nose.

I felt the remnants of his ruined eye splash into my face a split second before my nose broke. Blood exploded down my face and I cried out in sharp pain. A crippling dizziness took me and I tried to steady myself, images spinning.

I turned my head away as Tommy headbutted me again, this time the impact ringing across my temple. My body sagged against the wall as I felt the strength leave me. I exhaled a blast of air in stinging pain as my legs gave out.

But Tommy held me upright and I felt the grip around my hand tighten.

"Oh, you've been bad, Jack," Tommy snarled, his good eye blindingly bright.

He wrapped his hand around my fingers and pried them off the hammer. I heard it clatter to the floor and knew I was losing. Tommy slammed my hand up against the wall next to my head and bent three of my fingers back.

I screamed, a throat rattling cry, as he broke them, the snapping bones audible in my ears. Tommy leaned into me, breath hissing between his teeth, and then he twisted my broken fingers.

I felt blood erupt from the broken skin as Tommy kept twisting.

With a sickening, wet crunch he ripped my fingers off, a violent, cracking sound echoing through me in the form of a scream. Darkness pressed in on me as Tommy stepped back, tossing the torn fingers to the ground. I held my hand up to my face, howling, wavering, and saw a trio of gurgling stumps.

Without giving me a moment to recover, Tommy grabbed me by the hair and slugged me in the stomach. I dropped to the floor, pain spiking through my body in waves of burning fire. Everything began to dim as I collapsed, my breath a wet heave of desperation.

Tommy began to drag me down the hall and I felt myself being thrown again. I landed with a thud, head bouncing off the floor amid a pool of glass shards.

I turned over on my back, the ceiling a spinning, a blurring sky of shadow. Tommy loomed over me; he was a nightmare, half his face soaked in his own gory fluids. His empty eye socket was a cavern of darkness that revolted what little sense I still possessed.

"You don't get to win," Tommy panted, his fury electrifying the air. "Not back then…not now."

I coughed, a nail in my chest, voice a heaving dribble of air. "You don't…deserve…us…Tommy…"

Tommy knelt down on top of me, mouth twisted into a snarl.

His good eye blazed with blue fire and I saw him sweep his hand across the floor, collecting shards of glass in his palm.

"And you don't deserve your son," Tommy spat, raising his hand. I could do nothing but close my eyes as he slapped me across the face. A wall of pain plowed into me. The bits of glass he had been holding tore through my skin like churned earth. I felt the world go dark as my head was cracked sideways, the momentum from the blow stunning me into deep shock.

I could feel pieces of glass sticking to my face as Tommy rolled my head back so I was forced to look up at him. Warmth slithered across my cheek and trickled into my mouth, tasting like copper.

"My time here isn't over," Tommy growled, "not with so much still to fix." He raised a hand and ran it across his empty socket, wincing. "You took this from me. Tell me, Jack, how am I supposed to watch your son grow up now?" He gripped my head between his hands, voice changing. "Say...how about you give me one of yours?"

Realization shattered through the pain as Tommy reached for my left eye. I tried to bat him away, a sudden surge of energy and frantic horror at what was about to happen. Tommy's face was grim and horribly dark as his thumb found my socket.

I arched my back, trying to buck him off, but it was no use. I felt Tommy's thumb sink into the side of my eye and then he was ripping it out in an explosion of mind-numbing pain that shook my entire body. I thrashed and screamed until my throat went raw, a howling, terrified tremor of disbelieving torment.

Tommy held up my dislocated eye as lightning flashed from outside. Blood dripped from his fingers as he turned it over to examine it. He looked down at me as blood poured from my vacant socket and he smiled.

"An eye for an eye, Jack. Not a lesson I encourage…but appropriate nonetheless."

And then he slid my stolen eye into his empty socket. It squished around the burping yellow ooze and settled horribly into place.

Tommy cocked his head at me, the dead eye rolling to stare at nothing.

"Hehehehe…"

I rolled my head to the side, a broken, bleeding, fading mess of pain and torture. Every single fiber of my being screamed with searing anguish. The darkness pressed in closer and I begged to be enveloped by it. I couldn't beat this monster before me. I couldn't stop him. He was too strong…too relentlessly violent…what chance did I have? How could I kill something born from a nightmare?

And then the image of Mason filled my head.

I pictured how peaceful he looked while he slept. The gentle rise and fall of his chest. The untainted purity and innocence. An innocence that had been robbed from me, from my childhood. The same purity that had been ripped away from my family.

From Mom…

From Dad…

…from Katie.

And the same torment would befall Mason…

*No…*my mind groaned, *you can't let Tommy have him. Not again. Not another one…*

I vainly groped along the ground, my ruined hand clinking over the glass. Tommy towered over me, a monster of impossible power. My cheek rolled across the floor as my head fell, my lips pressing against the shattered pieces of the window.

In the darkness, I extended my tongue and bit down on a long shard, bringing it into my mouth. I closed my lips over it and pressed it against the inside of my cheek, ignoring the pain. I turned back to Tommy.

Mason…

With every beat of my heart.

Mason…

Mason…

I moaned and Tommy turned his eye towards me, smiling, "What's that, Jack? Something you'd like to say?"

I muttered again, dimly summoning the deepest reserves of my strength.

Tommy leaned down, "I didn't quite catch that, champ," he gloated.

"Fuck you, Tommy," I croaked, bringing the glass shard between my teeth like the tip of a knife.

Surging with sudden ferocity, I jerked my head up and buried the sliver of glass into his remaining eye. I dug my mouth into his face and jammed the shard in as deep as I could.

Tommy's reaction was immediate and immensely gratifying. He flew backward and tumbled off of me, screaming in shocked pain. As he fell, I saw my own eye roll out of his head and plop to the floor.

Glass crunched beneath him as he rolled, now lost in blindness and howling in crippling agony. Thunder exploded from the storm outside and a sudden wind blasted through the house.

I slowly rolled over onto my stomach, every movement bringing with it a jolt of fire. Gritting my teeth, I began to crawl towards the fireplace. I felt the tattered remains of my cheek flap across exposed muscle like bloody, shredded curtains. My empty eye socket was a pit of burning pain. My mutilated hand felt like it had been dipped in acid.

I reached the brick face of the fireplace, listening to Tommy scream at my back, and grasped for support with my good hand. Blood dripped from my face onto the floor as my fingers brushed against the rough surface.

Get up...get up...get up...

Blinking back a blast of dizziness, I panted heavily and managed to get to one knee. I paused, letting the room settle, and then I stood. I sagged against the fireplace for a moment and suffered a horrifying moment where I thought I was going to black out. When I was sure I wasn't, I looked at Tommy.

A flash of lightning exposed a ruined face streaked with dripping yellow ooze. He was on his knees, blindly groping, screaming, and enraged with furious pain.

I looked down and my good eye fell upon what I had been crawling towards.

I picked up the fire poker leaning against the hearth and advanced on Tommy, legs quivering beneath an onslaught of exhaustion.

Tommy flapped his arms and turned in my direction, hearing me approach.

I didn't give him a second to react.

I swung the iron poker as hard as I could muster, catching Tommy directly across the face. The poker's hook cleaved a piece of his jaw away and I heard it splat wetly against the far wall. Tommy dropped to the ground stunned as his face began to bleed more yellow.

Gasping, using the poker as a crutch, I hobbled to where he had fallen.

My voice was a rasping shudder as I looked down at him. "You don't get to have my son, you fucking monster."

Tommy, even through the pain, managed to jerk his head in my direction, raising his hands for one final lunge.

I didn't give him the chance.

Howling, I raised the poker and drove it through his chest. Tommy gasped and his body spasmed as the poker passed through him and thudded onto the floor, pinning him where he lay. Yellow fluid exploded from his mouth and began to spread across his chest.

Wavering, weak, I went and retrieved the hammer. I came back to Tommy and stood over him, my own consciousness threatening to leave me. I shook the encroaching black away and raised the hammer over my head.

I nailed Tommy to the floor, each clang of the hammer blasting through my skull. Tommy squirmed and writhed beneath me, his hands weakly grasping at my pant legs. I kicked him away and then stepped back, the poker planted firmly into his chest.

But I wasn't finished yet.

I limped into the kitchen, praying to stay awake, begging not to pass out. I reached for the stove and turned on the gas burners. Immediately, a nauseous odor filled the air. Without pause, I scrambled through the cupboards until I found a bottle of liquor I had seen previously when I had gone for a glass of water. Taking it, I returned to my victim. Holding the bottle with my good hand, I unscrewed the cap with my teeth and spit it out. Then, I upended it over Tommy, splashing it across his face and into his empty eye sockets. They filled like muddy pools.

"Jack..." Tommy called to me, his voice hoarse, "You need me...Mason...needs me..."

I threw the now empty bottle at his face and was rewarded with a weak exclamation as it shattered across his chin. I stared down at him, the monster from my childhood. The shadow across my life. The source of so much torment and misery.

And now he lay broken beneath me.

I turned away, limping for the hallway, feeling myself growing increasingly weak. Mason...I had to get him out of the house...had to get him...to safety...I was so...close now. I stopped and steadied myself against the wall, fighting again against a sudden, rearing darkness.

Come on, Jack...almost there...

I made it to the end of the hall and pushed the door open. Mason was huddled on the bed, crying, his face flush. He looked up at me, his eyes wet and terrified.

"Da!" he sobbed, scrambling for me. I opened my arms and he rushed into them. I picked him up, struggling against an onslaught of pain and dizziness. Mason embraced me, weeping, his little voice strained with fear. He lay his head on my shoulder and I hugged him tightly.

"We're leaving little man," I whispered. "Me and you."

Together, we hobbled back down the hall, a laborious trek that cost me the last bit of my strength. I looked into the living room at Tommy impaled to the floor. One hand groped blindly at the air, weak, but alive.

I reached around Mason and dug out my cigarettes from my pocket. The battered pack was a crumpled mess, but I managed to find one that wasn't ruined. I brought it to my lips and ignited it.

Mason clutched me tighter, his face buried in my shoulder, as I inhaled.

It was the most delicious thing I had ever tasted.

"Goodbye, Tommy," I whispered.

I flicked the cigarette into the living room and it landed on Tommy's legs. I stood there for a moment and allowed myself the satisfaction of watching him catch fire. The liquor goaded the flame into spreading and soon Tommy's entire body was a roaring, blazing inferno.

Faintly, I could hear him screaming, a whispered, terrible thing filled with unimaginable pain. I pressed Mason tighter against me and turned to leave. I pushed the front door open and we exited into the night.

The rain battered the both of us, washing the blood from my worn, beaten body. I made it to the field across the street before my legs gave out. Mason rolled into the wet grass beside me but jumped up almost instantly. He stared down at me with concern, his eyes widening as lightning illuminated my torn, ruined face.

I lay on my back, staring up at the sky, giving into the darkness. I reached into my pocket, feeling weightless. With a shaking hand, I pulled out my phone and dialed 911.

As the operator answered, the house exploded.

Chapter 13

I became slowly aware that I was still alive. Sound melted gently into my ears and sensation bled back into my body. I could hear people talking above me, far, far above me. It was a muffled, urgent conversation. I tried to open my eyes, but found the darkness massively dense. I focused on breathing instead.

Inhale…

…Exhale…

Inhale…

…Exhale.

Yes, that was a little better. Something cool rested against my face, specifically my left eye.

Oh no…

Memory began to filter in through the haze, a violent, horrible recollection of what had happened. My eye…I was missing an eye…someone took it from me…but who?

Tommy.

I gasped, bolting awake in an instant, fear consuming me in a sudden rush. Light blinded my good eye for a moment and I blinked, growing dizzy. I had to get up, I had to make sure…the boy…my son…what was his name…

Mason.

I felt his name rise on my lips and I croaked, struggling once again to ascertain where I was. Where was Mason? Was he safe? Christ, was he SAFE!?

"Jack, relax," a concerned female voice urged. "You're ok. Everything is ok."

Mom? Was that Mom?

I opened my eye again, slower this time, and the world came back, gentler now. I was in a bed. A hospital bed. Nurses swarmed around the room checking machines, leaning over me, asking me questions I couldn't process.

I reached out and tried to bat them away, searching for my mother's voice. As I raised my hand, I froze. I stared at it, a lump of bandages engulfing it from view. Something was wrong with it. It felt like something was wrong with my hand.

Tommy.

"Mom?" I croaked, throat dry, lips chapped. "Mom, are you there? Mom, where are you?"

The nurses were pushed aside and my mother's face blurred into view. Her eyes were red as if she had been crying. Her voice was pale, her skin tight against her cheekbones. Her bottom lip trembled. Then, her cool hand was on my face, beneath my still seeing eye.

"I'm here, Jack," she whispered. "Thank God you're ok…"

"My hand," I said, "he ruined my hand…"

Mom took my wrist gently and lowered it back down to my side. "You're alive, Jack. That's all that matters to me." She leaned down and kissed my cheek, her familiar scent bringing with it a flurry of memories like a gust of autumn leaves.

"Tommy," I said into her ear, voice rasping, "Tell me he's dead. Tell me he's gone. Please, Mom."

She turned her eyes to me and nodded. "He's gone, son."

I felt myself sinking into my pillow. "Where's…Mason…? I need to see…him…make sure he's ok…"

My mom smiled down at me, her eyes welling with tears. "He's ok, Jack. He's resting, but he's ok."

I blinked back looming darkness, my mind slipping back into unconsciousness. "He's…my son…I have a son…"

Before I could gauge my mother's reaction, I was gone again.

Five days later I was released from the hospital. I walked out into the parking lot, my mother on one side, Mason on the other. I held his hand in my own. The one that still had all five fingers. Mason was talking nonstop and I smiled as the sun winked down at the three of us, warm and welcoming. I adjusted the eye patch across my face. That was going to take some getting used to.

We climbed into my mom's car and she began to drive us back to her house. I flipped the visor down and inspected my face in the mirror. As I did, I saw Mom shoot me a worried look. It wasn't anything I hadn't already seen before.

My cheek was healing as best it could, a shredded mess of scabs and eventual scars. It looked like someone had run over my face with a lawn mower.

I closed the visor.

"You ok?" Mom asked, reaching over and squeezing my arm. I looked into the backseat and smiled at Mason. He smiled back and looked out the window.

I sighed and turned back to Mom. "Are you?"

She said nothing for a moment, focusing on the road, and then softly, "So much has happened, Jack…so much death…your father…" She fought with herself valiantly. "I'm going to really miss him."

I nodded, voice soothing. "So am I, Mom. So am I."

She wiped a tear from the corner of her eye and put on a brave face. "But this little man in the backseat…what a blessing he is to our family. Despite everything that has happened, despite all we've had to endure…our family is still here," her eyes turned dark, "and that monster isn't. We're the ones who get to keep living."

Tommy Taffy.

I turned and looked out the window, the events of the past couple days washing through me. When I had called 911, they tracked the call and sent a couple squad cars to investigate. What they found was a smoldering house, a bloodied, unconscious male, and a crying toddler at his side.

What they didn't find…what they never found…were any traces of Tommy. His body, along with what remained of Rez…had vanished.

When they questioned me after I had recovered, I told them the truth. I told them what happened. I told them that a man had invaded Liz's house, murdered my friend Jason, and killed the mother of my son. I chose to omit the details on Liz's death. No one needed to know she had killed herself. What good would that have done?

I described my eventual confrontation with the intruder, how I had been injured in the struggle, and how I had finally killed the bastard. But they couldn't confirm that part because Tommy had simply vanished.

When they told me this, I kept my mouth shut.

After all…what evidence is there of a dream beside your own haunting memory of it?

Later, I found out that there was still an ongoing search for the bodies of Liz and Jason. I didn't know what Tommy had done with them, but I suspected they would never be discovered.

I turned away from the window and my thoughts. I looked back at Mason and then my mother. Our eyes met and I gave her a weak smile.

"We're going to be ok," I said gently.

Fighting tears, she pursed her lips and nodded.

"No crying," Mason said quietly from the back seat.

Mom and I laughed, the tension broken.

And so here I am, at the end of my story. When I started this, I hoped it would purge some of the horrors I endured. I hoped it would somehow give me closure on the entire ordeal. I'm not sure if it has. I guess time will tell.

Me? I'm doing just fine.

Mason lives with my mom most of the time. I get over there as often as I possibly can, when I'm not working. They're my life now. I won't abandon them. I won't hide from my responsibility. I am a father now and it's my job to make sure my son is taken care of.

He's helped Mom's mood miraculously. After we laid my father to rest, she clung to that little boy and I felt an impenetrable bond form. I'm glad for it. I'm glad to see her smiling again. I'm glad to see life back in her eyes.

And Mason…my little Mason.

He has become an unexpected ray of sunshine in my life. I can't say the storm clouds have vanished, but that little boy sure did push a few of them away. He makes me happy. He makes me want to be a better person. After I finish this, I'm going over to Mom's house for dinner. I bought Mason a baseball glove. I think he's going to like it.

As for Tommy Taffy? Well…as far as I'm concerned, that monster is gone.

But the memory of his reign hasn't left me. I don't think it ever will. Maybe it's not supposed to. Sometimes, when I'm all alone in the darkness of my apartment, I think I hear him laughing from inside the walls.

Christ, I need to wrap this up. There's probably a million more things I could say, but it won't do any good. It's over and I want to bury it in the past where it belongs.

I'm tired of being afraid.

I'm tired of thinking about him.

The nightmare I'll never forget…

Tommy Taffy.

About the Author

Elias lives in New England and can usually be found writing in front of his computer, wondering if this time he's gone too far.

When he's not writing, it's usually because he's snuck away to salvage whatever excuse for a social life he currently has on life support.

He believes the horror genre has grown stale and is doing his best to breathe new life into it, one story at a time.

Find him on Twitter @eliaswitherow and on Facebook at facebook.com/Elias-Witherow-831476890331162/.

YOU MIGHT ALSO LIKE:

The Black Farm
by Elias Witherow

Severe(d)
by Holly Riordan

The Worst Kind of Monsters
by Elias Witherow

THOUGHT
CATALOG
Books

Thought Catalog Books is a publishing house owned by The Thought & Expression Company, an independent media group based in Brooklyn, NY. Founded in 2010, we are committed to facilitating thought and expression. We exist to help people become better communicators and listeners in order to engender a more exciting, attentive, and imaginative world.

Visit us on the web at *www.thoughtcatalogbooks.com.*

Collective
World

Thought Catalog Books is powered by Collective World, a community of creatives and writers from all over the globe. Join us at *www.collective.world* to connect with interesting people, find inspiration, and share your talent.

Made in the USA
Monee, IL
05 October 2024

67262158R00163